# ILLEGAL LIAISONS

Published by New Europe Books, 2013
Williamstown, Massachusetts
www.NewEuropeBooks.com

Copyright © Grażyna Plebanek 2013
Translation © Danusia Stok, 2013
Cover image: *Dirty Windows* © #2 1994, Merry Alpern
Interior design by Liz Plahn and Justin Marciano

Translated from the original *Nielegalne związki* © Wydawnicto W.A.B, 2010
First published in English, in the UK, in 2012 by Stork Press

ISBN: 978-0-9850623-6-1

Cataloging-in-Publication Data is available from the Library of Congress.

First edition

Printed in the United States of America on acid-free paper.

# ILLEGAL LIAISONS

Grażyna Plebanek

*Translated from the Polish
by Danusia Stok*

**New Europe Books**

*For Halina, Anka Ś., Jan, Wojtek, Maciek*

**book one**

# 1

*Brussels, 2007*

HE WOULD HAVE RUN THE RELAY – work, home, family – without stopping, had not the old edifice squeezed between insignificant buildings allowed stained-glass light into his soul. Jonathan enters the church and feels the sickly-sweet smell of candles rouse his sleepy cock. She is already there.

Jonathan pauses, his knees weak. The girl is walking down the row of pews toward him; he sees the outline of her slender figure in the semi-darkness, her long hair flowing in a movement rarely seen in this world. Jonathan does not get caught up in lame comparisons because the smell, warmth, and outline of her breasts beneath the blouse and her long legs – not the most shapely yet disarmingly coltlike – below her skirt, enfold him just as the girl – woman really, yes, true woman – plants a kiss on the corner of his lips.

"Hellish idea," thinks Jonathan, pressing the lemon-scented body to him. Meanwhile his hands move up and close over her taut buttocks.

"Communion of bodies," thinks Jonathan.

"Andrea …"

And in his mind he adds, "May it last forever."

When he returns from Ixelles one and a half hours later, speeding the car in his mind, he feels more powerful than the four-year-old Toyota. He would readily ram a hole in the floor with his foot and get home by the *Flintstones* method; bubbles of joy burst with a silent "puck" until Jonathan bursts into laughter.

He keeps recalling the last hour over and over again.

The prelude: he and Andrea leave the church, bodies rubbing against each other. They climb into his car; Jonathan switches on the indicator and joins the line of cars. The gear lever is in his way as his hand hurries to slip beneath the passenger's skirt. When he reaches the strip of skin above her stocking, Jonathan gasps. He miraculously overtakes a motorcyclist and slips his hand between the girl's thighs. He is nearly in the place he wants to be.

Although, in truth, the prelude was different. Just as he was going out to meet Andrea, Megi leaned out of the kitchen.

"Jonathan? Get some money from the cash machine on your way back from the gym, will you?"

He nodded, adjusted the gym bag on his shoulder, and was gone. An expression of indifference, an intake of breath as though he could roll up the scent of eau-de-cologne trailing after him and squeeze it into his gym bag, as far away from his wife's nose as possible.

He quickly pushed the front door open and stepped out into the street. A last inquiring text and the screen flashed in reply – she, Andrea, was already waiting for him.

The voices of his children reached him from the window. Jonathan hunched his shoulders and walked briskly to the car. His daughter had almost given him away once, when she had asked why he was wearing his best T-shirt to the gym – the one Megi had bought him in New York. Another time his son had cuddled up to him and, stroking his clean-shaven cheek, had asked, "What's happened to your prickles, Daddy?"

Jonathan threw the gym bag onto the back seat and drove toward avenue Emile Max. The blossom on the trees was splendid, some white, some cherry-colored; fallen petals covered the street in a damp carpet, lined the bends in the road, camouflaged the dirt. When, the previous day, he had passed this way with his children, Antosia had removed her shoes and run barefoot while Tomaszek had run over the froth of blossom with the wheels of his bike.

Jonathan had promised himself that he would photograph the trees before the petals fell. He had, of course, forgotten and now he had only one day, two at most, to capture this fragile beauty.

He drove and tiny, everyday recollections pecked at his memory. He passed the roundabout, parked in a side street behind the church and got out of the car. He was on edge. If only the smallness of family life would let him go! He had come here to meet his lover.

The apartments on Dailly Square basked in the warmth of the setting sun as he returned from meeting Andrea, and a lipstick-red blaze colored the roof tiles. Jonathan turned right and parked in front of his house. He grabbed the handles of his gym bag and cast a searching glance over the interior of the car: the children's seats were covered with biscuit crumbs, an empty juice carton lay in the middle, a forgotten drawing – everything looked as it should.

The smell of dinner reached him at the threshold. His wife had not had time to change after work. She was wearing slippers but beneath her apron was a suit skirt from which dangled a "leash" – an identity tag for entry to the European Council. It crossed his mind that Megi was a modern wife: aromas from the kitchen did not overpower the smell of ebonite that usually surrounded her when she came home from work, an aroma characteristic of office-workers who spent their days at a computer.

Jonathan smelled of another woman so he darted upstairs.

"Did you get the money from the cash machine?" – the question stopped him when he was already at the top. He slapped his forehead; Megi pursed her lips. Jonathan turned and locked himself in the bathroom.

Throwing off his clothes, he smiled at the mirror. Before stepping into the shower, he licked the taste of his lover from his fingers.

# 2

THEIR START IN BRUSSELS, two years ago – one of many beginnings, which were not really the beginning of anything but served as convenient memory props. The recollection of two small keys handed over to them by the owner of the apartment – Jonathan had gazed at them in amazement. He thought that the rooms – almost four meters high, with arched, vaulted, and palatial windows ending in intricately grated panes – deserved the kind of keys that dangle from a witch's belt in fairy tales.

Megi locked the empty apartment and slipped the keys into her handbag. They made a round of "their" new area, stopping at the window of a pharmacy, at a display where keys and glass are cut. They picked up a take-out menu from a Chinese restaurant and sat down over coffee at the café in the square.

"*Café au lait, s'il vous plaît,*" Megi ordered.

"*Lait russe,*" the waiter corrected with a smile.

Megi glanced meaningfully at Jonathan but he was not looking at her. Elderly people sitting at the neighboring tables (later he found out that there was an old people's home around the corner) were reading French newspapers; the waiter took orders in Dutch; a guttural Arabic followed the children who had laid siege to the playground beyond the trees. The wind played with the folds of the long garments worn by Arab women pushing prams, and licked the chocolate bellies of black mothers followed by the eyes of Polish workers.

"Did you hear that? They call coffee with milk 'Russian milk,'" Megi's voice broke through the multilingual hubbub.

Jonathan smiled absentmindedly. He had forgotten what beautiful backsides black women had!

Jonathan had known from early childhood that journeys meant parting. His mother had first left when he was seven years old. She had been offered a placement in England and disappeared from his life for a couple of months. At the time, it had seemed she had left for good.

One day he had gone to see her with his father. The visit had flown by so quickly that he didn't remember any of it; yet he had never forgotten the parting. They had stood at the departure desk in the airport. Jonathan, who held on to his mother's hand as hard as he could, had felt she did not want to let him go. His father had stood nearby clearing his throat pointedly now and again, but Jonathan had ignored him. His mother, too, had not let go; she looked as though she wanted to incinerate herself. Then his father had summoned an air stewardess with his eyes and put his arm around his wife with a decisiveness which was unusual to him. His mother's grip had weakened, so Jonathan held on even harder. The air stewardess kneeled down in front of him and said something like, "Oh!"

He wouldn't have noticed her – he was in despair, and his mother's hand, slipping away, was growing damp in his hands as if it, too, were crying – had it not been for the stewardess's eyes. They were sky blue, crystal clear, full of northern brightness. Still kneeling, she had taken his other hand – she had had enough tact not to press her hand into the warmth left by his mother's touch – and silently stroked him on the cheek.

Her eyes had so riveted Jonathan's attention that his father had quietly managed to persuade his mother to disappear from the departure lounge unnoticed. When they sat Jonathan down at the round window of the airplane, he was no longer crying. He was soaking up the brilliance of the sky which was merely a faint reminder of the other woman's gaze. From that moment, his mother had ceased to be his entire world; and he avidly began to track down eyes of sky blue.

Some time after this, his parents divorced; his mother married an Englishman. When Jonathan finished primary school, she had him join her so that he could attend an English secondary school. His father agreed, even at the price of not seeing his son for an indefinite period. He desperately wanted Januszek (that is what the boy was called before his English buddies, unable to pronounce his name, had christened him Jonathan) to be a citizen of the world and not of a country constantly invaded by its neighbors.

A few years later, both parents used the same argument and, once he had finished school, pressed him to study in France. There, he found a second pair of intensely blue eyes – he met the Swedish girl, Petra. The first time he saw her, she was hanging onto the back of a friend, too drunk to stand upright. She had the face of Grace Kelly, straight nose and classic, arched eyebrows. A shiver ran down his back when she looked at him – icy irises, misty with an excess of alcohol. He helped to lay her down on the couch in the student hostel, and stretched out next to her.

He didn't sleep that night, only watched her and dreamt of putting his lips around her clitoris. When he could no longer bear the girl's heavy sleep, he touched her lips with his fingers.

Nothing happened between them that morning but from then on, Jonathan didn't leave her. Everything about her excited him, even the fact that she wouldn't let herself be fathomed. Taciturn, reserved, only in bed did she turn warm. She wasn't very keen on experimenting but when he took her on all fours, she stuck her rump out like a cat until her thighs trembled and a quiet whine escaped her lips. As soon as she climaxed, he would slip out of her, turn on his back and gaze into her pupils, the cold blue of her irises becoming black.

Every night he warmed the angelically pale, slender body until it had started to tire the girl. It seemed she welcomed her periods with relief, so as to be able to forbid him access, but blood didn't put him off; he liked the heightened sliminess of her vagina, the metallic scent mixed with the smell of sex. He pumped hard until his skin grew damp and, seized with tingling excitement, sucked her tongue with abandon.

In spring, Petra was on edge for a month, didn't allow him to touch her; finally, she told him she was pregnant. For an instant, he imagined a tiny person with blue eyes, but Petra wouldn't hear of it. He helped her a little after the abortion; the girl's face, as usual, didn't betray much, only her eyes looked as if all color had seeped from them.

They remained together another two months. Petra's beauty inspired general admiration, and Jonathan was prompted by an atavistic instinct to keep an eye on her. On the other hand, he already knew what she was capable of in bed.

After graduating in France, Jonathan went to Poland for a holiday. He lived with his father, visited relatives, enjoyed the taste of Polish sausages and the accessibility of Polish vodka. He felt "warm" in Poland. People opened up the moment they ceased to smell deceit in his accent; they rubbed against each other on buses and trams, yelled and hooted, sweated in anger at the government and at their neighbors, and laughed at drunkards anchored to bus and tram shelters.

He was about to go back when he met Magda at a party. Younger
by a year, she was just writing her Master's dissertation. She had brown
eyes and full lips. Although he had had a good number of girls before
– there was even a time when he was attracted by neurotics as fragile as
chipped vases (he tried to put them together but as soon as he left they
fell apart again) – she was exceptional.

It was because of Magda – nicknamed "Megi" by his buddies because
she was Jonathan's girlfriend – that he stayed in Warsaw. He found a job
as a journalist and began to earn good money with which they rented a
studio apartment. They got married; in 1998 Megi gave birth to Antosia
and four years later to Tomaszek.

When they left Poland in 2005, Jonathan had already acted out
several stages of adult life. He had chanced upon a turning point in
history, and when capitalism had opened its jaws to young, unaffected
people with a knowledge of languages, he had begun to earn decent
money working first as a translator, then as a journalist. He had taken
out a loan at the right moment and bought an apartment; later, when
he was selling it, the price of real estate had gone up and Jonathan had
made a fair profit.

He also had a few irrational phases behind him. Although an
unbeliever, he feared that – having been born on December 24 with
a name beginning with "J" – he would not live to see his thirty-fourth
birthday. Things turned out otherwise, and Jonathan, who had a son at
this critical age, became euphoric and made a decision that his friend,
Stefan, said was a result of postnatal shock – he resigned from his job on
a widely read newspaper in order to stay at home with the child.

Care of the newborn turned out to be the hardest task he had ever
undertaken. He tried to focus on nothing but that, yet when he was
offered an article to write, he kissed the hand which offered it. Then
came another offer and another; finally, he started translating. Soon it
was clear that he was backing out of paternity leave. And since his wife,
counting on him, had gone back to work six weeks after the baby was
born, they had to hire a nanny to look after Tomaszek. The woman's
wage was almost as much as Jonathan was bringing home as a freelancer.

For a long time Megi reproached him for not staying with the child
like she had, sacrificing two years of her career for their daughter. It was
easy for her to talk. She claimed it hadn't been easy but, as Jonathan saw

it, she had blended effortlessly into the landscape of the sandpit. After a month of changing diapers, he, on the other hand, felt his buddies were no longer treating him as one of their own, and that the mothers, rhythmically rocking their prams, did not see him as a man.

Yet there was something at which he had succeeded. During his failed paternity leave, he had written a book. It was a children's story, born of the rapture he felt for his daughter and son, seasoned with a sense of guilt that he was unable to give them one hundred percent of his time even though women could – some men, too – and even though it was growing fashionable throughout the world.

He wrote another story to go with the first and then a third; and before he knew it he was being invited to literary evenings where mothers of gap-toothed fans pressed books at him to sign. And somehow, without great plans, he had become a writer of fairy tales. As a counterbalance, he dressed, at the time, like a war correspondent, until he found out that camouflage waistcoats were a hit in health spas.

# 3

WHEN THE ALARM RANG, Jonathan hoped for a moment it might be Saturday. The smell of breakfast and the barely perceptible scent of Megi's perfume drifted upstairs. The front door slammed. Monday.

He dragged himself to the bathroom. He was tall, slender, with his mother's dark hair, which he didn't like to cut. He pushed it back, put his glasses on and, although his jaws had grown stubble overnight, he let it go – he didn't have the energy to shave.

With a sense of duty unusual for a seven-year-old, Antosia got up without having to be told off; Tomaszek allowed himself to be carried to the bathroom then stood in front of the toilet bowl. Peeing with his eyes shut, he cursed the fate of a preschooler. By the time Jonathan came to make the children's beds, his son had crept back to his room and buried himself beneath the duvet.

"Tomaszek," Jonathan stood over the small mound, hands on hips. "Get up!"

"Tosia's in the bathroom," came from beneath the duvet.

"Antosia, out with you!"

"I'm looking for my bobby pin! He's hidden it."

"Then take another one," shouted Jonathan.

"I don't want another one. I want the one he's hidden!"

Jonathan fished his son out from beneath the duvet.

"Tomaszek, give Antosia back her bobby pin."

"What bobby pin?" The boy's gray eyes opened wide.

Jonathan started to laugh, and Tomaszek, giggling impishly, jumped beneath the duvet again.

"Get up, we're late." Jonathan tried to keep a straight face. "To the bathroom, quick march!"

"But she's in there."

"Antosia!"

"I'll come out when he's given me back my bobby pin!"

Half an hour later, they were caught in a traffic jam. A single line of cars crept along the avenue de Roodebeek – both sides of the street were being repaired – and they picked up speed only once they had dived into the tunnel. Getting on to the Montgomery roundabout was like driving a car at a fairground, with everyone barging into the first free space in the outside lane.

Jonathan kissed Antosia goodbye in front of the school then ran with Tomaszek to his classroom. Tiny Asians, white children, and a few Africans were running down the corridors. Jonathan glanced at one of the mothers, an Italian with a shapely bust beneath her tight blouse. Someone started talking to him: a Canadian woman wanted to arrange for her son to play with Tomaszek in the afternoon. She was not pretty, but Poland for her was not simply associated with plumbers; a lawyer, like Megi, she had read Kosiński and Kapuściński.

Seeing the farmer from Ohio approaching, Jonathan leaned over to her. The other rooster in this henhouse, the American had informed Jonathan of his Polish roots on the day they met. He knew the word "dupa" [ass], wore glasses and a hairstyle with a painfully neat parting; the mothers whispered that he was a retired prison guard from Ohio.

Jonathan said goodbye to the Canadian woman and made his way to the parking lot. He didn't turn the key in the ignition immediately; he didn't want to go home. Their possessions had arrived and stacks of boxes were waiting for him in the apartment. He unpacked some every day, yet the stacks didn't seem to diminish.

He pulled out of the parking lot only to stop again at a bistro in the nearby square. He bought a coffee and booted up his laptop. One email, from Stefan.

Before opening it, he looked around cautiously. Jonathan's friend – one of Megi's colleagues from student days who, like her, had got a job at the Commission and moved to Brussels – usually attached pages of porn to his emails. This time, too, a pair of breasts loomed on screen. Jonathan closed the laptop a little – he had told Stefan so many times that he was an ass man, that he preferred shapely backsides and long legs.

After a while, he peeked at the photograph. He distrusted men who claimed not to look at naked girls because they found them crude, or to watch porn films because the dialogue was boring.

In the end, he beckoned to the waiter. He felt guilty – Megi was working hard at the office while he was sitting in the sun, looking at porn.

WHEN THEY HAD BOUGHT the air tickets from Warsaw to Brussels in the spring of 2005, a weight fell from Jonathan's shoulders. For the past ten years he had been living in one place. He had allowed himself to become domesticated by his love for Megi. He didn't complain but his hankering after travel felt like a gunshot wound. He anticipated that moving to another country with a family of four would resemble Circus Knee on the move but was still tempted by the vision of a sailing ship promising freedom.

In 2005, Megi had received a gift from fate: an offer to work in Brussels. She had, in fact, been preparing for the EU exams for a long time, and had passed them; even though her relatives, who wanted to see in her above all a wife and mother, were prone to put the Brussels offer down to coincidence and to what Uncle Tadeusz liked to call 'sheer luck'.

When Megi found out that she had passed the exams and been offered a job – thanks to which she could support a family of four in the middle of Europe – she initially cowered, as though she had shouted and brought down an avalanche. Then she locked herself in the kitchen for a few evenings and jotted down arguments for and against. Jonathan, who knew all too well that trying to persuade Megi to do anything could bring about the opposite effect, chose to wait. Finally, she scrunched up the pieces of paper, sat down at the kitchen table, and called Jonathan. A few days later, they invited their more distant family to tea in order to inform them – amid the sweet fumes of apple pie – that they were moving to Brussels.

The first to take offence was Uncle Tadeusz; this was not, in his opinion, what true patriotism should look like. He pronounced the word like "patriotis," and Jonathan would have readily bitten him in his fat leg because, ever since Jonathan had resigned from his job, the uncle had been casting doubt on his masculinity. "Real men don't act like that," grumbled the pensioner, while other relatives asked, "What do you want to go live among strangers for?" and, "Why go to that Belgium?"

Megi and Jonathan left behind the Wedel chocolate cakes – "so that you have something sweet to eat in Belgium" – entrusted the children to their grandmother, and one spring day in 2005, stood on an unfamiliar square, squinting in a light familiar from great Flemish paintings. The moment was like a safe haven in his memory, a moment of respite, until daily routine re-asserted itself.

# 4

A FEW WEEKS AFTER the move, the rhythm of work was regulating Megi's new life; Jonathan, on the other hand, was still all over the place. Too many boxes and numerous domestic duties, to which he was no longer accustomed in Warsaw, fell on his shoulders, as if in revenge for his escape from paternity leave. Slowly, it dawned on him that the travels he had been used to in his youth and after which he hankered, were now different. The sailing boat had turned out to be a barrel-shaped barge.

The apartment, inundated with cardboard boxes, began to force him out into the city, but the paths outside were not yet smooth. Jonathan, who had enjoyed the life of a freelancer in Warsaw, decided to seek a permanent job. He had to tame the city not as a tourist but as a resident. And, more importantly, most of his income as a journalist had been cut off when he left Poland so he had practically nothing in his account. Jonathan discovered he didn't like taking money from his wife's account. It made him feel – what, precisely?

He didn't analyze his state of mind too deeply; he wasn't one to delve into himself to such an extent. He sent his CV out to umpteen places and soon emails started to arrive, until one day he came across a letter that excited him. It wasn't an attachment from Stefan but an offer of work – riveting to the last paragraph. When he reached the bit about pay, he groaned with disappointment.

He went home to put up some shelves but the thought of the strange job did not leave him. Every now and again, he grabbed a notebook and, using one of Tomaszek's crayons, jotted down ideas that came into his head. Unable to bear it any longer, he phoned Megi. He bounced off her answering machine and pressed the next number on his list – Stefan's.

They had met in Warsaw over ten years ago. Stefan, a regular at the parties thrown "chez Kic," the student hostel on Kicki Street, ran into Jonathan who was staying there unregistered. Their last student kicks brought them together and at every occasion they exchanged stories like the one about Stefan trying to deflower a young lady from the depths of Poland, in the dark mistaking her tights for her hymen.

Jonathan would have called Stefan his best friend had it not sounded in Polish like an avowal. The institution of best friends seemed bookishly pretentious to him (Winnetou and Old Shatterhand), which is why he just called Stefan, Stefan.

They arranged to meet on rue Franklin. Already late, Jonathan rushed, ignoring his cell phone as it swelled with messages from Stefan. At last, in the garden of a little eatery, he caught sight of a well-kept figure constrained by the discipline of a suit, and with fair hair scarcely anyone knew was thinning.

"I'm going to become an alcoholic because of you." Stefan pointed to the empty glass of beer and gestured for another.

"It's the nanny, she couldn't find her way." Jonathan collapsed into a chair.

"Pretty?"

"She's got a gold tooth."

"My aunt had gold canines." Stefan lost himself in thought.

Jonathan silently raised two thumbs. He had got the nanny's details from a Polish plumber but this was not what he wanted to talk about.

He had just opened his mouth to say something when a round from a machine gun resounded.

Stefan dug out his cell and read the text.

"Kalashnikov fire?" Jonathan leaned back in his chair. "Poland, the Christ of Nations, as our poet says?"

Stefan made nothing of it and slipped the phone into his pocket.

"It goes off when there's a text from Monika."

The waitress stood their beers in front of them.

"How is she?" Jonathan reached for his packet of cigarettes. "Found a job?"

Stefan fished out a bit of dirt from his glass. Monika, Stefan's wife of over ten years, was born twenty years too late. In the '60s she would have been, as Jonathan's father said, to his son's linguistic horror, a typical dolly bird; twenty years later, next to her long-legged, blonde classmates, she looked middle-aged.

Stefan had gone out with her during his first year of studies but could not endure the monogamy. When they met again, two years after college, Monika consoled him after a heavy-going relationship he had had with a domineering French philology student. She fell pregnant. Stefan treated her honorably: he proposed and she accepted.

After their daughter's birth, Monika brought her mother over to help with the child; the mother lived with them, taking turns with several aunts. The elderly women all dunked pieces of bread roll in milk in exactly the same way and smoked forty cigarettes a day; Stefan could not tell them apart. The two-room apartment grew gray from smoke and Stefan's pleas to smoke on the balcony because of the child met with a shrug. Stefan, who was not sure which of the aunts he was addressing, soon hung a notice up in the kitchen prohibiting smoking in the apartment. The notice disappeared, and the apartment continued to turn gray with smoke.

Stefan had no access to his daughter. The short, buxom women with tight perms kept strolling with his child through the gardens of the housing estate, until he felt superfluous in his own apartment. Monika, meanwhile, had found employment with a leasing company and held a position the name of which nobody was capable of remembering.

When several years later Stefan was besotted with a colleague from work, Monika – with infallible instinct – fell pregnant again. The result was a son, Franek. Stefan bought a larger apartment because the number of carers at home doubled.

When offered a job in Brussels, Stefan deluded himself that he would go alone, but Monika packed up herself, their teenage daughter and the younger Franek, bade farewell to leasing, and was ready for the move. Stefan merely managed to negotiate that no one from their village should accompany them.

"Monika?" Stefan glanced at his cell. "She's not found any work yet. It's hardly surprising, she doesn't speak any languages."

"And how are things with you at work?" Jonathan quickly changed the subject.

Stefan came to life. He could talk for hours about work; he observed and played out personal relations with a passion. He pointed out his empty glass to the waitress and started to summarize the latest reshufflings in the Directorate General for Enlargement, where he was a senior administrator. All that Jonathan remembered was the abbreviation used for the place where his friend worked – "enlarg" from "enlargement,"

When Stefan paused to drink, Jonathan confessed.

"I've been offered a job."

"In the Commission?"

"No."

"Media?"

Jonathan remained silent, building suspense.

"They want me to run a course in creative writing."

Stefan squinted. His pale eyes, which usually expressed a certain wickedness that women found attractive, showed careful thought.

"How much?"

"Don't ask." Jonathan lowered his head.

"That bad?" Stefan reached for a cigarette. "What does Megi say?"

The previous evening flashed before Jonathan's eyes. Frequent dealings with his wife's answering machine had led him to hope that the modulated voice of the machine might have undertones of sexual promise. In reality, instead of arousing the imagination, it pushed his thoughts into a gutter as narrow as a sledge track. Megi had finally answered late into the evening but her voice had sounded distorted and distant. She was still at a meeting that was meant to finish past midnight. She could not talk for long. She merely asked about the children and Jonathan sensed some of the energy, bubbling in him since the morning, turn into anger. He pressed the cell button hard, bidding goodbye to the word "wife" with his eyes.

"We didn't even have an opportunity to talk," he muttered. "Megi works till late."

"Someone has to," laughed Stefan and Jonathan stared at him thoughtfully. Everyone had faults and Stefan's was a lack of tact. "Anyway, if the pay's poor, don't bother. Look for something else."

"But it's interesting! I can put the curriculum together myself. It grabs me."

Stefan thanked the waitress with a nod as she stood a beer in front of him.

"How old are you? That's what can grab you." He indicated the girl as she walked away. "Work sets you up. You've got a degree, experience as a journalist, languages. Am I to tell you what to do? After all…"

He stopped as his cell started ringing in his pocket.

"I'm at work," he said into the phone. "Dinner. Business. What do you mean you don't understand what the mail from school says? All right, I'll be finished soon."

He hung up, downed his beer, and turned to Jonathan.

"Think of a sensible job. Oh, and the vice-head of the task force is holding a party on Friday. Megi's probably got an invitation. Make sure you come!"

# 5

JONATHAN'S THOUGHTS rarely turned to the first time he had met Andrea. The moments in which they later immersed themselves occupied more space in his memory; and they had leapt into something more intense – they insisted – than ever before.

Jonathan's memory turned out to be a clever device that didn't prompt comparisons, at least not when he was with Andrea. She was his goal, his oxygen, and his delicacy; he mounted her, lived by her breath, eagerly licked the nipples adorning the olive-skinned spheres of her breasts. Images of the bodies of women with whom he had been in the past, including the pale recollection of his wife's body, lay forgotten at the bottom of his memory.

Jonathan set out to climax with Andrea carrying no burdens, only his ego, which never physically let him down – something that filled him with pride. When later they lay side by side – and these were limited minutes of pure happiness, which disappeared as soon as they parted – Andrea, as women are wont to do, would say something like, "I remember the first time I saw you." In her postcoital stupefaction, she could think of nothing else. She, so intelligent, witty, wise, wanted to whisper only about them. And so Jonathan, who had a similar vacuum in his head, hid behind the smoke of his cigarette and murmured, "Yes, yes, I remember."

The truth came out when it turned out that "when I first saw you" meant something different than him and to her. Andrea counted their days together from their first meeting, he from their first lovemaking.

"Two different calendars!" shouted Andrea, knitting her dark brows. Did they have anything in common whatsoever? She was angry but a moment later forgave him, and Jonathan suspected that the abyss which proved his masculine lack of sensitivity in some way excited her.

Jonathan did, in fact, remember the first time he saw Andrea but he didn't tell her because he didn't want her to have any power over him. He had already realized that she could be cruel when she caught a whiff of blind attachment. He didn't want her to wave a sheet stained with blood, his blood, in front of his nose, so he let her refresh this "forgotten" memory for him.

Each time she spoke about the first time, Andrea added something new, some element she had previously overlooked. In this way she constructed their mythical beginning. Jonathan, meanwhile, silently struggled to hold on to his own. Frankly, he was afraid of her myth. He sensed that in repeating her story, his lover was spreading her web around him. And he was scared of it, just as every man is scared when he suspects he's being trapped, even though all she tied him with was the thread of a story.

When he thought about his first meeting with Andrea, Jonathan tried to recall facts: the well-kept apartment with its stained-glass window over the stairwell and enormous hall ending in a garden. As always, the size of living areas in Brussels staggered him. Unfortunately, the large room reminded him of a toilet bowl festooned with dried turds, and Jonathan would readily have scoured the knick-knacks and growths of souvenirs with steel wool.

He took a glass of champagne from the tray offered by a waiter and merged in with the crowd. People stood in groups in the middle of the room, some dressed in suits, others in jeans, yet Jonathan sensed that they were not quite as at ease as they pretended to be. He was just about to share his thoughts with Megi, who had come up to him with a glass, when she grabbed him by the arm and pulled him toward the nearest gathering.

"This is my husband, Jonathan," she introduced him.

"Delighted…" Jonathan shook hands with the slim man.

"This is Ian, who looks after European parliamentary relations in the organization of employers."

"My pleasure…"

"This is my husband, Jonathan. Jonathan, meet Peter. Peter is the spokesman for…"

"Aha…"

"I'm Megi, and this is my husband, Jonathan. We've been in Brussels for over a month. No, we haven't seen the Atomium yet. Jonathan? Have you met Margit? She is deputy spokesman for…"

"For?"

"At the European Commission."

"In the European Commission …"

"From the Commission …"

"Excuse me a moment, I've an urgent call." Retreating, Jonathan reached into the pocket of his jacket.

He leaned against a table laden with snacks, mown down by social apathy. A private apartment and waiters, people in jeans but on stiff legs, a host with the handshake of a wet fish and a hostess with the face of Cinderella's sister. Were they having a good time here, or working?

He grabbed a carrot and nibbled it quickly.

"You're not from the Commission?" The question sounded like an affirmation.

Next to him stood a woman he didn't know.

"It's that obvious, is it?" he sighed.

She laughed and held out her hand.

"Andrea."

Much later, he noticed that her hands were different from the rest of her body; they were wide, as if older, which she tried to disguise with a neat manicure. He hadn't noticed at the time because Andrea was only just emerging from a haze of unfamiliarity. Tall and slim, she turned to take a canapé. Her buttocks were small and so round that he wanted to knead them.

"And don't worry about those people." She smiled, pointing at the undulating human circle. "Look, those on the outer circle are trainees…"

Jonathan looked at the twentysomethings whose faces were turned toward the center of the circle.

"… those closer to the center are higher-ranking officials. See the bald one on the right?"

"The bullet head?"

"He's sharpening his teeth for the position of minister's adviser. While the fat one with a muff of hair is angling for the still warm place of a colleague who was promoted to another department."

"And the man everyone's looking at?" asked Jonathan, indicating the center where a tall, slim, gray-haired man was standing. The charisma emanating from him could be felt even at a distance.

"He's the head of cabinet for the Justice Commissioner." Andrea smiled.

"He's boss of them all?" Jonathan was lost.

"He's their god."

The circle shuffled as the head of cabinet for the Commissioner retreated, shaking the outstretched hands as he went.

Andrea glanced at her watch.

"It was nice to meet you," she said.

Jonathan felt an unexpected wrench within, a child's voice screaming, "I want!" Perhaps it was the trace of a Swedish accent in her practically perfect English?

"What do you do?" he asked in desperation.

"I work for Swedish television. And you?"

"I write."

"Articles?"

"Books."

"Ohhh!"

Jonathan slipped his hands into his pockets. He loved this sort of reaction. He knew from experience that he ought to enjoy it to the full because it generally preceded another, less desirable one that began with the question: "And what do you write?"

"Fairy tales."

He usually bore the phase of "losing face" manfully but this time he added equivocally, "I was recently offered a job to run a course in creative writing in Brussels."

"Ohhh!"

"But for financial reasons I suppose I ought to try for a place in the Commission …"

"Your course sounds more interesting."

"You don't want to know how much they pay."

"You wouldn't want to do what you don't like."

He squinted at Andrea and saw more of her: brown hair and beautifully sculpted lips.

"Look at that pâté," she said, and he reluctantly turned his eyes to the table. "Some people love it."

"It's *foie gras*."

"I think you'd feel like those overstuffed geese in the Commission."

He turned his eyes from the pâté and looked at her again. Final promises to phone were being exchanged among the group of officials but he was suddenly short of words. The silence between them grew thick.

"Are you…" Jonathan began but right then somebody stopped short beside them.

They both turned. It was the head of cabinet for the Commissioner.

"Simon, meet Jonathan." A professional smile appeared on Andrea's face. "Jonathan is a writer and a lecturer in creative writing. Jonathan, this is Simon…"

The man's handshake was energetic. Although Jonathan knew nothing about male beauty, he immediately knew that this man, although over fifty, put most men in the shade. And that his high rank had little to do with it.

"Andrea, we should be going," the man said in excellent English.

"An Englishman, from Eton," Jonathan quickly surmised.

"… Simon," Andrea finished, "my partner."

That night, Jonathan reached for Megi but he didn't like the taste of her lips. They ended swiftly; Jonathan got up and went out on to the terrace for a cigarette.

He gazed at the clouds rolling over the dark mass of sky. He had immediately taken to the weather in Brussels, warm with an undertone of damp. He loathed southern climates, the vertical sun and blind stubbornness of heat.

"Simon, my partner." There was not a single woman at that strange party – and that included Megi – who had not stared at the man. Jonathan stubbed out his cigarette. Childish unease signalled its presence again, the tiresome "I want," just as when Andrea had been leaving with Simon and Jonathan had taken the chance to look at her beautiful backside again. And now the sway of her hips was irking him like the hook on which a stupid pike – Jonathan – had let itself be caught.

Daily life slotted back into its course. Jonathan unpacked more cardboard boxes until he felt the days themselves had become rectangular. Reach for a box, open, pull out the contents... Finally, the vision of a trip to IKEA acquired the exotic taste of escape and Swedish meatballs offered an opening into the wider world. Sitting at a plastic table, he savored the thought of the jaws of their home in Brussels, hungry for equipment and objects, snapping at a safe distance.

On the way home, he stopped off to buy some bread rolls. Megi couldn't get used to croissants and preferred ordinary bread, while the children loved the little rolls with a slit down the middle which they had immediately called "bums." Jonathan asked for six bums and a take-out coffee.

He was just leaving the counter when he started. He had "met" Andrea a few times since their first meeting – running across the road, glancing at her watch, getting off a tram. But it was never her. He didn't blow the impression she had made on him out of proportion; he often allowed himself to fantasize about women he hardly knew, rewrote scripts for which in real life he had neither time nor courage. It was one thing for his cock to dive into the hole of an appetizing thirty-year-old, another to wrestle with questions about whether the sex would lead anywhere.

Jonathan's principles, too, acted like a bucket of cold water. He was too young for a bit on the side; that was fine for old men needing to invigorate themselves or bores with the mentality of elderly pensioners. Women found him attractive; he'd had quite a few before Megi and knew he could have one at any time. And even though monogamy wasn't easy, when fantasies of other women – or the women themselves – became too pressing, he repeated Stefan's maxim: "If you can't knock her up, forget her'. In his case, "can't" had meant "didn't choose to."

As for an honorable attitude to a woman who belonged to another man, he had to admit that abstract male honor stood on a par with the fear of catching HIV.

When he saw Andrea, real in the light of day, he assured himself it was the sight of a familiar face that made him happy. As a seasoned traveller, he believed that a new place only became home when you bumped into people you knew on the street. And there – a few weeks and he was already meeting someone!

She noticed him, stopped hesitantly.

"Jonathan," he jogged her memory. "We met…"

"I remember. Fairy tales – and a creative writing course."

She was wearing a pale blouse and a skirt with a slit that aroused his imagination.

"A croissant, please." She leaned over to the salesgirl.

"A croissant at twelve?" he asked. "Isn't it time for something more substantial?"

"I'm just off to lunch. I've got to eat something before."

"You must be going to lunch with dwarves if you've got to eat first."

"There you go, you're already writing fairy tales!" Tiny wrinkles appeared around her eyes and disappeared. Jonathan thought he would like to gaze at that smile for longer. There was something exciting about her face, both sexy and intelligent.

"I'll write one if you promise you won't touch the poisoned apple on the way," he muttered.

Andrea glanced at the croissant with suspicion. Her blouse was covered with crumbs as she bit into the pastry; a few fell down her neckline.

"I've got some rolls for a rainy day should anything happen." He lifted the bag of "bums'. "Would you like one to take with you in case the dwarves serve in-flight portions?"

She shook her head.

"My dwarf's from the Commission. I want to get him on my program. I don't eat much when talking business."

"I get angry when I don't eat."

"That's incredible, I'm just the same! Other people seem to cope with hunger in a civilized way but I get livid. I've even got a complex about it."

"You shouldn't," Jonathan reassured her. "After all, we're beasts of prey. The skin of a lamb but beneath lurks a wolf."

"Sounds like a disease," she grimaced.

"*Homo homini lupus* in Latin."

She smiled again and he remembered the coffee he was holding. He drank a little without taking his eyes off Andrea. She pushed the hair from her forehead with a gesture that told him she didn't mind his gaze.

"Do you live nearby?" she asked.

"A few streets away."

"How's your creative writing course going?"

"I'm working on a survival course at the moment. I mean, we've just moved." He indicated the jeans in which he had kneeled to assemble the wardrobes, beds, and shelves.

"And you're no longer looking for a job in the Commission?"

"I haven't even started. Since you said I'd feel like a goose…"

This time she didn't smile, as if the joke had run off track and was bouncing over a road full of potholes.

"I've got to run," she said, glancing at her watch.

"I've overdone it," he thought.

And then something happened that made the hairs on his hands stand on end. Andrea pulled herself upright, shook the croissant crumbs from her blouse, and walked up to him to say goodbye, kissing him in the French manner on both cheeks. But Jonathan forgot how many times they kissed in Belgium and after two kisses leaned over for a third; she, disorientated, paused as she turned her head and, instead of offering her cheek, touched his lips with hers. Jonathan's reflex was to move his lips a centimeter (something shouted silently in him, "I want!") and their lips joined, quivered with warmth and moisture and started to search for each other.

The following morning, after taking the children to school, Jonathan sat down in a café and checked his email. Those organising *L'Atelier d'écriture* had invited him to an interview in a week's time. Megi said he should try as long as he could manage to fit the job around his domestic duties. He couldn't count on her – she had masses of work. He congratulated himself on having already at least found a nanny.

He was opening the document with the notes he had taken with the course in mind, when Andrea appeared in his thoughts. The film of their meetings began to roll again; the recollection of her warm lips sent a hot wave through him. It was unusual in that this film had no continuation, unlike his transitory fascinations with other women during his recent decade of monogamy. What would have been the beginning of a script leading to explicit consummation broke off at an innocent kiss. It left him in a rapture he could not recall – or perhaps he hadn't felt before.

He flicked at the casing of his laptop. There was something narcotic about the woman; the very fact that he was dreaming about the smell of her and not her rump was a bad sign.

His cell rang. Jonathan started, immediately on edge.

"It's me," he heard.

"Megi?" He barely calmed his voice. "Your number hasn't come up."

"I'm calling from work. Listen, I'm not going to manage to take Antosia riding today. I've got to hand in the report by tomorrow."

"I'll take her, no problem."

"Thank you, darling!"

Pssss… The air started to go out of his scented visions of Andrea.

"Are you there?" asked Megi.

"I love you." He heard his own voice.

"And I love you," she reassured him hurriedly. "I've got to finish. Got a meeting."

Jonathan arrived at the school too early. The playground was still empty, although a hubbub had started in the building like in an enormous beehive. He sat down on the wall next to a few mothers.

"… a trip to the farm, they're asking parents to help look after the children," a beautiful Italian was saying in a heavy accent. At a distance it sounded as though she were speaking in her own language. "But I can't go. I'm frightened of poultry and farm animals."

"Do you swell up?" The Japanese woman spoke English like a five-year-old, syllable by syllable.

The Italian fell silent for a moment, disorientated.

"I'm not allergic," she explained. "I simply panic."

The Japanese woman froze and Jonathan observed the Italian; madwoman or not, she really wasn't bad.

"And I find live fish repulsive." A third woman joined in, her accent flat, Finnish. "And stuffed animals."

"I dislike open spaces," admitted the Japanese woman, "and closed rooms."

Jonathan considered the technical aspect of this paradox and heard the familiar voice of the farmer from Ohio.

"*Dupa* [ass/pussy]," the American greeted him.

"Good afternoon," replied Jonathan, making room for him on the wall.

"How are things with you?"

"Great. And you?"

"What a day, what a day…"

"We're looking for parents who might be willing to go with the children to the farm," the Italian began, as she approached them with the Japanese woman. "The school's arranging a trip but they need someone to keep an eye on the children. With all those animals about. Maybe you could help?"

"Me?" the farmer made sure.

"You," the Japanese woman nodded. Unintentionally, the concentration with which she spoke English made her sound cruel.

Once in the car, Jonathan asked the children how school had gone. They started telling him as he wondered how old Andrea could be. Probably over thirty, the age at which true women blossom, when the manner of a woman is superimposed on the looks of a girl – the thing that excited him most.

He overtook a Peugeot which was manoeuvring clumsily and registered the noise coming from behind.

"Stop arguing," he muttered automatically.

"Then tell him to stop copying me!"

"I'm not copying her." Tomaszek was cross.

"And what did you do today, son?" Jonathan changed tactics.

"We copied squirrels," answered the boy.

"Ha, ha," said Antosia. "Hiding nuts?"

Jonathan pulled away from the lights. Andrea was shapely and slim while also being so appetizingly full-figured that he wanted to squeeze her.

"No, no!" Tomaszek grew more and more annoyed. "We walked behind them, you know, behind them…"

"You followed them?" Jonathan prompted.

"Exactly!"

He didn't even know whether she had any children. He knew it had not left a trace on her figure; nowadays forty-year-olds looked better than twenty-year-olds. Megi, having given birth twice, had a better figure than before. Why then, when thinking about his wife, had he for some time been changing the letters in the word "sexy" to "sensible"?

Andrea had small breasts and beneath them a narrow waist and round hips.

"Daddy, the lights."

"Yes, yes, the lights."

"They're green," Antosia explained patiently. "You can go."

"Oh, right!"

Objectively, it was easy to admire Andrea. She was beautiful, intelligent, witty, and delicate. Her legs were not very shapely but they were very long. The few wrinkles only added to her charm. The trophy wife of the guy chased by most of the women in the Commission.

She could have anybody. He was an idiot to think about another man's wife so much.

"So what did the squirrels do?" he asked.

And at that moment a text from her arrived.

When the front door banged shut and the children ran to greet Megi, Jonathan went downstairs and kissed his wife on the cheek. "You haven't put the shelves up, you haven't made sure Antosia is doing her homework, you forgot to buy the meat for tomorrow…" he heard.

He discreetly hid the cell in his pocket. He knew the text by heart anyway: "Enjoyed talking to you, Andrea."

That night he slept with his hands behind his head, his underbelly restless. Why had he flirted with Andrea? Why had he thoughtlessly replied, "Would willingly do so again"?

# 6

*L'ATELIER D'ECRITURE* was located in a nineteenth-century apartment. The way in was up some stairs, passing the stone sculptures in a little garden.

The woman who met Jonathan had silver-gray hair and spoke perfect French. She set a few subtle traps in their conversation but luckily he knew the French idioms and the books she mentioned. He threw in a handful of titles on literary theory, quoted the contents of articles he had recently read in professional publications until her face lit up. She was over fifty but so attractive that her gray hair seemed merely flirtatious.

"You've got a group of seven. That's how many registered but things can change. People generally drop out during the course." She got up and held out her hand to him with a smile.

"Thank you, Mme Lefebure."

"Cecile," she corrected.

Leaving *L'Atelier d'écriture* Jonathan made his way along the main axis of the city straight to the stone arch crowned with a sculpture of galloping horses, which stood on the wings of pavilions housing museums and a nightclub. Despite the monumental grandeur of the building, the area was cosy. Mobile stalls selling waffles were parked on the square, cyclists circumnavigated the arch, strollers sat eating sandwiches and reading on the grass and on the steps.

Even though it was autumn, the grass in Cinquantenaire Park was as green as the parrots squawking, in the branches. It was a mystery how those exotic birds could survive European winters and yet they were still here, losing their emerald feathers, which on days like these merged with the background.

Jonathan's cell beeped in his pocket. He stopped; pigeons scraped at his feet, ruffled in a frenzy of love. Megi was texting him to call. He deleted the message and stared at the one that had arrived the previous day – from Andrea.

Since that first text, messages had filled their small screens more and more frequently. The dramatic tension was like a game of cat and mouse – once he was near her, then she was almost touching him. He remained cold blooded and planned several moves ahead, interweaving wit with tenderness, compliments with elliptical statements, so that even he thought himself attractive. He hadn't seduced anyone for years and now ideas were popping up with the force of popcorn fried in oil. How it drew him in!

He looked around the park, semiconscious. On the right, a deep blue patch flashed by – a group of cadets from the nearby military academy warming up. They ran with a spring, half-boys, half-men. White and black, they passed elderly gentlemen dressed in white, *à la tropique*.

Jonathan squeezed his cell, sweetness running through his body. He didn't see the birds in their love dance on the path. To write or not to write to Andrea? He should phone Megi; she had asked how the interview had gone. "Best wishes to the most beautiful woman in Brussels from a new lecturer in creative writing," he typed on his cell. He broke out in sweat and cancelled the text. A moment later he wrote the same thing adding, "PS You've probably not eaten yet."

He put the phone away and strode briskly ahead. "It's only a game, we're not really doing anything." He slowed his breath. The wind tore at the flags overhead as he crossed to the other side of the arch. The beep of a message. Andrea had written, "I bite but not too hard…"

Stefan lifted weights with loathing. He was sceptical about physical exercise but liked women and that was what brought him here, against his hedonistic nature. With uncomfortable movements that didn't seem to belong to an intelligent human being, he lifted barbells to prevent an invisible wall building up between him and the opposite sex, like a Venetian mirror used by the police to help victims identify their assailant while remaining unseen by him. Stefan was the victim, beautiful girls his assailants. They tempted him, showing off their suntanned legs, flat bellies, and cleavages while he trembled lest excess kilograms hide him from their sight.

Jonathan sweated on the treadmill next to him. This cheered Stefan, gave him someone to talk to and allowed him to maintain some remnants of dignity in his own eyes.

"And so, did she get through to you?" he said from beneath the barbell.

"Who?" Jonathan roused himself from the stupor of his warm-up.

"Andrea Kunz, the chick from Swedish television."

The treadmill ran away from Jonathan. Despite the rising temperature of their text messages, he hadn't yet asked Andrea how she had got his number; one doesn't ask women such questions.

"She said she was doing a program about house husbands," panted Stefan, lifting a weight. "Did she ask you?"

Jonathan stepped onto the treadmill and fell into a brisk stride.

"No, we've only spoken over the phone. She needed a pithy quote."

"She's pithy herself," Stefan puffed and put the bar-bell aside. Jonathan was still striding with the springy pace of a stroller in a hurry.

"Remember when we just finished college?" Stefan wiped the sweat from his brow. "There were so many pretty girls around! I fucked them but what I really dreamed about was a flawless beauty. There were a few. They flashed by as if they'd arrived from another planet. The better ones didn't come to the Kic. They were somehow inaccessible. Like the chick who later emigrated to France, remember?"

Jonathan nodded. That was before he had met Megi. The girl had been phenomenal. He'd even managed to get hold of her phone number but when they'd met – he was passing through France – he'd been disappointed. He'd forgotten to tell Stefan.

"I approached her once, after a couple of beers," continued Stefan, "and said, 'You probably think I'm too short for you'…"

"Were you mad?"

"… and she looked at me like this, up and down, and said through her teeth, 'I do.'

Stefan smoothed his fair hair until Jonathan stopped laughing.

"Then I avoided beauty," he went on, "and screwed girls who were simply pretty but had small flaws. But they immediately wanted to get married!"

Jonathan slowed the treadmill.

"I remember," he muttered. "And then there were only ugly and desperate ones left."

"You were already living with Megi while I had just met Monika for the second time," sighed Stefan.

Jonathan bit his lip.

"And a good thing too, old man," he assured him, accelerating.

Stefan looked at him blindly.

"I regret – to this very day – that I didn't really go all out to get a perfect chick." He made his way to the rowing machine.

Jonathan stopped and again the belt nearly threw him. He gave up with the rest of his warm-up, followed Stefan and squatted next to him.

"How's that?" he asked.

"Be happy you've got Megi," Stefan murmured, struggling with the adjustable saddle. "You don't have to think, 'I'm nearly forty and still up for it.'"

"How's that?" Jonathan repeated.

But Stefan had already started to row on the spot.

Jonathan stopped at the lights and watched the tram drive away. The electronic sign *Louiza* changed from French to Dutch and back again. There was something charming in the name, the giddiness of a woman who could be a queen from Europe or a teenager from New Orleans, hide her cheek with a fan or conceal the large teeth of a smile with her hand.

An affair on the side for a tepid marriage, erection lifting.

Another tram pulled up, flashing the sign *Montgomery*.

There was, however, the matter of honor, a basic principle he'd carried away with him from books he'd read as a boy: do not take a woman away from another man.

He pulled the cell from his pocket – Andrea hadn't written anything that day. Very good; he, too, wouldn't write. After all, nothing had happened between them; he hadn't even suggested they meet. It was only a game, neither foreplay nor anything criminal.

His eyes followed a bus with a NATO sign that changed into OTAN, short for *Organisation du Traité de l'Atlantique Nord*.

Perhaps it would all somehow peter out of its own accord. Please!

# 7

JONATHAN RINSED HIS RAZOR, splashed his face with water and patted the rest of the Victor & Rolf scent into his skin. Megi clattered some cutlery downstairs, no doubt cleaning it; they had taken it out of the boxes just that day. She'd also found the dinner set they got as a wedding present from her family: plates covered in a floral design, more suited to a grandmother's household than a young family's.

He brushed his hair and put the brush back on the shelf below the mirror. Sometimes he caught himself doing little things that reminded him of his father, an unpleasant feeling that he counteracted with a shrug of the shoulders. But the fear remained – like that in dreams about going back to school.

He opened the bathroom window and took a deep breath as he looked out at the Brussels street. He had more hair than his father had even in photographs when he was young. The latter had grown bald quickly and Jonathan hoped this was not a question of genes but of getting up for years at daybreak in order to go off to the same socialist institution. It must have been difficult for him to bring up an only child alone.

Jonathan pulled on his jeans and fastened his shirt. Megi bustled around downstairs preparing the Saturday party. She'd invited her new colleagues from work and it was important for her that all went well. Jonathan had promised to fry salmon in dill sauce, his culinary masterpiece.

When he went down, Megi looked at him from over a pile of plates. In a pair of tight jeans which highlighted her bottom and with her hair, straight from the stylist, cut in a bob in order to show off her neck, she looked like a girl.

"Jonathan?" she hesitated. "Would you please not ask anyone your usual question, "But what is it exactly that you do?""

"It makes it easier to find a subject in common," muttered Jonathan distractedly, taking the dill out of the fridge.

Megi left the plates and watched him. Jonathan was once more struck how the color of her irises could change from – theoretically warm – brown, to cold, almost graphite.

"You don't have any subjects in common." Her tone was calculated to cut any discussion short. "They have their own EU subjects, which are as finely set apart from normal, universal ones as those of astronauts. You're to rely on the knowledge I've been feeding you over the last few days."

"And what if someone tells me they're the head of the Eastern Partnership task force again? What does it mean? That he goes to the office and what?"

"Don't try to understand. Ask about general things."

"For example?"

"Oh, for God's sake, you used to be a journalist, do I have to tell you how to talk to people?"

Jonathan held the dill under the tap.

"My grandfather was a lawyer," he said, placing the bunch on a chopping board and picking up a knife. "My father's an engineer and my mother a physicist. The first defended clients in court, the second designs purification plants, the third researches."

"And now people work in leasing, audit, PR, and human resources." Megi, annoyed, blew at her blonde bangs.

"Those aren't professions."

"But you don't have to tell them that!"

Jonathan shrugged and pulled the rust-colored cuts of salmon out of the fridge. He seasoned them, laid them on baking foil, and doused them with wine. He washed his hands and walked up to the stereo. What music to choose? He ran his fingers down the records.

The intercom buzzed. Jonathan switched on the sound system, and Megi, on her way to the hall, glanced at him in surprise.

"Music from *Stealing Beauty*? But that's music for lovers!"

He did not have time to answer because at the door stood the head of cabinet for the Justice Commissioner, Simon Lloyd, and his partner, Andrea Kunz.

Jonathan kept glancing at the guests from behind the kitchen worktop. On Megi's right-hand side sat Simon, the focus of the gathered group. Rafał, who had hosted the party at which Jonathan had met Andrea, won Simon over within minutes with his knowledge of literature; his wife, Martyna, although she'd asked Megi at the door if she had anything for constipation, told interesting stories. Mainly about herself, but in three languages.

On Simon's left sat Przemek. Jonathan couldn't say much about him because they hadn't had a chance to exchange more than a couple of words. He remembered that Megi, who worked with him, had praised his open mind and nose for politics, which, combined with a knowledge of French and English, "boded well for Poland," as she said.

Jonathan tore his eyes away from Przemek's elongated skull and observed the sympathetic journalist who had come with his partner. Next to them sat a trainee who worked with Megi, and next to her, a Spaniard, an employee at the brewery. Stefan wasn't there because he'd had to go to Luxembourg on business.

"Have you been to Thailand?" Sentences flew across the table, too light to grasp.

"Yes, it's really super!"

"It is, isn't it? And Costa Rica?"

"We discovered a place last year…"

Jonathan looked at the Spaniard, who was getting bored because he didn't speak any Polish. Jonathan, too, was bored and was grateful to the fish for requiring so much attention.

"What about the Canaries? Because next year we can't…"

"Pretty bad. Besides, how much can one take?"

"Nothing's authentic there any more. Everything's touristy…"

"Yes, but basking in a deck chair by the pool…"

"Now, that's different."

When they switched to Commission jargon, Jonathan started to clear the table and the trainee took advantage of the commotion to move closer to Simon Lloyd.

"He's unbelievable!" he heard her say to the journalist's partner.

"'Unbelievable' why?" Jonathan, joining them, couldn't take any more. The trainee turned to him in amazement.

"My friend really wanted to work for him," she replied as if this explained everything.

Jonathan looked across the table but instead of Simon his eyes rested on Andrea, who was talking to the young journalist and Przemek. They were laughing, exchanging quick repartee.

"And what do you do?" Jonathan heard.

He turned his eyes to the trainee girl. Her face was shaped like a Kaiser roll; she was stocky but in her own robust way could be considered attractive.

"I write." Again he glanced across the table. Rafał had joined in Andrea's, the journalist's, and Przemek's conversation.

"And what do you write?"

"Books," he mumbled distractedly.

Instead of an "oooh!" a squeal resounded at his side.

"Well, I've never yet, never yet…" The girl put her hand over her mouth in an effort to control her joy.

"Never yet what?" Jonathan tore his eyes away from Andrea's group. "Never written anything? And do you want to?"

The girl snorted again but a moment later grew serious.

"Write? Come off it! But you know what I really want to do?" she asked, pronouncing "want to" as "wanna."

He nodded, confused.

"I want to open a retro clothes shop."

He was opening a bottle of wine in the kitchen when Andrea came up to him. She was wearing high heels and a slippery dress, beneath which her breasts were so clearly outlined that he was covered with goosebumps.

"Can I help?" she asked, sitting down on the stool at the worktop.

He took the rest of the glasses from the sideboard and thought that had they been alone he would have parted her thighs and slipped his hands up to her pubic hair.

"Will you pour me a glass?"

He shuffled from foot to foot; the physical reaction taking place in his trousers made it difficult to move. Andrea tilted her head. After all those text messages it suddenly seemed strange to him that she should be sitting here, so close yet so distant.

"We'd best think of a subject." She pulled back her long hair. Everything about her was polished and neat; only her hair lived its own, lush life. "Politics perhaps?"

"And not tourism? It's riveting." With his head, he indicated those gathered around the table.

She laughed and he gazed at her, trying to work out the mysterious link that raised her face, whose features were far from classical, to that of a beauty. Perhaps it was the smile, of which he could not see enough? Or perhaps the intelligence in her eyes, highlighted by tiny wrinkles?

"Andrea ..." He cleared his throat and assumed a completely different tone of voice. "Andrea. Where does the name 'come from?"

"I come from a family of Czech immigrants but was born and brought up in Sweden. When I ask for milk in a Czech shop they look at me as if I were quoting fragments from the old Czech Bible. Do you speak archaic Polish, too? When I first heard you I thought you were English, like Simon."

"No, I was a teenager when I left Poland. I even remember martial law."

"Tanks in the streets? My mother told me. I always thought she was still living Prague Spring..."

"Doesn't she like Sweden?"

Andrea shook her head.

"It's like in Kundera," murmured Jonathan. "There's no life after the fever of Prague Spring."

"The unbearable lightness... That's where her recurrent bouts of depression came from."

"And your father?"

Only then did they notice Simon's presence.

"Everything OK?" He put his arm around Andrea's waist and looked her intently in the eyes. His gray hair appeared ash blond in the evening light. He didn't look like a typical Englishman; slim, tall, he resembled a Scandinavian with the smile of a boy.

"We've somehow not had the chance..." he turned to Jonathan. "What do you do? Your wife mentioned you're a wonderful father."

"Jonathan lectures on a course in creative writing," Andrea threw in.

"You're a writer?"

"I've published three books."

"What about?"

"Fairy tales."

Simon glanced at him with amusement; Jonathan's fingers squeezed the neck of the bottle.

"I've got children, too." He heard the man's voice again. "They're already grown up, and studying in Durham."

When the guests had left, promising to return the invitation, Megi turned
to Jonathan:"Simon's girl, Czech or Swedish, you know who I mean?
She says she doesn't want to have children. She's so set on her career."

"She's still young," he mumbled, leaning over the dish-washer.

"She's over thirty! I already had Antosia and Tomaszek by that age."

"Simon's much older than her."

"He's incredible…"

"You find him attractive?" Jonathan dropped a dishwasher tablet
into the hollow of the lid and turned on the machine. "You always liked
older men."

"And she, Andrea," Megi said, ignoring his last comment, "must have
been one of those girls who didn't wear vests under their blouses and
were never cold. I remember those olive-skinned types, resilient to the
temperature. I envied them. My nose was always blue."

She removed the tablecloth and shook it out over the sink.

"Did you notice how obsessively Martyna talked about her 'close friends'?"
she said, throwing the tablecloth into the washing machine. "In my opinion,
you can have a few close friends, but dozens – that's misunderstanding the
meaning of the word."

Jonathan smiled to himself. He liked these moments after a party,
their spiteful comments, a safety valve for the sense of disappointment
they invariably felt on realizing that "grown-up" parties, as opposed to
those of students, had nothing much to do with enjoyment.

"Well, because how can you confide in twenty people?" continued
Megi, struggling with the lid of the washing machine. "'Listen, I got a
chill yesterday, and my boss is a prick.' I can tell you this but …"

She broke off.

"Where are you?"

"Here!" he shouted from the stairs.

"You off already?"

"Why?" He leaned over the banister.

"Oh, nothing." And a moment later she added, "Check that the
children haven't kicked their duvets off. Good night."

Jonathan stopped at the half-landing and rested his forehead on the
window. Megi scraped the chairs across the floor. He should have stayed
with her, talked, but something forced him out of the kitchen.

The window frames   moaned in a gust of wind. Jonathan
stared at the storm, fascinated by its intensity. He had always
wanted to touch the elements, the truth, vibrations. Traveling
had once given him all that, then the first years with Megi, and finally,
surprisingly, the children. They could be the sweetest things yet at the
same time drive him crazy. When he wanted to strangle them, they
stroked his jaw, clenched in fury, with their tiny hands.

Another strong gust thundered against the window pane. The
thought, *Andrea is an element*, came to his mind at once.

He woke up at the sad hour just before dawn and lay there listening
to his wife's breathing. She was snoring gently, as she always did when
sleeping on her back, one hand on her navel, the other behind her head.
The night was bright; the clouds swirled in tiers, masses of cotton wool
clambering over each other. He recalled how once, not that long ago,
they lay together like this and Megi, stretching out her arm, had pointed
to a gap in the clouds and said, "If I were a bird, I'd pierce that hole…"

It had excited him at the time; it was something new. When they
had met, she didn't belong to the so-called easy girls. He knew from
friends that she hadn't had many boys before he came along; it took a
long while for her to decide to go to bed with anyone. He'd asked her
about it once, used as he was to easygoing girlfriends in England, France,
Sweden and Spain. She'd explained something in a roundabout way
about her sense of self having been childish for a long time and having
instinctively protected it from criticism or attempts to dominate it; that
she preferred to mean a great deal to a few than nothing to many.

She had, in his opinion, been a little stiff in bed as a twenty-something,
and motherhood had turned her into an almost prudish lover. She only
changed when going back to work after having Antosia. He'd sensed
she really was aroused by sex. He'd even asked her what had happened.
She'd replied that she felt her otherness, her boundaries and was finally
ready to transgress them.

Jonathan buried himself in the sheets but his head, instead of hum-
ming with sleep, was getting lighter. He sighed and reached for the
notebook next to their bed. He might as well make use of the time to plan
a schedule for his writing course. He was to present it at the beginning

of August, a month before sessions started. Cecile Lefebure had given him a free hand in the choice of subject.

'"The semantics of love', he scribbled. A moment later, he crossed out the quotation marks and put the notebook aside. He slipped out from beneath the duvet, crept into the hallway and wrote, this time on his cell, "Will you meet me, beautiful?"

A week later he drove Megi to the airport. The road led past the barrack-like buildings of NATO with its flags fluttering in front. Before they reached the underground parking garage, the road climbed up and they could see the tails of parked airplanes.

"Have you got your passport?" asked Jonathan, switching off the engine.

"Yes," replied Megi, unfastening her seat belt.

"Wallet?"

"Purse."

"Cell phone?"

"And a pair of warm panties." She laughed. "That's what my granny used to ask before any trip. She even managed to accost you once, do you remember? And you still married me."

A moment later she added impatiently: "So I've got my underwear then. My thongs…"

Jonathan still didn't say anything. It was dark in the car; he couldn't quite see her face. A sense of otherness hung in the air for a while, stirring the tip of his cock. He moved closer to her when suddenly the lights of an approaching car lit up the interior of the Toyota and he saw the familiar eyes of his wife in front of him.

"You're going to be late," he muttered and climbed out.

When he returned to the parking garage alone, a message beeped on his cell. His mouth instantly grew dry with emotion but it was only a text from Megi: "Plane full of priests. Think they'll bring me bad luck?" "It's nuns who bring bad luck," he wrote. "Men's eternal fear of women," the reply came back, with a smiling face attached.

Waiting for the babysitter, Jonathan tried to take notes for his writing course but couldn't concentrate. Sentences gave way under the pressure of thinking, the children made a racket and Megi had already phoned three times asking about some trivialities, quite as though she were keeping an eye on him at a distance.

Jonathan pulled out his phone and once again read Andrea's message – she was waiting for him on Saint-Boniface Square. He needed to leave in ten minutes but the babysitter had still not arrived. He brushed his teeth for the second time, went back downstairs, and started reading.

Anaïs Nin was to be an important figure in his course so he was going through her *Diaries* again. *As a child I was really worried when I found out we have only one life*, he read. *I wanted to compensate for this by multiplying my experiences.*

"Will you play Yu-gi-o with me?" Tomaszek rested his elbow on Jonathan's knee. The four-year-old body radiated a puppy-like expression, knew nothing of conventional distance and, with its gestures, showed how strongly tied it was to the bodies of its parents.

Jonathan ruffled his blond hair.

"There's something I've got to do. Ask Antosia."

"Tosia!" yelled Tomaszek. "Will you play with me?"

Jonathan hunched in on himself. He shouldn't be going to see her, giving his children the slip in order to meet a woman he didn't know. He had such a wonderful family, a great wife – that ought to be enough. He raised the book to his eyes and they fell on the text: ... *compensate for this by multiplying my experiences.*

"You've got three lives left," Antosia haughtily informed her brother over the cards.

Tomaszek groaned and thumped his elbows on the table. Jonathan looked at his son with compassion. Antosia was a ruthless player, didn't allow anyone any handicaps. He returned to his reading: ... *When I was happy, in a state of euphoria, as always at the beginning of love, I felt I had received the gift of survival...*

"There, I didn't die!" Tomaszek howled nearby.

... *in the fullness of many elements....* Jonathan read to the end before closing the book, resigned.

He remembered the details of his first *tête-à-tête* with Andrea: the photograph of a bagel and cappuccino behind the window of the café, on a level with the image of froth, a fly buzzing, trapped behind the glass; an old man having difficulty opening his trunk, a beggar with a dog.

Jonathan was on his way to his rendezvous and the treadmill of the pavement was fleeing from beneath his feet. The reverse gear of common sense grated in his head but his legs gathered speed. Within, born from self-hatred, a new life was sprouting.

At last, the church. Despite the darkness, he caught sight of her at once.

She tasted of cool fruit.

# 8

WAKING ON THE CUSP of night and day usually swept away any useful thoughts and left shreds of panic – the heating was malfunctioning, his son might be cold on his school trip, his daughter might fall for some dickhead in the future. The flutter of such thoughts blackened the hours between four and six in the morning when Jonathan would fall into a delicious snooze, interrupted three-quarters of an hour later by the sound of the alarm clock.

That summer, his waking up reminded him of Christmas when he was still a child – the gnawing anticipation, dreams swirling in the imagination of uninhibited reality. He was so excited that even though he tried to close his eyes, he couldn't. He got up and silently, so as not to wake the household, crept downstairs where his present awaited – a text from Andrea.

He'd grown dependent on seeing the little envelopes flashing on his cell, waited for them day and night; his mouth grew dry when he saw them and his hands shook. In the evenings, he waited for his wife to go to bed, then sat on the sofa and sent messages from the darkened room. In the mornings, he found it hard to wake up and swayed on his bed, his sleepy eyes roaming over the photograph on the wall, which he'd taken on his visit to Gotland with Petra. A house as crooked as the Tower of Pisa – he'd recorded it at the last moment. When they'd returned a year later, the house was no longer there.

At night, Andrea wrote: "You have the code to enter my dreams. . . ."

"Can I enter them as I stand?" he wrote back.

"And are you standing…?

"In my boxer shorts."

"To attention?"

"Straight as a rod. For you."

He curled up on the edge of his bed, in the morning. The glass over the Gotland photograph reflected a red tile from the apartment roof opposite. The loft window always opened at the same time, someone would lean out, start to bustle around, and soon the shape of another head would appear. Jonathan knew what was coming: as he climbed into his car with the children to take them to school, the neighbors, the couple opposite, would stride off to work in their suits.

It was practically all women at the first session of his creative writing class.

The older ones sat in a group by the door, the younger at the head of the long table by the window. The two men – one a balding thirtysomething, the other gray-haired – sat a fair distance from each other.

Cecile introduced Jonathan: the author of three books, a journalist with a degree in literature, a Pole who'd gone to school in England, studied in France and had been living in Brussels for the past few months. Jonathan nodded, his eyes on Cecile's long neck, adorned with a red necklace.

"…will in a moment introduce his schedule for the course in creative writing," she concluded.

Jonathan opened his laptop and rose to his feet.

"Good morning," he began. "I'm very pleased to be able to put forward a program that, at this stage of my life, I believe to be the most interesting. I hope it will also inspire you."

He looked around at the faces turned toward him. Attentive eyes and encouraging smiles; one of the young women kept nervously pushing back her hair as it fell over her forehead, the balding man mechanically drew circles on a sheet of paper.

"Before I introduce the subject of the course, I'd like to say a few words about myself."

He leaned over his laptop and the photograph of a gap-toothed little boy appeared on the white screen behind him. The older women laughed, the younger ones exchanged glances. The men looked at Jonathan questioningly.

"Thank you for the excellent introduction." He turned to Cecile. "After so many kind words all I can add is that... the lad behind me is also me."

The women smiled, the older man adjusted his glasses. Jonathan pointed behind and said: "I had fewer teeth ... "

They laughed; the thirtysomething put down his pen.

"... and fewer nasty experiences. Drugs, of course." He waited for them to relax completely, then grew serious. "But I hold on to this photograph and, what's more, look at it sometimes. Why? Because so much is happening around us. We rush to work in the morning, to collect the children in the afternoon, do the shopping on Saturday, organize family outings on Sunday. Or we feed the cats and stress about foreign language exams. From time to time we meet people we really like. Too rarely. Just as we all too rarely calmly breathe the air that reminds us of past holidays, too rarely do we simply sit and gaze aimlessly..."

He cast his eyes over the gathering; they were listening to his every word.

"I believe it's important," he continued, pointing at the smiling, gap-toothed boy behind him, "not to lose sight of oneself. And in writing, that, I believe, is what's most important."


"Two beers on Luxembourg Square?"

"I don't know what time Megi ..." began Jonathan.

"Three beers." Stefan's voice sounded decisive. "Come earlier and you'll make it for happy hour, beer's half price."

Luxembourg Square, a cosy square surrounded by low-rise buildings, was crammed with office workers. Black specks in suits moved around between tables and trampled the scrap of lawn which had automatically become the smoking area. Jonathan locked his bike and made his way to O'Farrell's.

Stefan, who, judging by his spaced-out eyes and gargantuan smile, must have drunk a fair amount, edged closer to his friend.

"You know Rafał, the last party was at his place."

Jonathan nodded.

"Yes, he came to dinner. When you weren't there." Jonathan tried to make it sound like a reproach.

"His wife's terrible." The drunken "sss" drew the attention of the other customers.

"What's that?" Przemek leaned over toward him.

Jonathan remembered how he had tried to make fun of Przemek, saying that, professional or not, he thought the man was slippery. He teased Megi because he knew Przemek was after her, but she was annoyed when Jonathan made fun of her new colleagues. With his perfect English and French, he had no idea – in her opinion – what it was like to be constantly accosted by colleagues "from the West" about where to find a "cheap Polish housecleaner." "You don't know what it feels like when they say Poles can be intelligent, too." She was furious. "It's covert racism!" Which was why she was all the more impressed when Poles consistently and obstinately climbed the Commission ladder.

Jonathan sympathized with her patriotism but couldn't work up any enthusiasm for Przemek. "He's the sort of person who sees life as a transaction," he argued.

"What's terrible?" Now Rafał, too, was leaning toward them.

Stefan opened his mouth but Jonathan gave him a warning tap on the shoulder.

"He doesn't know what to say," he winked at the others.

"I'm celebrating my birthday next Saturday," the Indian woman sitting diagonally opposite said. "Will you drop in?"

"Can I bring someone?" sputtered Stefan.

"Of course you can. I'd like to meet your wife."

"Wife?" Stefan's finger shot up. "What the hell are wives for?"

Jonathan reached for the peanuts and caught his sleeve on Rafał's glass. The beer spilled in a frothy puddle.

"Sorry, I'm terribly sorry," Jonathan pleaded as he got to his feet. "I'll call the waitress. Stefan, we're going!"

Jonathan struggled across half the city with a drunkard and a bicycle but, finally, managed to deliver Stefan home. Freed from the weight of his friend's body, he felt surprisingly unsteady on his feet, as if standing on rickety scaffolding. And what if both of them were going through a stage of accosting younger women? Every man at some point experienced the irrational fear that he might not get it up one day, but did the way they were behaving mean that the serpent of anxiety had slipped from their minds to their bodies?

He mounted his bike and pushed at the pedals. He rode clumsily, uncertain whether it was the effect of the beer or the vision that he was fleeing: he and Stefan, their shoes and false teeth highly polished, cravats around their necks, sitting in a sanatorium and boasting about the number of lovers they'd gone through while they still could …

When Megi left for Luxembourg on business, Jonathan already had a babysitter lined up. It was only so that he could go to the gym to get the strength for a Sunday full of paternal duties, he repeated to himself. He even took his gym gear but, spraying himself with his favorite scent, he no longer deluded himself – his body knew perfectly well what it wanted. He left, waving goodbye to Antosia and Tomaszek, unable to force himself to give them a hug. He was leaving them, going to Andrea. He felt contaminated.

There was a smell of incense in the church, candles blazed, but the pews were empty. Jonathan grew apprehensive. He had walked with a sure step but, in his mind, saw himself going home. Over the swirl of uncertainty, fear, excitement, and lust drifted the rhetorical question, "What for? What for?" But now, when Andrea had not come, he desired her with childish greed.

She emerged from the shadows of a pillar and a wave of heat ran through him as though he were a teenager. A few minutes later they were driving through the city in solemn silence. Jonathan had imagined many times what they'd do if an opportunity like this finally arose – Simon gone to England, Megi staying the night in Luxembourg. And now his fantasies dissolved, the glow of text messages extinguished. Erotic anticipation had turned into a barrier between driver and passenger.

He didn't try to slip his hand beneath Andrea's skirt. This was entirely unlike the times they'd met over the past weeks when, drunk with frustration, they'd caressed each other in churches, back streets and empty parking lots. Now, she stared at the passing brasseries while he, with the care of an old man, drove the car across the roundabouts of Ixelles.

Entering Andrea's apartment, Jonathan was struck by the smell of Simon's cigars and the gnawing thought that he'd never yet been unfaithful to Megi. Sometimes they attracted each other, sometimes repulsed, but until now he'd never gone with another woman, even though opportunities had arisen.

He stood there as if in a waiting room, shifting from foot to foot. Suddenly he felt Andrea's fingers on his lips – and sucked them with the instinct of a newborn baby. She was familiar, tasted like a wild apple; she was unknown, the tart smell of her perfume excited him. Her lips were full, moist, her pussy warm.

She drew him onto her – for a brief moment they were still separate beings – but then Andrea wrapped her legs around his hips. Listening to her guttural groans, Jonathan climaxed and in his head clattered the startling thought, "What a relief, what a relief…!"

# 9

THE SECOND LESSON in creative writing was like the first day of school. Grown-up pupils pulled out their notebooks or brand new exercise books when Jonathan entered; they listened attentively and jotted down a reading list. He gave them homework – they were to dig out their oldest memories of love.

On his way back, he breathed in the warm smell of the city. The arch in Cinquantenaire Park blazed in the light of the setting sun. Erected in triumph at Belgium's conquest of the Congo, its symbolism reminded him of the Palace of Culture in Warsaw but was aesthetically far more pleasing than the Russian gift. Perhaps because the history of Belgium meant little to him.

He reached Merode roundabout and walked toward the park. Cars sped along the tunnel beneath him. They were going toward the arch but never reached it; they didn't spring from the tunnel until past the Schuman roundabout. On the square by the arch, some Arabs were testing the power of their mopeds. The room of students flashed in front of Jonathan's eyes again, giving him an instinctive feeling of contentment. Something told him he had drawn them in, that he was going to succeed in picking out, from the skeins of their emotions and the density of their patterns, the threads of the stories they were determined to spin.

He didn't get his hopes up that there might be a real writer in the group. To him, they looked more like people who wanted to write about what hurt them. He suspected they'd cry with anger if personal fragments didn't fit in with their work, but such were beginnings. That was why he had immediately placed a mirror in front of them – their own memories. The sooner they began to delve into themselves, the better. Best they began that very day, in the enthusiasm of their September start.

He entered the park. Trees muffled the din of the mopeds; birds rounded off their conversations before the fall of dusk. His phone vibrated with two text messages, one after the other. "How did it go?" and "I long for your hands... I want them on my hips." He immediately replied, "I'd take your hips and lower them on me."

After his first night with Andrea, when he got home in the morning, the nanny leapt from the sofa, her hair dishevelled. He paid her and peeped in on the children. Tomaszek was asleep with arms outspread trustingly; Antosia was on her side, collected and intent, even in sleep. Jonathan went down to the kitchen and poured himself a whisky. He rarely did so; Megi didn't like alcohol on his breath at night. But his wife wasn't there now, not in the house, not in his thoughts. His skin, clothes, and hair smelled of Andrea; his thoughts clung to her, danced around the moments spent together, stroked that other reality.

He was surprised not to have a mental hangover. First times tend to be disconcerting, which was why he sometimes ended up that way. With Petra it had been different, and then with Megi. And now with Andrea. Their moves, which that night had replaced the web of meanings spun by text messages, were simpler than words but didn't seem awkward to them. Thanks to the haze of enchantment that engulfed them from that first, accidental kiss, they lay together unashamed.

He knocked back the rest of the whisky and smiled at his reflection in the kitchen window. He hoped Andrea felt the same – tingling in the tiniest parts of the body and corners of the mind, excitement that was not relieved by orgasm. Although he'd had her four times that night, he was still burning with desire to be with her.

He went to bed and fell into a shallow sleep, longing for their recent closeness. He awoke in the delirium of memory: her arching hips, his intoxication as he climaxed, the taste of Andrea's lips, those above and below. The following day he was still elated by the electrifying recollection.

It wasn't until Megi returned that he took fright. Because although he'd slipped back into every day life with his usual facial expressions – grimacing in anger as before at the children's disobedience, the windshield wiper not working in the Toyota or the long list of shopping – he was someone else after that night in Ixelles. His body was now entangled with another body. He had another woman. Their night, the hours of deep penetration and provocatively slow nearness, made Andrea seem no further than a centimeter away in his thoughts.

# 10

AFTER FOUR DAYS of her cousin and husband staying with them, Jonathan realized Megi felt like biting someone. It was not that she disliked Adelka. They were more or less the same age, the children got on somehow – especially ten-year-old Paula and the slightly younger Antosia – while the husband was what was called a nice guy. But when they'd announced their arrival, Megi – who in the past would have been pleased that her relatives had forgiven them for "leaving their homeland,"proof of which were the emissaries – was on edge and close to being rude.

"It's understandable," Jonathan reassured her as, locked in their room, they ignored the morning bustle as their guests prepared to go sightseeing. "This is your daily life, work, family. You get up at six every morning while they've just come to laze around."

"But she's my cousin. What's suddenly made me like this," said Megi, wrapping the duvet around her.

"Calm down, they're leaving in two days."

"Oh God, two more days!"

Jonathan laughed, then immediately turned serious. Megi really was heated up. Hardly surprising: the move, a new job, new colleagues, stacks of migration documents to fill in and formalities to sort out, all this in at least two languages – and now guests!

"As it is, I admire you," he said. "I've always admired you. You've got so much patience with people."

"Even with Aunt Barbara!"

Jonathan nodded. He'd observed Megi struggling with herself for years. He didn't really know how to help because he didn't like analyzing other people's personalities or individual behavior. Even in his stories he adhered to a behaviorist view. He didn't make notes about his characters' traits; if a hare or elephant got mixed up in something, it came from the story.

Jonathan preferred to think in images about people around him, which is why a scene from ten years ago now appeared in front of his eyes: Megi – tall, slim, running about carrying plates, unaware of the sexy sway of her hips. It had been a couple of weeks after their wedding, and Megi – brought up without a father, according to her relatives – had insisted on making dinner for them.

Jonathan couldn't tear his eyes away from her and finally grabbed her in the kitchen, slipping his hand beneath her blouse. She scolded him and he looked at her, astounded. He'd fallen in love with a great girl brought up by strong, wise women, and here was this little bourgeoise, worried that Aunt Barbara was grumbling about the veal!

For a while Megi had scrupulously remembered the name days of her uncles and aunts, and even her mother, whom the family had crossed off because she'd dared to get a divorce. They'd been prepared to accept her now – until Aunt Barbara tried to introduce her to her daughter's mother-in-law as a widow. "I'm a divorcee," Megi's mother had corrected her. What was worse, when asked when she was going to marry her fiancé, she'd asked, "Which one?"

Jonathan, who was also "stranded" – his mother had married again and his father was living with another woman – adored his mother-in-law and wouldn't let himself be carried away by his wife's romantic visions of the supportive clan. He'd decided to wait out the period of heightened socialising that the wedding had brought down on Megi. To expect a group of people tied by blood always to stand like a wall behind them was, he believed, childish. He was right. A wall did quickly spring up but between them and her relatives. Jonathan's and Megi's absence at a cousin's wedding, belated greetings, an inappropriate present, not calling back or calling at the wrong moment – and the rubbish already began to stack up.

He now stroked Megi's fair hair. He'd fallen in love with her because she was beautiful and had the makings of an individual, not a cog in a mixer, blending family celebrations.

"Even with Aunt Barbara," he repeated after her.

"Shhh, they'll realize we're not asleep." She put her hand over his mouth just as Adelka's face appeared in the door.

"Magda dear, where is the colander with the small holes? So, off in forty minutes, are we?"

Adelka found Grand Place small while Robert paid no attention to the buildings because he was telling Jonathan about the sick system of promoting employees in his bank.

"If he got a new Toyota Picasso at the start why can't I choose a car? Why do I have to drive around in what's practically a wreck?"

"Look at this Art Nouveau building." Megi indicated the narrow building with windows shaped like portholes covered in seaweed.

"It must be dark in there," Adelka pondered. "Italy's got better ones but you can't really live in them either. Stucco's all well and good but I need a new bathroom. Oh, I didn't tell you in the end about the tiles Robert's found for our kitchen! You know how much they cost?"

"There's a very good café here. Shall we go for a coffee?" Jonathan suggested, catching his wife's grateful eye.

They returned from dinner just before midnight. Jonathan avoided the tunnels so as to show his guests the Avenue Louise lit up.

"Chanel," squealed Adelka in the back. "And Dior!"

"That's all women think about," muttered Robert, leaning over to Jonathan. "So when are you going back?"

"In about ten minutes?"

"I'm talking about your country."

"Poland? But we've only just left!"

"You're right, must make some money to take back with you."

"I don't want to go back," Jonathan let slip. "Well, certainly not now anyway."

"Look, Adelka, Tommy Hilfiger." Megi's voice reached them.

"Well, brother, you're lucky your wife brought you here, then," Robert said, bridling.

When they got back, the babysitter, exhausted with looking after the three children, needed someone to drive her home.

"I'll go," Jonathan was quick to volunteer.

He dropped the girl at the seedy end of rue Dansaert, which was famous for its expensive shops, and turned back to the city center. His cell beeped – he was to be in Ixelles within ten minutes. He made a sharp turn right.

He'd be late coming home. What would he tell his wife? He'd think of something. That there was a traffic jam. Or a detour. That he'd got lost – after all, he didn't know the city all that well yet. "Sorry, Megi, I got lost," he repeated as he sped over the limit to Andrea.

On Sunday, Megi drove their guests to the airport while Jonathan gave the children their supper and put them to bed. Once they were asleep he stretched out on the bed in the conjugal bedroom and gazed at the sky through the loft window. Two stars shone brightly, moved toward each other – no, they were airplanes.

He closed his eyes. Last night's quick rendezvous with Andrea, and then the next; lust pressed them more than time. She'd pulled a condom on to him, murmuring with feigned gravity, "Securing a condom is probably more effective on a cock that's thicker at the base, not one shaped like a baseball bat."

They'd made love with such force she'd scratched his sides with her fingernails. With her, he discovered new depths of erotic imagination; he wanted things that had never entered his mind before. Instead of pinning reality down with "to do" notes, he jotted down ideas in his memory to try out with Andrea. She was his inspiration, so unremitting that he started to wear his shirts pulled out over his trousers in order to hide his frequent erections.

The church bells chimed. They arranged to meet in churches because hardly anybody went there apart from them. The temples of their love. They would meet there and then go to her place. Even now, on hearing the bells, the head of his cock stirred gently in his trousers.

He reached for his notebook to make some notes for his course but again he was distracted by the recollection of how they'd fucked on the leather sofa in Andrea's apartment. She hadn't wanted to make love to him in the bedroom and he hadn't insisted – the smell of Simon might have had an adverse effect on his erection.

When she returned from the airport, Megi sat on the edge of the bed and smoothed the bedspread.

"You know, my grandmother used to treat the marital bed with great respect?"

"Your grandmother?" Jonathan's eyebrows shot up. "That somehow doesn't fit with her. She was no traditionalist."

"I told her once that a friend of mine from school was having an affair with a married man and they met at his place. And Granny replied, "In the same bed as the other woman?" And I said, "Granny. She's having an affair with a married man. Do you understand?" To which Granny responded, "Yes, she is. But in the marital bed! Can't they do it somewhere else?""

Jonathan put his notes aside. Megi had started unfastening her blouse seductively – she must have seen the cock promisingly stiff in his trousers. She slipped her bra straps down but the more naked she was, the further he retreated into himself. He came, finally, despairingly, with his face hidden in her bust.

# 11

THE APPLES stood in a black bowl, their red skins gleaming. The richness of their color came from the rays of the setting September sun, which peeped into the room where Jonathan held his course. The stripes on the bowl spiralled to infinity and were as effective as a professional hypnotist. With difficulty, Jonathan tore his eyes away from them and looked at the seated group.

Their international character reflected the variety of Brussels's inhabitants. Of different races, cultures, descent, they all came from somewhere else; most of them were still en route. They had stopped here for a year or twenty; time would show whether they'd be able to give up further wandering and decide to set down roots.

Jonathan pushed the list aside; he knew their names by heart.

"Geert," he turned to the gray-haired man dressed in a jacket with beige patches at the elbows. "I wonder why you write."

Geert blinked and adjusted himself on the chair; his wire-framed glasses made him appear concerned.

"Why do I write?" he repeated like a child wanting to gain time. "Ehhh... That's a difficult question."

"A bit like asking, 'What's your favorite book?'" The black British woman, Kitty, joined in. She was plump, her tight black curls swirled beneath a colorful headscarf; the green eyes set in a dark face were surprising. "I never know what to say."

"Nor do I," agreed Ariane, an attractive German of over fifty. "Almost as bad as, 'What's your favorite color?'"

"Black," muttered Geert. "Why do I write... Because there's a story I want to write. Have to."

"It's important for you, is it?" asked Jonathan.

"Yes. Very... For me, that is, because I don't know what..."

"Why is it important?"

"I don't know. It's hard to say in a couple of words." Geert now spoke faster. "It's important because in a way it's there... That is, somehow I keep dwelling on it." He looked helplessly around at the gathered group. "It's the base on which I built the rest."

"The rest? Other stories?"

"My life."

A steady tapping could be heard in the silence – a fat autumn fly bounced against the window. Thirty-year-old Jean-Pierre, sitting on the other side of the tables, sprawled out on his chair, frowned in concentration. The fly took off and collided with his bald pate.

Geert sat with lowered head. Jonathan opened his mouth but Ariane was there before him.

"I can understand that perfectly well," she told Geert, who raised his worried eyes to her. "My story's also got layers that I want to write down. My daughters say I've lived through a lot and am very good at talking about it. But they don't have the time to listen. They say I should write it all down. I've even started doing so but it's an uphill struggle. I used to be able to write quite well – got top marks at school – but then, working for so many years as an architect, my pen got rusty."

"You want to get going as a writer?" prompted Jonathan.

"Refresh my skill." He noticed that her French was precise, avoided vulgar influences. "Somehow I've got to put across what happened. There are so many stories."

She laughed, revealing her even teeth. Geert blinked; Jean-Pierre adjusted himself on his chair. Jonathan stopped himself from laughing at the sight of the males instinctively reacting to Ariane's sexy smile.

At this relaxed moment, Geert's confession seemed out of place.

"I have only one story."

"And I don't have any," Kitty interrupted. She had a rattling accent; Jonathan automatically scanned England in his head, searching for the girl's roots. "Fiction puts me off."

"Why?"

"I used to be a journalist," sighed Kitty. "I worked in a press agency first, then on a daily paper. There's a terrible emphasis on facts there."

"And truth." Jean-Pierre draped himself over his chair in a Byronic pose.

"Not necessarily." Kitty frowned.

"You've had enough of facts?" Jonathan broke in.

"I want to slow down. I adore Virginia Woolf. I can read her for hours. *The Waves* or *Mrs Dalloway*, it's all the same. In it, a day seems like an eternity."

"And eternity seems like a day," finished Nora, the oldest of the participants.

"Yes." Kitty studied Nora carefully and repeated, "Yes."

Jonathan looked at those gathered. There was a silence between them – one that was not embarrassing, since it reflected common thought. When Jean-Pierre started to wriggle restlessly in his chair, Jonathan pointed to the bowl.

"Help yourselves to the apples. They're good for concentration."

They ate, exchanging remarks that grew less and less formal, got to know each other. There was laughter first on one side of the table, then on the other; the anxious Geert looked at Ariane with increasing confidence, Jean-Pierre gesticulated in Kitty's direction. A moment later, he looked around for a trash can. Not seeing one, he glanced enquiringly at Jonathan.

"Exactly," said Jonathan. "The apple cores."

They looked at him curiously.

"Take a good look at their shape."

Ariane swept her eyes over the others, joined in embarrassment; Geert bestowed on her a saddened gaze. Jonathan laughed.

"You must think I'm the crazy Miss Trelawney, if you've read *Harry Potter*. You're right, a core is a little like tea leaves, but see for yourselves the shapes you've created."

Jean-Pierre rested his back against his chair and was the first to stretch out his hand with the apple core. A moment later it was Kitty with the expression, "What the hell!" Before a minute was up, everyone was examining what remained of their apples, exchanging comments and giggling nervously. Jonathan leaned over the cores with childish curiosity.

"One side bitten right down, the other not touched, beautiful, Geert. And here? The whole apple bitten round but you can't see the seeds. While here, we have a fine piece of work, gnawed right through, pedantically..." He went on while they laughed and exchanged remarks.

Finally, he pulled himself up straight and stood behind the table.

"That was simply a quick hands-on lesson, intended to enable us to see how we get to the center."

"I didn't get there. I only ate the skin!" Jean-Pierre raised his hand.

"And that's the next question: what, for each of us, constitutes the center?"

An hour later, Jonathan was in the park, kissing Andrea's lips. Their bench was tucked away; the last rays of sun slid down the trunks of the chestnut trees. He took her face in his hands; they sat now, forehead against forehead, the girl's eyes full of sun, almost amber.

He went home thinking about Andrea, moved and aroused.

The sight of Megi bustling about, in turn, awoke in him a growing tide of tenderness. He helped her out by serving supper, aided Antosia with her homework, and put the children to bed.

During the night, the warmth of her body in the dark, and an erection that again appeared at the recollection of his meeting with Andrea that day, made him press his hips against his wife's buttocks without thinking. Willingly, she stuck out her backside and he entered her. Instead of Megi's back he saw Andrea's eyes before him, lit by the remains of the sun. He felt himself growing flaccid, so he quickened his pace. Megi arched her back; tears gathered in the corners of his eyes. He was giving her remnants – his woman and best friend; instead of an apple he was pressing a core into her.

The week before Christmas, Megi's colleagues from work organized a party that Jonathan called a Commission Christmas party. He didn't quite know why he had to go to it – he was neither an official nor a Catholic.

Megi, who had been baptized, received first Holy Communion, and been confirmed, had become increasingly independent in her outlook as the years passed; Aunt Barbara called it "leaving the Church." Megi needed the elevation of religion, jokingly calling it "a hunger for mysterium," but had ceased to find herself within the Catholic Church. The clergy irritated her; sermons didn't interest her; and the chasm between her and the community of childless men continued to surprise her.

They had thought that in Brussels, a city with a hodgepodge of denominations in an otherwise lay country, their religious beliefs wouldn't matter. They were happy not to have faced the dilemma of their friends who'd remained in Poland – whether to send their children to religious lessons simply to stop them from feeling like outsiders. The communist schizophrenia, where one thing was said at school and another at home, was repeated in their children's generation. "As if the Polish mentality couldn't stand life without authorities." Megi screwed up her face. "As if the people were writing a collective dissertation where nothing that's theirs comes from them, it's all 'op. cit.' and 'ibid.'"

They walked now lost in thought, Jonathan squeezed into a black jacket, Megi with an angry expression. From the frying pan into the fire – in Brussels, too, their compatriots were drawn to the Church. Office workers sang in choirs, their wives taught religion, and their sons served as altar boys.

"I wonder what their daughters do," muttered Megi.

"Whose daughters?" Jonathan came to.

"Remember confession? A childhood nightmare! The best way to shrink the shoots of budding womanhood."

"Then why the hell are we going there?" Jonathan stopped short.

"I've told you a hundred times," she hissed impatiently. "I've had enough questions about why I don't go to Mass! How many times can I say I'm unpacking crates?"

"Can't you tell them you're a nonbeliever?" asked Jonathan, but Megi ignored him.

The host of the Christmas party, Ludwik, greeted them at the door. Jonathan noticed that he leaned to one side, which made him look subservient but could have been the result of neglected scoliosis.

"We already know each other." Ludwik shook Jonathan's hand when the latter tried to introduce himself.

The Christmas dishes were topped with a typical parsley garnish. Nobody had touched the food yet; they all stood around with glasses in their hands. Rafał and Martyna were deep in conversation with people Jonathan didn't know. Przemek was gazing across the room at Megi with genuine admiration.

Somewhere at the side Jonathan heard Stefan pontificating. He noticed, from a distance, that he was adamantly gesticulating at a pretty girl. Monika was nowhere in sight. Jonathan hesitated but Stefan beckoned for him to come.

"Meet Victoria."

"Jonathan!" He heard before he managed to extend his hand to the girl.

Monika stood in front of him. The black dress, short hair dyed red, and the dark shawl over her shoulders made Jonathan greet her like an aunt he'd not seen for a long time. He asked after the children and Monika answered with a few smooth sentences. As usual, she had phrases suitable for the occasion at hand; listening to her, Jonathan thought that Megi was right when she called Monika a black hole – topics, devoid of angles, were sucked into conversational nothingness in a flash. "If one were to believe what she says," he reflected, watching Monika's lips moving, "one would think there's no friction in her life." He nevertheless generally defended Monika when anyone criticized her in public. Beneath the ready-made formulae he saw the girl he'd known for ten years and who had once come to him, lugging a suitcase in one hand and holding a baby in the other. That one and only time Jonathan had been forced to mediate between her and Stefan. Before a year had been out, Franek was born.

"Stefan, may I?" Monika smiled at Jonathan, and pulled her husband aside.

Jonathan glanced at Victoria standing next to him with a hesitant smile.

"What do you do?" Desperately, he filled the awkward silence.

"I'm a *fonctionnaire*. I work with..." For a while, she went on about her position and about the connections between people he didn't know and, since he didn't pick up these threads, she grew bored of him. Desperately, he tried to throw the ball into another court.

"Have you read *The Arrangement* by Elia Kazan?"

"Was that on the reading list?"

When Stefan appeared with neither glass nor wife, Victoria was no longer there.

"What's a *fonctionnaire*?" asked Jonathan. Coming from him the word sounded like the name of an insect repellent.

"A position in the Commission for which you have to ..." began Stefan. Jonathan stood with the face of someone who's had a crowbar forced into his brain, making the mechanism grind to a halt. In the end, Stefan waved it aside and went to get something to eat; Jonathan followed him. But on the way he stopped short – he had caught sight of Andrea.

She was standing in the door, eyeing the place and the gathering people. She hadn't exposed her legs or bust yet there was, as usual, something intense about her appearance that turned heads. Jonathan wondered by what miracle such a woman had noticed him. Before he had time to move in her direction, she was sucked into the circle standing nearest the door. Regret racked him. He couldn't go up to her, kiss her, introduce her; he could only watch from afar as she stood there unattainable – and alone. Simon had gone to England to visit his children before Christmas; Jonathan knew that better than anyone because just three hours ago he had made love to Andrea in her apartment.

When he finally managed to get to her, their host sprang up between them.

"Ludwik." She pecked him on the cheek, glancing over his shoulder at Jonathan.

Ludwik watchfully followed her eyes.

"I'd like you to meet Andrea Kunz," he said. "An excellent journalist working for Swedish television."

Jonathan's mouth grew dry. He had just caressed her yet he couldn't get rid of the feeling that was always with him when they were together – arousal and stage fright shook him even when they had worn themselves out with love.

"And this is Megi's husband," concluded Ludwik.

It was as if someone had struck Jonathan. Ludwik greeted other guests, introducing Andrea to them, while Jonathan turned away and started to study the apartment. The interior looked as if the owner had wanted to kill himself: white and beige cut through here and there with flashes of metal fittings and surfaces; everything closed, fitted, nothing protruding. "He must think that by getting rid of old dishcloths and shoving the rubbish into hermetic cupboards he's going to smooth out his own mucky insides," Jonathan thought vindictively and muttered to himself: "Perhaps the son-of-a-bitch hasn't got a soul."

"What's that?"

Megi was staring at him, half amused, half unsure whether she'd heard correctly.

"Want some fudge?" Jonathan answered with a question.

"Not now but thanks for buying it. You know how much I love it."

"Are you enjoying yourself?"

Megi shrugged.

"Day and night discussions about work. 'That document, Megi, which category did it belong to?'" She grimaced, parodying the way Przemek spoke. "'*White paper, yellow paper, non-paper?*' I want to go home!" she ended and slipped her hands around his waist, beneath his jacket.

Instead of returning the hug, Jonathan stiffened. Andrea was watching them above the guests' heads.

"I wonder where Simon is?" muttered Megi, following his gaze.

Andrea was now laughing with the rest of her crowd, throwing back her long, glistening hair.

Jonathan pushed Megi's hands down.

"Simon?" he repeated mechanically.

"Simon Lloyd, they came to our place, don't you remember? That's Andrea there, his woman, partner, or whatever they call her. It's hard to find a name for a concubine who's over thirty. Everything sounds so infantile. But they're quite a couple. Simon, well … And she, although no classical beauty, is as radiant as an icon. She has some sort of distinction, style. She's certainly not common."

"Let's go and eat something. Aren't you hungry?"

"I've already eaten. I'm going to say hello to her. Have a *kabanos*, they're pretty good." Megi kissed him on the cheek and made toward the circle where Andrea shone and which was mainly made up of men. Jonathan saw, from where he stood, that some of them reacted to Megi's appearance but a moment later all stared at Andrea again. "No one can share the spotlight with her," he thought with a strange pride yet simultaneous stab of disappointment that they weren't looking at his wife in the same way.

Without much thought, he pushed his way toward them.

"Simon?" Andrea was saying. "In England. Gone to visit his children."

"So you've got a free pad!" smiled Megi.

"What's that?" Andrea raised her eyebrows.

"It's a Polish saying. I meant that now you're alone you can lie in bed as long as you want and parade around in your pajamas. I envy you," sighed Megi. "I've not had the house to myself for years."

Andrea looked at her as if she hadn't understood that either.

"I'm going to get myself something to eat," she said after a while. "Can I bring you anything?"

"No, thank you, I've already eaten," Megi replied for the second time that evening.

Jonathan almost ran alongside the apartment façades. Street lights were reflected in the windows and in the stained-glass trimmings on doors that looked more like ornate church doorways than stairwells. Metal stirrups, which protruded from the walls and served for wiping shoes, assumed the forms of Art Nouveau. Pavements glinted with dampness; the first snowflakes of the winter stuck for a moment then instantly melted. Winter hung in the air but did not stay for long.

He turned into a one-way street and reached the military school. The cadets must have gone home for Christmas because the historic building stood in darkness; only the flags swayed lazily. He ran across the street to a fence. There was nobody there the day before Christmas

Eve; the arch towered over the silent park and the green parrots had hidden themselves away.

Jonathan left the playing field to the right, ran a few meters, and turned down a dark pathway leading beneath the arch. He stopped at an ancient chestnut tree and lowered Andrea's hood. The temptation grabbed him to kiss her with open eyes so that he could see her eyebrows, forehead, the snowflakes perched on her hood. He slipped his fingers beneath her hair and held her head. He wanted to suck in all of her, swaying with passion – in her, on her.

# 12

HE PASSED CHRISTMAS, which they spent in Poland, mainly in the company of his cell phone. The family discussed politics, not asking about their life in Brussels, and only occasionally, returning from the balcony where he'd slip out under the pretext of having a cigarette, did Jonathan hear Robert say that Belgian women were ugly and Adelka claim authoritatively that the clothes were too expensive. Megi compulsively looked after Antosia and Tomaszek, who were irritable because of the changes. Later, they distributed the presents they'd brought from Brussels and returned laden with gifts they'd received in return.

"Are we a couple of scout leaders or something?" moaned Megi the day before going back to Brussels. That evening her mother had taken the children to the theater, giving them unexpected freedom that they didn't know how to enjoy. "We rush around dealing with everything, look after the kids, and fake a smile. What's happened to wallowing in bed, eating mandarins, reading, making love?"

When they returned to Brussels, Megi ordained a real Christmas, as she called it. When he got back from the gym, Jonathan drew with Antosia and played with Lego with Tomaszek; in the evenings he and Megi listened to music or watched films.

"See how good this is? See?" Megi sat on the sofa, cracking nuts and radiating pride. She didn't put it into words but Jonathan suspected she was finding it hard not to say, "See? It's me who brought you here!"

The theme of the New Year's ball was decadence. Jonathan pushed the information out of his memory and on the morning of the last day of December bore the brunt of his wife's anger as she claimed she had reminded him numerous times. Jonathan was shaving when Megi knocked and walked into the bathroom; and was still naked with only the white shaving foam on his face when she blew up.

"I told you, reminded you, called, warned..." Megi yelled. Jonathan didn't say anything, just took sharper and sharper turns of the razor across his face until he exploded.

"You should have written me a note!"

"And what am I, some sort of mute that I've got to communicate with you in writing?"

Megi's face reflected in the mirror was crooked, and Jonathan thought that this was not a good morning.

"You know writing gets to me quicker," he tried to justify himself.

Megi threw her arms up and with a flourish rested them on her hips.

"Then it's just like work! So maybe you can go there instead of me, eh? People send each other notes in the Commission, didn't you know? So what sort of document am I to send you, *white paper, yellow paper*?"

"Best a *non-paper*," he growled and leaned over the sink to rinse the white mask off his face.

Megi fell silent, and Jonathan thought how uncomfortable he felt standing with his backside sticking out in front of an embittered woman. He was gripped by an irrational fear of being spanked.

"But you do realize," she said more calmly, "that something like that really does exist?"

He turned to her, water dripping from his face.

"What? Non-papers?"

"A non-paper is also a document." Megi tightened the cord of her dressing gown. "Even nondocuments are about something. So, since I told you a hundred times to hire a costume..."

Jonathan watched her lips moving at great speed and thought that this was a battle he'd lost even before starting. Not only had he forgotten about the fucking fancy dress but he was standing here stark naked. On top of that there was nothing at hand with which he could defend himself. Even his cudgel was useless – hanging there pitifully, reflected in the mirror, as crooked as his wife's face.

Andrea's red dress perfectly summed up the theme of the ball and her derisive eyes were the best counterpoint to it. Following her with his gaze, Jonathan subconsciously noted the number of men doing the same and the vigilant presence of Simon, who had his arm around his woman's waist. He looked tired and Jonathan almost felt sorry for him, but the redness of Andrea's dress was the stronger force.

The sight and smell of his lover made him dizzy and he lost his guard; he got carried away talking to her, brought her wine, followed her when she went to talk to someone, or stood and watched as she danced. Her hips moved in the same lazy way when she danced as they had so recently when she'd sat on him. She danced and he couldn't tear his eyes away from the sight; he saw nobody else, only those swaying hips of hers and her twinkling smile. And even though he knew that she was smiling to herself as she always did when she immersed herself in making love or dancing, in his eyes the entire room revolved around Andrea.

At one moment, she stretched her arms out to him, placed his hands on her hips and they twirled, lost in each others eyes – Simon, Megi, and all others had fallen from the red orbit.

The redness of the dress washed away the contours but didn't blur the picture. Martyna, her weasel-like eyes sparkling behind a carnival mask, drew on a cigarette as she peered into the room through the windows of the terrace.

"Have you seen Jonathan and Andrea?" she asked Monika. "What's going on between them?" Przemek, wearing the costume of a Turkish pasha, nudged Rafał who was busy fishing out a piece of carp from the platter.

"Poor Megi," lamented Martyna, passing Monika the cigarette lighter. "Maybe it's only a passing fancy," muttered Monika. Her corset kept slipping down so she had to grip the contraption and hoist it up.

The trainee who dreamt of opening a retro clothes shop stood in the kitchen doorway wearing the costume of an undressed pussycat. She attracted men's attention but only until Andrea, dancing with Jonathan now, appeared.

"Has she gone mad, she's got Simon!" The girl shook her head. "Perhaps she's drunk?"

"Who's drunk?" asked the Spaniard dressed as Zorro, struggling with a corkscrew.

"Pity poor old Simon," mumbled Rafał, carefully turning the sliver of carp around in his mouth. He wasn't dressed formally, having thought people weren't really going to dress up. "She was always like that, remember?" The eastern ornaments clattered as Przemek shrugged his shoulders and scrutinized the table, annoyed that he'd tried everything.

"But who is this guy to make Andrea want to dance with him like that?" The trainee touched her eyelashes to make sure they hadn't come unstuck. "He's only some writer, Megi's husband."

"We're going after the toast. I've got a flight tomorrow. I promised my wife I'd spend the weekend with them." The cork squeaked in the Spaniard's hands as he sweated beneath his cape.

"What a slut," stated Martyna, stamping the cigarette butt out on the terrace tiles. "She hasn't got any children so she's making the most of life." Monika blew smoke mixed with vapor toward the sky. The cork popped from the bottle and the Spaniard smiled roguishly beneath his moustache.

"A lot of guys have had her ..." Przemek stretched out his ring-covered hand for a pickled mushroom.

"You too?" asked Rafał placing a carp bone on his plate. Przemek-pasha laughed. "I don't like furniture from flea-markets or women past their prime."

"What are you staring at?" asked Stefan.

He'd just left the bathroom where he'd spent some time fishing out his monocle, which had fallen into the toilet bowl. He hadn't noticed that he'd accidentally opened the door when leaning over the toilet bowl and now looked around hoping nobody had witnessed this nineteenth-century dandy's humiliation.

"Sparks are flying between them!" Rafał put down his plate with what remained of the aspic.

"Sparks?" Stefan looked around.

The couple on the dance floor moved in an off hand manner that to them must have seemed smooth and graceful but to observers might have appeared obvious, blatant. Stefan carefully scanned the dancers and observers.

"They're drunk, that's all," he snorted disdainfully, wondering whether to insert the monocle back into his eye socket, but unable to bring himself to do so.

"You think so?" Przemek's eyebrows shot up. "I saw them walking down the street once suspiciously close to each other."

Stefan was more annoyed than he'd been a few minutes ago in the toilet.

"And Martyna told me that she once saw them leaving somewhere together, a church I think it was," added Rafał.

"Jonathan in a church?" Stefan wiped his brow with a napkin decorated with golden letters: *Happy New Year*. "He's an old atheist, even a chick like Andrea couldn't get him to go to one!"

Rafał laughed but Przemek froze with a strange expression on his face. Stefan followed his gaze – two feet away from them stood Megi. Her bobbed haircut was ideally suited to her Roaring Twenties costume but the golden cap, which until then had added a decadent charm, now looked like the tilted hat of a clown.

For a moment, nobody said anything. Only when a strange smile appeared on Rafał's face – something like an attempt to sympathize beneath which lay uncensored joy – did Megi turn and leave.

"Bloody hell," said Stefan.

"What's happened?" asked Martyna, joining them by the table.

Rafał leaned over to his wife's ear. Stefan made his way toward the dancers. He tapped Jonathan's shoulder and whispered something to him. As Jonathan went to where Megi had disappeared, Stefan walked Andrea to the terrace. He pulled some Gauloises from his frock coat and passed them to her, but she refused with a wave of her hand. He must have said something amusing because she burst into laughter, a little exaggerated.

"Her last fellow said she had a drink problem." Rafał lowered his voice as he poured himself more punch.

"Man problems, more like," muttered Martyna.

"Let it be. The girl's just got drunk, that's all." Monika waved it aside.

"She's one thing." Przemek adjusted the Turkish fez slipping down to his ear. "But that husband of Megi's! With a wife like that …"

Jonathan stood outside the toilet waiting for Megi to emerge. He stood close enough to hear her open the door but far enough not to have to explain why he was keeping an eye out for his wife.

When Stefan had warned him that Megi had heard something and wanted to go, he'd left Andrea and run after his wife, only to see her disappear behind the bathroom door. He knocked. "Engaged," came the answer.

She'd already been there for a good while as he stood outside, paralysed with regret and sadness. He wanted to hug her, explain everything. And kill those gossips. He glowered at the circle of Megi's colleagues – they were talking about them. A wave of anger surged over him and just as it had swelled so, unexpectedly, it began to subside – how could they help it, the poor bores? They had nothing better to do.

He had to explain everything to Megi. He had to tell her he didn't want any other woman except for her (which he didn't, other than Andrea). He simply had to say he'd got drunk.

*Megi stands in front of the sink and looks at the mirror cracked with age.*

*"Bloody hell!" She slaps the sink.*

*Her golden cap slips down to her eyes but all she can see is Andrea's dress; beneath her eyelids crumples the red mist of fury.*

*She wants to run out to them, catch the woman by that long mop of hers. That's what she wants to do, but she holds on to the sink, holds on with all her strength. Finally, she leans over it as if to vomit.*

*"Easy, easy." A voice in her speaks but soon grows silent as if it, too, was scared of Megi. Everybody ought to be scared of her, everybody! That whore, those gossips, Jonathan!*

*"Easy, easy," whispers Megi, as if she were steadying a horse. The beast in her still bridles, but a tiny bit less.*

*"Easy…" She hears her voice and slowly, very slowly, sits down on the closed toilet seat.*

*"When did it start?" She forces herself to think; the chronology is to help get a hold of what is seething within. "Is it because he's sitting at home with the kids and is bored?"*

*Images leap in front of her eyes. Megi on maternity leave, day and night at home; Jonathan at work or in the gym. Megi at the time: hips still narrow but a belly that after the birth resembles an elongated bread-bin suspended over her hips. Jonathan: accepts her body during the pregnancy and birth, but once she's a mother suddenly no longer wants her.*

*Another image: her aunt, staying with them for a few days and poking her nose into everything, points at the hook in the hall.*

*"Don't you think that's a good place for you to hang Jonathan's clothes?"*

*"What clothes?" Megi doesn't understand.*

*"For work. So they're there waiting for him in the morning. Shirt ironed, tie, trousers, socks ... "*

*"Pants."*

*"Underwear, certainly," says her aunt without a smile.*

*Next scene: Megi in a suit, already at work, slim again. The crop rotation of work–family suits her, independence carries her away. Men look at her, pick her up, a married woman, a rose without thorns, who can be had without responsibilities. They want her, many of them – except Jonathan.*

*Someone knocks at the bathroom door.*

*"Engaged," Megi answers back.*

*She places her hands on her skirt and sits on the loo like an old woman in a doctor's waiting room. And thinks about how the other guy had picked her up – or, in fact, she'd picked him up. Not long afterward Jonathan, too, had come back to her. When she got pregnant they decided Jonathan would stay at home with the child. But Jonathan couldn't bear it and chickened out of paternity leave.*

*Megi raises her hands. Something is tickling her and her face is still stiff and a little wet; she hadn't noticed the tears.*

*Jonathan ... When they do make love it's so good ...*

*Megi adjusts herself on the convex toilet lid. They've both changed; she, too, is no longer the twentysomething who is slightly rigid in bed, "likes" various positions in order to make herself more attractive to the boy. Now sex really does arouse her. So why is he now...? Why are they passing each other by again?*

*Or maybe it's not her body but something in her character that's started to repulse him? Maybe she overlooked his feelings, didn't notice on time that he didn't share her joy at being a parent? Maybe deep inside he remained still that other boy, in defiance of all those who – including her – had demanded he be enthusiastic about being a father. Had that been the beginning of their otherness, the tearing apart of the entity that had been put together during the first years of their relationship? Beginning... Does such a thing exist?*

*The music falls silent or seems to. A quiet voice whispers within, "But what, in fact, has happened? He got drunk, the woman led him on. And people gossip." Megi has heard a lot about Andrea in the Commission canteen – that she has guys on the side, that she doesn't want children, that she's a career woman, that she acts as if the older man isn't enough. That she's a whore.*

*Megi bends back her head. The apartments in Brussels, with their high ceilings edged with stucco, pride themselves in being old. She would also like to be like that some day.*

*Breathe in, breathe out, breathe in – nothing's happened – she's got to get rid of the thoughts flitting through her mind, dancing like ghastly butterflies.*

Jonathan stared at the bathroom door. How long could a woman spend fixing her make-up and brushing her hair? His wife's hairstyle was tidy as opposed to Andrea's hair, which was free to the elements; it was precisely this aspect of feigned neglect that drove him to frenzy.

Damn Megi's hairstyle! He had to convince her he was drunk.

"Megi." Seeing the door open, he rushed forward.

She didn't look at him but neither did she push him aside. Slowly, he took her by the hand; with the other, he raised her chin.

"I got drunk," he said with a foolish smile.

# 13

JONATHAN CLIMBED as though he were mounting the stairs of a lighthouse. Their house, attached on both sides to the neighboring houses, was like a tower, seductively pretty with its stairs like white teeth. Over the last few days he'd mounted the stairs so many times that his calves hurt. Meanwhile, his cell phone remained silent, hidden beneath the marital bed. Text messages arrived from Stefan, questions from his mother, an amusing remark from his father but, since the New Year's ball, nothing from Andrea.

Had he studied the messages he sent her, he would have realized he resembled himself from the final days of secondary school. He'd believed, at the time, that dignity came second to feelings and that the woman he loved would understand. Since then the notion of "the woman he loved" had evolved, stretched beyond mere desire. This was colored by the half-bitter, half-amused realization that there was no love without play, and not only foreplay.

Now he was behaving as though he were retarded. And, to his surprise, he sometimes found a masochistic pleasure in it. Up and down he went on a swing, throwing his legs out then drawing them back beneath the seat, his hands loosening their grip on the rope, a pulsating ball tightening then opening in his stomach. The movement robbed him of reason. Just as in childhood he had raced his friends, so now he felt he was swinging harder and harder, up and down.

While he kept checking whether the woman he loved had tossed him at least a few crumbs of reciprocated feelings, Megi was taking down the Christmas decorations with the children. They were having great fun as always. Ever since Jonathan had told them that in Sweden people sang a valedictory song to the tree, each year Antosia, Tomaszek, and Megi had tried to compose a song worthy of their Christmas tree. Jonathan went downstairs just when they'd given up, as usual, and began to howl *Wlazł kotek na płotek i mruga* (The cat has climbed the fence and sits winking), a popular Polish children's song. They giggled and the dry needles fell, shaken by their intertwined arms as they circled the tree.

"... sits winking!" yelled Tomaszek and tumbled over.

Megi halted to pick him up, herself weak with laughter.

"Sing, you dope!" Antosia, for whom rituals were very important, was cross.

"Mommy, she called me a dope." Tomaszek pointed an accusing finger.

"Antosia!" Megi's expression was far from stern.

At that moment she caught sight of Jonathan.

"Come and help us," she groaned, heaving up her laughing son.

"Do-pey, do-pey," chanted Antosia to her brother.

"Don't say that," said Jonathan spontaneously.

He walked up and pulled Tomaszek to his feet. As he took him by the hand he was horrified at how small and fragile it was. He covered it with his own and grasped Antosia's hand, soft as a puppy's paw. Megi grabbed the children on the other side and together they formed a circle around the Christmas tree.

Jonathan wanted to weep so he pressed his face against a branch, hissed "Auuu!"; they laughed.

Jonathan stirred the pot, roughly shaking logs of carrots. The thick mass floated to the surface. He'd learned how to make Polish *krupnik*, thick barley soup, from his mother. Chicken in beer sauce, a speciality of Nick's, his mother's English husband, was roasting in the oven. For dessert, in keeping with French custom, there would be cheese.

Jonathan had taken refuge in cooking when Andrea's silence had become unbearable. He'd already gone through the stage of hoping that she would write to him, of worrying that something had happened to her, of being frightened that he'd offended her, furious that she treated him this way and, finally, of feverishly trying to arrange "accidental" meetings. Now he was going through a stage of blunt despair.

The children were on their Christmas holiday and his writing course was to resume after the break. Megi had been working exceptionally long hours recently, while Antosia had caught a cold that she quickly passed on to her brother. Jonathan stayed at home with the feverish children, tied down because their nanny had gone to Poland.

He dished out medicine, cooked, pressed food into the noneaters, read to them and, during their brief naps interrupted by blocked noses, checked whether a text message had arrived from Andrea. So long as the children were poorly, he concealed his frustration and forged it into patience, but when they picked up, he was drained.

When one day Tomaszek, still grumpy and afflicted with a head cold, approached and started to tug at Jonathan's T-shirt, demanding that he play with him, Jonathan, who was just taking the dishes out of the dishwasher, couldn't stand the weight of the little person clutching at his feet any longer. He took a cup from the dishwater and flung it against the floor as hard as he could.

Tomaszek froze, looking at the swing of his father's hand, at the plume of sharp pieces. A long while passed before he overcame his fear and started to cry.

Antosia ran downstairs and stood at the door, staring owl-like at her brother and father. Jonathan was still standing over the shell of the broken teacup, his face white, his hands clenched; Tomaszek was shaking with sobs which were becoming less and less like those of a child and more and more like those of an animal.

Jonathan couldn't bring himself to hug him, afraid that if he took him in his arms the child would fall apart like the teacup. Antosia ran up to her brother and put her arms around him; he clung to her tightly.

"Daddy?" whispered the girl.

Jonathan hid his face with his hands.

"I'm sorry, sorry …"

He felt as if he'd had an accident. If he yelled, "I'm going through a difficult period!" they wouldn't have understood anyway. He really was going through a difficult period – one of lying in wait for a call from Simon's woman, the bitch in the red dress, the reason his children were having a bad time with him.

When Saturday arrived, Megi took over the domestic helm and Jonathan pretended that he'd caught a cold from the children. He ached all over; he wanted to cry, didn't eat, forgot to drink. When he slept, he slept like a log. Blessed sleep, terrible awakening when persistent images invaded him again – the magic of secret meetings, the best sex of his life, soaring, starry lightheartedness. And the thought that all this had fallen apart. He no longer had Andrea. She was having a good time somewhere else with someone new, someone better placed than him.

Then had come the phase of blunt stupor, which led him to the kitchen. Since he couldn't escape from home he decided to discover its creative aspect – cooking. He anointed the chicken with herbs and in his heart cast a spell over all those who could send him text messages not to do so – except for Andrea. The worst moments were when, with a pounding heart, he opened the envelope only to come across a stupid joke from Stefan.

The approaching spring loosened the beaks of birds; they began to sing but the sound only irritated Jonathan. Others waking up to life, he felt, was unfair when he himself was unwell (he felt left out). He had had no idea that the wound of rejection could go so deep; he couldn't cheapen his experience by thinking of it as Stefan described it – a couple of fruitful fucks with a good piece of ass such as Andrea. And what, it's ended? Everything comes to an end.

Why couldn't his thoughts stop there, give his mind and pride a break? Unfortunately, they didn't. A behaviorist at heart, he demonstrated an unexpected determination to drill and bore away at the shaft of suppositions until he felt himself falling in head-first.

Why had she ditched him, and without a word? Was he lousy and if so, where – in bed, in life, in conversation? Images from their meetings appeared before his eyes; obscured the car window as he drove. He shook his head like the dog he was beginning to resemble – shaggy, bristled, with hungry eyes.

He discovered a strange dependence on things he hadn't had the chance to notice before. Such as the fact that routine was a savior. However crumpled he may have been on leaving the house to take the children to school, he returned in a better condition – fleeting conversations calmed him and the gaze of women for whom he was one of few men they saw at this hour, eased his pain.

In spite of this he felt ill. He was undergoing an enforced detox, with no anesthetic or therapist to help. Stefan, although he tried, couldn't put himself in his position because for him women were like stunning clothes – he kept trying new ones. Jonathan wouldn't have been able to talk about this to his father or mother. If anyone were to understand him it would have been Megi.

Jonathan exchanged a few greetings and goodbyes in the school parking lot and got into his car. He watched the women disperse to their cars and realized that he drifted among them like a helpless teenager. Pain was tearing at him, respecting no boundaries.

But he had children now! The thought appeared so suddenly that he even pulled himself up straight. For a moment he couldn't understand what this realization was supposed to mean; finally, it dawned on him. He turned the key in the ignition and drove out of the parking garage too fast.

He raced ahead, angry at the red lights, overtook old men in their cars, grumbled about "snails"; he raced, red in the face, with seething insides and the feverish thought, "She's got to tell me, I'm an adult, a father, damn it!"

It wasn't yet ten when he came to a halt. He glanced at Andrea's window and saw that the bedroom curtain was still half-drawn – a sign that she was in the bathroom. He instinctively hunched in on himself when he saw Simon leave. The latter looked well-off in his trench coat, carrying a briefcase. Jonathan shook the trouser legs of his jeans as though to give them an elegant crease. For a while, he observed Simon in his rear mirror, and when Simon disappeared round the corner, Jonathan climbed out of the car.

He was just about to press the intercom when an elderly woman in a headscarf à la Queen Elizabeth emerged and held open the door. He thanked her, a little taken aback. His legs carried him to the second floor where all he had to do was press the bell.

"So, how are you?" asked Andrea, standing in the doorway, barefoot and wrapped in nothing but a towel.

He was going to lay it all out for her, throw it in her face, but all he managed to do was cross the threshold. And when she placed her hand – her peasant's hand, so different from the rest of her subtle self – on his arm, he caught her by the waist, carried her into the room, and threw her on the sofa. She unzipped his fly and helped him lower his trousers – just halfway down his thighs because his cock was already digging into her velvet pussy surrounded by neatly groomed hair, was slipping in and halfway out, until she shouted; he thrust into her a few times and ejected a charge of fear and joy, rejection, and blessedness.

They didn't manage to talk afterward because Andrea was afraid Simon would return; what they had done had been terribly careless, without a contraceptive at that. Luckily she'd taken the pill and was having her period. The sofa was sticky with sperm and blood when he drowned in Andrea once more, licked her clitoris until she groaned his name.

When later he was going home, waves of bliss mixed with the taste of menstrual blood flooded him, his head aching with jealousy that Simon always had her like that. Tiredness and arousal merged and didn't allow him to enjoy fully what he'd just done. It had been one of those strange elations – bereft of lightness, effervescence, ecstasy. A difficult, lame elation. Yet elation.

**book two**

**1**

*Brussels, 2007*

THE SCULPTURE ADORNING the lofty arch in Cinquantenaire Park
glistened in the sun; Jonathan raised his eyes to catch the rays falling
on the horses' manes and the figure of the woman driving them.

Jogging had become routine for him in Brussels. He couldn't resist
the sweetness of the climate, the soothing warmth, and didn't mind
the rain and drizzle. Running ordered his stormy emotions, calmed
his thoughts, and offered a relatively flat path along which glided the
joy of his recent lovemaking. His body, oiled by the rapture he had just
experienced, moved harmoniously; he ran and his energy, instead of
being depleted, increased.

His passionate intercourse with Megi that morning had surprised
him. And yet, over the past few months it had become more and more
frequent. Jonathan was getting used to the thought of duality giving
him strength. His strength didn't wane from making love to his wife in
the morning with the prospect of doing so to his lover in the afternoon.
Quite the opposite: the anticipation of complementing the morning act
wound him up to such a degree that the horses on the arch seemed like
the first step in a flight to heaven.

# 2

*Brussels, spring 2006, a year earlier*

WHAT WAS SUPPOSED to have been the brutal end of Jonathan's relationship with Andrea had become its true beginning. It was then that things really started to boil; and the two of them were always on the boil, on a high flame, sparks flying. They tempered the seething roar in view of what people might think.

From the time he'd intruded on her and demanded an explanation, they met whenever they could. They discovered bestial rutting and slow lovemaking, rubbing bodies to the rhythm of music, and arousal to make the ears burn, skin tingle, and groans erupt. Jonathan tried to catch the essence of love but whether he sunk into the words of a song or the smell of his lover, he couldn't get a hold on it. He became entangled in trivialities, alarmed by the obvious; he rejected popular ways of thinking, what other people might think, and flew – whether up or down, he didn't know.

He no longer woke up at four in the morning, the hour of anxiety, but earlier, a couple of hours after falling asleep. He was bursting with ideas. Experience had taught him not to try to remember them – what remained in the mornings was a murky puddle of guesses – so he'd get up, sit on the edge of the bathtub and jot down strange thoughts about luminous tails. Other thoughts he tapped into his cell phone, quietly in order not to wake Megi. When the screen lit up with the night's reply, his blood pounded, his throat grew dry – this was how his body answered Andrea's signal.

He isolated himself from Megi. He surfed the internet whenever possible, read newspapers, or pretended to prepare material for his creative writing seminars. Once he had struck up with Andrea again, his wife's body became that of a stranger; he was astounded she even existed. Only the children survived the ravages of his emotions. He rediscovered them, observed their changing moods, euphoric expressions, tiny manipulations, outbursts of contagious happiness – and in them recognized himself as he was with Andrea. "Andrea's Jonathan" also

flared up and sulked, wanted and took or received "a slap on the hand."
Paradoxically, he understood his children much better now.

Love, that spring, tasted differently to different people. Jean-Pierre wrote
about his former girlfriends, concentrating on sensual experiences. Jonathan
felt he'd been given a Swedish quilt sown from scraps of material – colorful,
warm, and useless.

"And what happened with Fabienne later?" he asked, pointing to
the name of the first girl on the list of the author's juvenile fascinations.

"I don't know." Jean-Pierre shrugged.

"Then make it up," said Jonathan.

Ariane described her infatuation with a certain sailor. There were
numerous expressions denoting aesthetic admiration for her white and
his black skin; yet just as the beginning of the story foreshadowed a long
piece of work so the end shrunk hastily. When Jonathan drew Ariane's
attention to this, she nodded in acknowledgement: she had so many
stories she feared she wouldn't have time to tell them all.

"Choose one," Jonathan advised but Ariane wasn't convinced.

"One? Why one? Why this one in particular?"

Kitty wrote about love for a child. Tenderness seeped from every word
until all those present smiled at the successive diminutives. Looking
at her, it crossed Jonathan's mind that women submerged themselves
in motherhood, became the yolk kneaded into a cake mixture. For
homework, Jonathan advised Kitty to write a similar text about herself.

"But how?" she asked.

"The same as here." He tapped his finger on her piece about love.
"With the same tenderness."

A skeptical smile appeared on Kitty's face but Jonathan didn't budge.

"Try, at least give it a try. In a few years your leaven will be ready."

"Leaven?" Her eyes opened wide.

"The beginnings of a new love. People really need it. Parents." He
smiled.

Nora's story was an enormous tapestry, an epic framework, ready to
be filled with characters. Jonathan had few comments; he waited to see
whether Nora would populate her story with small, precise individuals
or focus on one, clear character.

The problem was Geert. His story began in a childhood spent in the Congo, gave a vivid picture of the landscape with all its smells, gusts of wind, rustling grass … and there it floundered. Geert couldn't write any more. Jonathan examined the barely sketched emotions and tapped the French text with his pen.

"Have you tried writing it in Dutch?" he asked.

Geert shook his head.

"French is closer to me. I went to school in Liège when we got back from the Congo, then studied in Paris."

Jonathan read through the conclusion again.

"Maybe you could do it in English?"

Geert nodded but looked surprised.

"It's not my language, I've got no feel for it."

"That's precisely why." Jonathan handed back the paper.

He was tempted to prescribe the same for himself – a cunning way to see his own emotions simplified – but after some thought decided he would be like a barefoot cobbler. Deep down, he didn't want to detach himself from what had besotted him, he wanted his head to remain knotted with emotions, his head between Andrea's thighs.

He thought the next seminar should be on theory. They'd written as much as they could and now they needed inspiring reading, a breather, the fresh air of letters not their own. He glanced at his watch. It didn't grow dark in May until late, but now the light in the park was fading, fortunately. He said goodbye to his group and on his way home turned down a dark alley. There, beneath a familiar tree, waited Andrea; he practically broke into a run, regardless of how undignified he appeared. Before catching sight of the slender figure concealed by the shadow falling from the branches, he shook with impatience. Presently he would reach out for her, his complementary reading matter, his air.

One day at the beginning of June, Jonathan woke up at dawn. The summer rays of morning drilled into his sleepy eyes and, out of nowhere, a conversation with Andrea flashed through his mind. She had stood leaning against the wall with her trousers halfway down her calves while he kneeled in front of her, digging first his eyes and then his tongue into her pubic triangle. Andrea started to groan; it was obvious that her reaction was so strong it even embarrassed her.

"See how I react at the very sight of your head there." She tensed. "Instinctively, like Pavlov..."

Jonathan hadn't been sure whether her English was unclear under the circumstances, or whether Andrea had left the dogs out because she hadn't heard of them. And although, at the time, he'd pushed the thoughts away, in the early morning light they floated up from the bottom of his mind with a considerable "pop!" Yes, it was between Andrea's thighs that "The Pavlov Dogs" had been conceived, the characters of the book that was to bring Jonathan popular success.

The Pavlov Dogs quickly started to live their own lives, complicating Jonathan's paternal and amorous existence. He couldn't let go of the storyline sprouting in his head; he sensed that if he didn't catch the gift offered to him by fate, it would disintegrate. So he scrupulously divided his day into segments for individual chores: caring for the children and taking them to school in the morning, shopping, paying bills, and replying to emails from school – a speciality of that establishment (Jonathan was regularly urged to join the flamenco club); preparing material for his writing course, articles, gym. And meeting Andrea.

After some thought, he designated the hours before lunch for his writing, which was why the pattern imposed by Andrea – that it was she who decided when they should meet – soon became a hassle. He swung between dozens of interspaced activities and she arbitrarily told him to present himself just as he was going to school or sitting down to write.

"I work as well," he whispered into her ear after making love. "Let me know a bit earlier if you can."

"I will," she murmured, brushing aside the mention of his work with a smile.

Then she again specified the time and place of their meeting at the last moment and Jonathan performed miracles to get everything done. He drove to her, irritated, his male pride hurt; he returned panting and happy, worked up by the thought of the steering wheel sticky with the combination of her juices and the gasoline that had dripped on to his fingers when he'd filled the car at the last moment, worried that the tank would run out before he got to school.

He was tempted to say "no" to Andrea once, but never dared. She didn't like to hear how Jonathan combined his commitments as a parent and working writer, how much planning this juggling required. She didn't have children – he justified her – so didn't bear them in mind; and when he forced her to do so she must have thought the kids could cope by themselves, requiring help only on the rare occasion of something like the washing machine or dishwasher breaking down.

He tried to go back to the old-fashioned custom of it being he, the man, who proposed the meetings, but Andrea's stubbornness was like a rubber wall. He had to admit to himself that it undermined his self-confidence more than the lambasting of Uncle Tadeusz, the hot-tempered defender of "real men." "Couldn't we meet an hour later?" texted Jonathan. "Sorry, but I'm working," replied Andrea invariably. When he couldn't accommodate himself to her schedule, she retracted her proposition and he broke out in cold sweat – in the end, she'd find herself someone who would have no problems fitting in with her.

He flinched but went, risking arriving late at school, bungling the preparation for his course, not noting down the ideas that came into his head. He never regretted it afterward – both long intercourse and quickies guaranteed him a dose of pure happiness for a day, a day and a half, and the fact that Andrea felt the same prolonged the ecstasy that they celebrated with text messages. Clearly it was to be – the time had come for him to grab several important things at once.

Andrea had her own theory about sex, and although Jonathan considered it a little girlish, he listened with pleasure as he did to everything she said. She claimed that one could foretell sexual compatibility by first kisses. If there was something in the first touch of lips that broke through otherness, what followed ought to be positive. But if there was a shadow of distaste, unease, a feeling that this was not it, it should end there.

"Does that mean that all the lips you've touched worked out well?" he asked naively.

She hid her laughter beneath her hair.

"I understand, you had to learn somehow," he muttered.

He was angry at himself for being jealous of her past. This was something new, undesirable. Up until then his partners' past relationships had not mattered to him; he had recognized that the past was their own business, and together with Stefan ridiculed men who felt threatened by a woman's sexual experience. Just as they did the myth of deflowering virgins – they associated it with bad-quality sex.

So where did this unexpected jab of jealousy come from? Did it confirm his commitment or desire to own "his woman"? Was he a man in love or an embarrassing idiot?

Andrea interrupted these soundless ruminations, snuggling up to him and recounting the story of their first kiss once again. The accidental brush of their lips had given her the premonition of what could happen to them in bed; in the crowded café a world of experiences unknown to her – at least with such intensity – had opened up. The coincidence had been a unique gift to them both, something which, in another configuration, they couldn't achieve. That was why she'd written to him first.

Before he left, she showered him with caresses and tender words and, although she was better with the first, he was also sensitive to the latter; at this point in his infatuation he was moved by his lover's charm. He walked around dazed with admiration, lust, and an incessant desire to be close. This last feeling was so strong that the very thought of parting – which was becoming unavoidable due to approaching holidays – transfixed him with pain.

At the same time he felt that, despite passionate lovemaking, he was not as close to her as he would like to be, that he was still unsure of her feelings. He was disorientated by the fact that their liaison was different from anything he'd known – too intense for a passing affair, too secretive for a future relationship.

He didn't intend to tell anyone about Andrea; he merely mentioned something casually to Stefan because he had to give vent. Despite good intentions, Stefan didn't show he understood the gravity of what had happened in Jonathan's life and put his condition down to the atmosphere of the city where bureaucrats landed up without their wives and, in clubs, found women willing to spend the weekend, the night or even shorter periods, with them.

"A colleague of mine in the department has three girls here," he informed Jonathan as they watched a school game in which Franek, Stefan's son, was playing.

"Do they know about each other?" asked Jonathan, sitting down on a bench damp from the morning mist. Franek, a round-faced ten-year-

old, marched toward his teammates with a solemn expression, unsure
of his capabilities but determined not to make a fool of himself in front
of his father.

"Think what you're saying," said Stefan, his eyes following the boy.
"Anyway, you know him, he was at the New Year party. The guy's got a
wife and children in Spain, like every decent Catholic. And three girls
here."

Jonathan leaned back on the bench and scrutinized the assembled
parents: mostly fathers although a few mothers were there, too, surrounded by flasks and bags of clothes for the players to change into.

"Where did he get them, the chicks?" asked Jonathan, sensing that
what was important was slipping away from the conversation.

"As if there weren't enough opportunities!" Stefan peered at him from
beneath the baseball cap he wore for the occasion in the belief that it
suited the father of a ten-year-old footballer. "We're spoiled for choice
here, every color under the sun, young interns and older goods whose
husbands stayed at home. And if the worst comes to the worst, there's
always a club like the Madou to pick up a quickie. Everybody knows
that you're only there for one thing. A quick glance, chat up, details
fixed, and it's yours."

"What's mine?"

"Whatever you want. What you've got."

# 3

THE PAVLOV DOGS slipped unnoticed from Jonathan's story into his family
life. After Antosia sneaked a look at the notes spread out by the computer, he
had to explain what he was writing about. From that moment the children
started to think of adventures for the dogs, tried out names, and Tomaszek
even tried drawing one. The creature looked like an elongated pregnant cow
but Jonathan told the boy that the animal was beautiful and could be the
leader of his mongrel pack. And, much to his own surprise, that is how he
started to imagine his protagonist.

The dog, which he intended to have been left an orphan by its owner,
imperceptibly became an aggressive, bristling creature. Hungry, its head

injured by a brick that some drunks had hurled at it, it had learned the first essential thing about survival: to avoid dog catchers.

Megi attempted to join in and invent adventures for the dogs but her imagination lacked the panache of both Jonathan and the children. On hearing that Tomaszek had suggested one of the bitches should be in heat, she strongly protested. She controlled herself only when Antosia came up with the idea that the dog should wear underwear on her "difficult days"– like her classmate's bitch.

"Flowery ones, you know Mommy, the wild flower pattern? And they've got to be long, halfway down the thighs, the dog's thighs that is, you get it?"

"Yes, I do," muttered Megi, gathering peelings into a newspaper. "Longer ones, à la bloomers."

"That would be, like, good," agreed her daughter, who had caught on to Aunt Barbara's expression and didn't want to stop using it despite countless admonitions and threats.

The following morning, Jonathan drove from school with his hands gripping the steering wheel so hard they grew damp. Andrea wanted to meet him that day so he had shaved carefully and, in the evening, caught up with what he'd planned to do in the morning – in a word, he'd done everything so that he could see her once he'd taken the children to their lessons. Yet, she'd given no sign of life since that morning!

Outside the school, he texted her asking if their plans still stood. He waited half an hour in the car, and texted again, this time asking if everything was all right.

She didn't reply.

He began to drive home with one eye glued to his cell phone. He drove and hated himself for what he'd grown inside – a tangle of burning jealousy, gnawing expectation, a sea of lurking tears. He didn't cry because he didn't usually cry – the routine of daily life helped him to rise above the grit of emotions – but when left alone after taking the children to school, he felt close to imploding.

He wanted to think about something else – a beer with Stefan, *The Pavlov Dogs*, a reading list for his writing group, politics, or the children – but he couldn't. Nothing, only the pain of uncertainty, a presentiment of rejection, spasms of imagination. He knew Andrea had taken a day off – a day off from him, too?

Between surges of emotion he noticed with horror how his moods kept changing: from morning euphoria when he picked his best boxer shorts, through pangs of guilt at hurrying the children into the car, to feeling the senselessness of his illegal liaison – because he had even arrived at the point of seeing it made no sense. He saved himself by listening to Tomaszek and Antosia nattering, enumerating in his mind what he'd achieved: his children's love, his wife's companionship, their common successes, mutual understanding. Yes, he imagined life without Andrea. There were moments he wished she wouldn't write to him any more.

But once he'd waved his children goodbye and exchanged a few routine greetings with other parents, the sight of the empty screen on his phone terrified him. He locked himself in his car and forwarded a question; he waited and urged her again. He started driving home but had to stop. When he made love to Andrea he breathed deeply, with his whole lungs; now he climbed out of the car, hunched and, pretending to examine his headlights, started frantically to catch his breath in order not to suffocate.

Suddenly, the trembling of his hands turns into the vibrations of his phone – Andrea sending a text to ask how he is. Jonathan leans on the car door, his arms hanging helplessly. Oh, no, he's not going to answer the bitch now, not after she left him waiting in fear, a laughing stock unto himself.

He climbs into the car and drives away furiously like many a poor guy who, racked by an excess of testosterone, wears down the car rubbers instead of latex ones. He speeds ahead; it's good he knows the way so well. He can afford to be reckless, although the family car screeches at the corners.

Jonathan firmly refuses to answer; meanwhile the cell beeps again. Jonathan slows down and reads: Andrea is tender and docile, apologizes for oversleeping but is climbing into her bath, and in a moment will rub oil over her body.

Jonathan stands at the traffic light; someone honkss. Ahead of him the road forks (yet it is only a regular crossroads) – left to his lover, right home. He stands at a red light, and now at a green, cars pass around him, he ought to switch on his hazard lights as the gesticulating drivers urge him to do but he stares at them dumbly; finally, someone stops, lowers his window and asks: "Çava?"

"Ça va," replies Jonathan.

He abruptly steps into first gear and drives into the left lane; cars brake behind him, honk furiously, but he slips across the red light.

Minutes later he is in Andrea's bed.

Jonathan stared at *Star Wars* even though the film didn't pull him in this time. He watched Antosia and Tomaszek ape a fight with lightsabers: the boy slashed the air abruptly, the girl moved gracefully, using Megi's dressing gown as a battle dress.

A wave of pride swept over Jonathan. Although Megi scowled, saying the film was stupid and too brutal, especially for Tomaszek, Jonathan smuggled in scenes from his childhood for the children, certain it was thanks to this that Antosia went horseback riding, rather than walking around in pink like the other girls in her class, and Tomaszek drew warriors and thought up wonderful stories.

The children's fight moved further down the room; Jonathan clicked the remote control so that Princess Leia appeared on the screen. Secretly returning to his erotic early teenage dreams, he didn't notice that Antosia, having conquered Tomaszek, had sat down in front of the television again.

"Daddy, not this boring stuff!" she moaned, while Tomaszek started bouncing up and down like a ball next to them, shouting: "Give us a fight, give us a fight!"

Jonathan rewound the film; Darth Vader's wheeze drifted from the screen. For a moment, he closed his eyes. Stirred sentimentally by Leia – his friends at boarding school had reacted in the same way – he thought back several hours to his morning with Andrea. He drowned in visions and when he emerged, realized his lover had not only replaced Leia but had also taken the place that had until then been reserved for Megi.

He pulled out his cell and quickly tapped: "You move me and I'm stiff for you." She swiftly wrote back; he got up and slipped out of the room.

"Aren't you watching with us, Daddy?" Tomaszek called after him.

"In a minute." Jonathan's voice came from the hall, muffled.

"What?"

"One moment!"

Megi returned from work just as he was coming downstairs, his phone buried deep in his trousers pocket.

"I asked you not to show them *Star Wars*," she said at the threshold. "And you weren't supposed to leave them alone to make sure they didn't see the heavy scenes."

"I went to the bathroom," mumbled Jonathan.

"Tomaszek pretends to be brave but he's frightened of all those hideous things. Don't you remember when he wet his bed a couple of times because of those horrible faces?"

Antosia stopped short and held out her sword, which just then stopped flashing, to her father.

"Daddy, has the battery gone?"

Jonathan tapped the sword and pressed the switch but the light didn't go on.

"Is it broken? Completely?" Tomaszek risked a new word.

"Will you fix it, daddy?" asked Antosia, squatting so that the dressing gown spread on the floor like a plumed headdress in front of her. "It can be mended, can't it?"

Jonathan walked up to the chest of drawers and found some new batteries; he unscrewed the flap in the toy. He glanced at Megi's tired face – he wasn't attracted to her, everything in him wanted Andrea. Could the pop-anthropological theory that men need to impregnate successive females be proving true? No, this was something else.

Tomaszek rolled the old batteries along the floor and leapt after them like a cat; Antosia didn't move, watching her father's hands. Jonathan pressed the switch – the toy flashed.

"Ha!" He slashed the air with the plastic blade.

"Thank you, thank you!" Antosia sprung from the floor.

Jonathan looked at the sword he held, its direction steered by his hand. In the same way, something in him directed the vector of desire toward Andrea. He felt himself drawn to her by a power as persistent as the call of water beneath the earth, a blind, eternal "I want," rooted in something mightier than him.

"Daddy, I want a go now." Antosia stretched her hand out for the toy.

Jonathan cleared his throat and handed her the sword.

Megi removed her jacket and threw it on the arm of the armchair.

"I met Monika."

"Ah! Did she draw you into the black hole?"

"Don't be silly. Didn't Stefan tell you?"

"What?"

"Simon's holding a party tonight."

"And ..."

"Simon Lloyd, the head of cabinet for the Justice Commissioner, the Simon who was here." She was almost speaking in syllables. "Don't you get it? They were here but they haven't invited us."

Her voice broke and Jonathan was amazed to see Megi cry. In her tights, skirt, and white blouse she looked like a frightened schoolgirl.

Before Jonathan managed to react, Tomaszek had run up to Megi and wrapped his arms around her hips.

"Don't worry, we'll invite you, we love you!"

"Yes, we'll throw a party for you." Antosia joined the boy.

Megi ruffled their hair and made toward the hall.

"Megi," Jonathan followed his wife hesitantly. "Don't worry."

She nodded and wiped her eyes.

"Przemek tried to cheer me up at work saying it might be because of our French. But that's a lot of rubbish, you speak better than that prat and his Czech-Swede, and I can get by, too. So why?"

Jonathan walked up to her and put her head on his shoulder.

"Don't worry, don't worry about it," he repeated, out-talking his thumping heart.

"It's not because so much depends on Simon, promotions and various ... It's just that I feel cut off, you understand, like a helium balloon cut loose from its string," snivelled Megi.

He stroked her hair, a little stiff with lacquer.

"Do you miss your family, friends?"

She pulled herself up and wiped the smudged mascara with her fingers.

"Are you kidding? Not them."

"Is it because you've never lived anywhere apart from Poland?"

Megi shrugged.

"It's not because of Poland! We're not immigrants, we're free individuals, we can buy pickled gherkins at the nearest corner. It's a sort of feeling, oh, I don't know? The umbilical cord being cut?"

"That you're suspended between one and the other? One thing's coming to an end, while the Other …"

"Exactly, a transition. And during the transition, total uncertainty."

Jonathan looked at her and raised his hand, which froze in the air. He clenched his fist and gently lowered it on Megi's shoulder. After a short hesitation, Megi replied with the same gesture.

They were still standing like that, staring at each other in silence, when whispering and clattering reached them from the room.

"What are you doing there?" Jonathan asked suspiciously.

"Ta-da!" Antosia stood in the doorway, ceremoniously pointing behind her.

Jonathan peered into the room. On the table stood little bowls of sweets, in the center towered Belgian chocolates and *ptasie mleczko*, Polish speciality chocolates.

"Sweets? Before going to bed?" Jonathan feigned outrage.

Megi burst out laughing; Tomaszek leapt from behind his sister and stood in line with her.

"Mommy's party!" He stood straight as a ramrod and looked at Jonathan. "Mommy's!"

As long as Andrea sought a reply, Jonathan didn't return her messages, but when finally she fell silent, he plunged into despair. He couldn't enjoy the regained clarity of his situation. He drove the children to school, came home, sat on the edge of the sofa, and stared in front of him. He craved the love of this one and only woman and, although Megi gave all of herself to him, his body howled for Andrea.

During the first days of blossoming summer, Jonathan cursed being in love, the plague that for months had given him wings but now devoured him, more biting than soap in a wound, salt on a cut, a blister in a shoe. He ceased jogging, did just what needed to be done, and only the Pavlov Dogs held him upright as they milled around in his head, ignoring his moods.

Jonathan sat and wrote but when he tore himself away from the laptop, the awareness of loss stabbed at him twice as hard. Unable to bear it any longer, he called Stefan. He briefed him about the metaphorical slap on the cheek his lover had dealt him – she hadn't invited them to dinner, which devastated Megi. He also poured out what hurt him most:

they had made great love that morning yet Andrea hadn't uttered a word about the party in the evening.

"To which I'm not invited," he fumed. "From which, in fact, I'm going to be excluded! And along with me, my wife."

It took Stefan a few seconds to assess the situation accurately.

"So, you're not going to have it off with Andrea any more?"

Jonathan moved his lips closer to the receiver and said, almost begging, "She's false and evil, do you understand?"

"Well, she's a fibber, that's for sure."

"Imagine if it was you she'd treated like that, not Megi. Should I go on seeing her? What about loyalty to friends?"

"Well, yes, I forgot that you and Megi are so close."

"That's not the point, that we're close," bridled Jonathan. "Wouldn't you ditch a woman if she'd treated Monika like that?"

There was silence on the line.

"No," said Stefan finally.

Jonathan lit a cigarette although he held to the firm principle of not causing a stink in the apartment.

"I think you've done the right thing," said Stefan after a while. "You've broken off with her, and … well, and good."

"'Good,' what do you mean 'good'? I can't even be happy I've ended it. I'm not in the least bit relieved."

Stefan started tapping something on his side of the line. Jonathan was just about to tell him to stop when Stefan said, "Remember when we were going to the Masurian Lakes, a policeman stopped us once and demanded a fine?"

"I remember, you bribed him."

"And he, being grateful, said to me, "Keep your eyes open on the bushes twenty kilometers from here. They're there, too. What if you come across an honest officer?'"

Jonathan stubbed out his half-smoked cigarette.

"You're a decent officer," declared Stefan. "You've broken off and stick to it."

"But I can't go on without her." Jonathan hardly understood what he was saying himself.

Stefan put his hand over the phone and answered something to somebody in French at the other end.

"What am I supposed to do?" asked Jonathan.

Something scraped in the receiver.

"Maybe fuck her one more time ..."

# 4

THE CAR RAN ALONG the motorway zipping western Europe away and unzipping its central-eastern part. Jonathan watched the receding landscapes in the mirror; the children, in the back seat, made a racket, then after stormy negotiations agreed to watch *Home on the Range*.

"Lord, what blissful silence!" sighed Megi now that Antosia and Tomaszek, headphones on, were staring at the small televisions attached to the headrests in front of them. "My neck was beginning to hurt with all that turning round passing juices."

"Best leave them in peace," muttered Jonathan.

"They'll kick up hell! I've got to shut them up somehow."

Megi pulled out some CDs and switched one on.

"Don't drown us out!" shouted Antosia.

Megi, resigned, pressed "stop" and inclined the seat.

"Racket or no racket, we're off on vacation." She stretched out her hand to stroke Jonathan's hair.

He shuddered, torn from his own thoughts.

"And you're still stressed with the city," sighed Megi and gazed through the windscreen. "Hardly surprising. We've had a difficult year. The move, a new job for me, and for you the children at a new school. You're brave to have taken such good care of them."

Jonathan nodded and slipped into a slower lane.

"I really appreciate it," continued Megi. "You've proved your masculinity."

"Masculinity?"

Instead of German valleys outside the car, he momentarily saw Andrea's shoulders revealed in her red dress.

"Any guy can take his children for walks at the weekends but not many can spend the afternoon with them, help with their homework, read to them, put them to bed."

"You think so?" mumbled Jonathan.

Andrea was now leaning her butt on the table edge. In nothing but stilettos; he'd already removed her Dress …

"… that the story's becoming clear." Megi's words reached him.

"Sorry, what did you say?" He leaned toward her, his alarmed eyes assessing the road. He shouldn't let himself get so distracted.

"It's great that your story's becoming clear! It's extraordinary how we live together, sleep in the same bed, yet you've got a life of your own like that."

The wheels scraped warningly along the white strip marking the road from the wayside.

"Shall I take over?" asked Megi. "Pull into a gas station. There ought to be one in five kilometers."

"No, there's no need. I thought the jerk behind was going to pass us."

Megi fell silent; after a while she settled her head on Jonathan's jacket, which she'd squeezed in between her shoulder and the window. Without her daily make-up and with strands of hair falling on her cheeks, she looked like yet another child in his car. Suddenly he thought that moments like these were necessary in order to be happy with one's lot, brief moments of separation beneath which lurks valuable intimacy. He wanted to say it out loud – he knew Megi would understand – but she was already asleep.

Again he saw Andrea. She lay beneath him on the crumpled bedspread. (She'd succumbed in the end, allowing him to make love to her where she slept with Simon, but refused to remove the spread so their smells wouldn't mix.) A huge wave of tenderness swelled up in Jonathan, flooded his nose and mouth; from his throat emerged a sound that was neither a cough nor sob. He glanced at the rear-view mirror: the children were avidly following the animated adventures of cows and bulls. He wiped his eyes with the outside of his hand and shielded his right cheek with it so that his wife, should she awake, wouldn't see it was wet.

By the sea, where Megi spent most of the time with the children so that Jonathan could have a break from daily responsibilities, he felt a little like a country dog that, let off its chain, doesn't dare venture far from its kennel. He ran along the coast trying to shake his head free of unwanted thoughts, but whether he jogged against the sun or left it behind him, Brussels – and the woman with whom he'd fallen in love – was always in front of his eyes.

He was tormented by the thought that his lover was not chasing after him as he was after her. Admittedly, she was tender when they met, admired – in text messages – his sense of humor, intelligence, the charm of an outsider, contagious sexual enthusiasm, and sophistication. And yet Jonathan sensed an imbalance in their commitment.

When it had dawned on him, he began to probe in an effort to extract as much as he could from her: he inundated her with compliments, provoked confessions, screwed her until she was breathless. He even dug his heels in a couple of times to keep her "on hold" and make her miss him – he didn't reply to a message, sometimes two, and waited. But when he let it go and stopped contacting her, Andrea also remained silent. She didn't ask, didn't sweet-talk him but accepted his decision. Then he was the one who couldn't stand it any longer and ran to her. He had once asked her why she did this, why she let him go. She hadn't answered. The worst thing about all this was the calm certainty that he was at her mercy. She kept dancing in front of him, the bitch in a red dress.

Only once did she come after him – after she'd omitted to invite him and Megi to the party in which mutual friends had been included. She'd apologized, written about some misunderstanding or oversight. But he'd lost his temper and remained unmoved in his silence for two weeks. "No, sixteen days," he corrected himself and accelerated his trot along the Baltic shore.

He returned to the rented room and took a shower. The children's scattered toys, his wife's drying swimsuit, the pattering feet of his mother-in-law who'd installed herself in the room next door, all jarred on his nerves. He liked Megi's mother a great deal but instinctively avoided her now – he was, after all, hurting her daughter.

He went out again, crossed the dirt roads and, clenching his teeth, assured himself what a good thing it was he'd broken up with Andrea. Good, very good. His long strides marked the rhythm: "Good, good, good."

He returned for lunch. He leapt up the stairs and neared the door. The children were making such a racket that it was obvious no adult was keeping an eye on them. He was about to peer in when he heard familiar voices coming from his mother-in-law's room. He glued his eye to a gap in the door. Megi's mother was sitting on the divan, her daughter had just emerged from the bathroom in a bathing suit he'd never seen before.

"Wonderful!" exclaimed Megi's mother. "Who'd have thought you'd had two children. Look how slim you are!"

"But doesn't this stick out, this here…?"

"Nothing sticks out. It lies on you perfectly, take a look for yourself!" She picked up the rectangular mirror from the sill and handed it to her daughter. "And don't be so silly. Enjoy what you've got. You're at a wonderful age." His mother-in-law sat down on the divan again, her thick hair fleetingly falling over her face. "The truth is that when I was young I was also blind to the way I looked, and only realized once I was over thirty. But I was happiest with myself in my forties, and later."

"Jonathan doesn't want me," said Megi suddenly.

Her mother didn't say anything.

"I don't even know when it started," Megi's voice faltered, as if she were in a hurry. "He doesn't fancy me, doesn't say I'm attractive. He doesn't say anything. He's there but he isn't there."

"Isn't?"

"Even physically."

Jonathan heard the divan squeak as Megi sat down next to her mother. For a moment they didn't say anything, his mother-in-law held her daughter close.

"I didn't think I could tell anyone," said Megi finally. "Jonathan is my friend after all, that is, my husband, man, but above all…"

"Fortunately he's one of those men you can usually depend on."

"That's true. Although he didn't stay home with Tomaszek, remember, when my maternity leave was over."

"But he's with them now. Being a parent is one thing, being yourself another. It's knocked into men's heads that, above all, they're to be themselves, the rest will be done for them by women anyway. That needs to be worked on if it's to change. It's already happening in your generation. You're friends, partners."

"Do you think so?"

His mother-in-law nodded and patted Megi on her bare shoulder.

"Don't worry, some things can be changed, fortunately. And those that can't…" She waved it off and got up to put the mirror back on the sill. "There, look at him!" She indicated the window. "For pity's sake, has nobody told him he looks like a tree trunk in those briefs."

*Megi sits in a fishing boat moored on the sand. She knows by heart the phases of the red sphere plunging over the horizon, the speed of the process, and the expression of reverence on the faces of those around her. Holidaymakers wade in the water, their hands behind their backs, which makes them look like conscientious penguins. Megi turns her eyes away from the disc of the slipping sun and gazes at the horizon where the sky meets the water in a gray embrace.*

*"Where are the children?" Anxiety needles her. "Ah, with mom!"*

*Mom … A couple of years ago Megi overheard some relatives grumbling in the kitchen about her mother. "Apparently the apple doesn't fall far from the tree," they griped, thinking she couldn't hear them. Megi stopped in front of the door but didn't hear the end; someone was approaching in the hall and she had to pretend she was rearranging the plates she was carrying from the table.*

*"Doesn't fall far…" It was true. She'd learned her maternal skills from her mother and grandmother. She, like them, looked after the house and nosed the little ones like a lioness – even if she did so through Jonathan at times. He was her eyes, her husband – well trusted.*

*The last spark of the setting sun disappears into the sea. The people disperse; the sky turns the purple color of end-credits.*

*"Where's Jonathan?" Another stab. "Running? No, he runs in the morning. At the café with the children? No, Mom's there … So where is he?"*

*Darkness and coolness draw over the sea; the beach around her grows deserted. Megi doesn't follow the others; she remains sitting in the blackened boat.*

Jonathan followed the edge of the sea, going against the crowd, which, having seen the performance of the setting sun, made its way to the exit.

Cold crept up on him, chilling his fingertips and raising the hair on his arms, but didn't force him to retire with the others. He strolled and thought about his cell phone. He would willingly throw it away. Now, with a broad swing like when skimming pebbles over water.

To his surprise, he recalled the way Megi skipped stones – and almost laughed out loud. It was a sight for the entire family; even the children proved better at the skill which, for some reason, she couldn't master. Megi would pick up a stone and take a swing but the stone wouldn't glide; in a strange flight resembling the trajectory of a sickle, it returned to the starting point, sometimes hitting Megi herself.

He'd taught her so many times how to skim pebbles, but she couldn't get the knack.

He kicked a piece of wood from which all life had been washed away by the salty water. He could teach her so many things! Be it only to make love like Andrea – unrestrained, indecently, sometimes even unaesthetically. To leave him breathless with desire.

He picked up a pebble and took a mighty swing. It was not a question of skill; Jonathan didn't believe in anything like objective sexual competence. What was most important in making love was intelligence, Imagination, and "chemistry," not necessarily in that order. There was also lack of inhibition, but this was a double-edged sword. He'd once had a girlfriend who admitted blatantly that animal copulation aroused her, and he was aroused by the fact that she'd told him. Yet when he was granting her request he'd felt a shadow of repulsion, which had appeared from he knew not where, and which had spoiled his enjoyment.

Jonathan hurled another pebble and when he heard the splash, far away in the dark water, he reached into his pocket and checked his cell again. The phone shimmered in his hand like a dead fish. He took a swing.

*Megi stands in the fishing boat and thinks about perverts. What if one is lurking in the forest by the path leading to the beach? A childhood terror brought up to date in the form of a goblin – a stocky monster with wide-set legs and narrow horizons?*

*Megi scrambles out of the boat and makes toward the dark funnel of the exit. There are two or three people on the beach; if something were to happen, they wouldn't hear her scream. She reaches the wooden walkway. Ahead of her is the dark forest and dunes, behind her a single, tall figure. "Shall I let him pass? Shall I run on ahead?"*

Jonathan made his way to the beach exit, which was barely visible against the dunes. Wading through the loose sand along the beaten track where the beach met the sea seemed too tiring. He glanced, yet again, at his phone which he hadn't in the end thrown into the water but hidden in his pocket with a groan of disappointment.

He walked ahead, moving away from the sea, following somebody's slight silhouette. He thought he would bury the phone. The struggle with himself to resist the temptation of getting in touch with Andrea who, put off by his silence, had given no sign of life, was finishing him off. In the end, he made a wager with himself: if he managed to write a message to Andrea before the slim silhouette ahead of him disappeared in the dark gorge of the beach exit, he would send it.

He pulled the phone out and began typing. He cancelled and wrote anew. He groaned and wiped his eyes, which watered from staring at the blue screen. He began again.

*Megi looks back, takes out her phone just in case, quickly searches for her husband's number, and positions her finger on "call". What had initially seemed a game of her own imagination, a controlled game of hide-and-seek — she and the archetypal pervert — has imperceptibly turned into painful anxiety.*

*The man walking behind her brightens the darkness with his phone. Megi quickens her stride. "Have your phone switched on, Jonathan, have your phone …" She shakes beneath her thin jacket and immediately reassures herself. "It must be switched on, he never parts with it."*

*With that thought in mind Megi plunges into the darkness.*

"Send." Jonathan's finger, damp with sweat, pressed the key on his phone while he raised his head. The message he sent was gliding just where he gazed – into the eyes of his lover, brown irises beneath dark lashes and hair so different from the delicate blonde hair of his wife, which their children had inherited.

So he was at Andrea's mercy once again.

He forged ahead through the dark forest, the rustling leaves deadening the footsteps of the woman before him. He reached the road lit by street lamps and hesitantly pulled out his phone. His heart thumped to the beat of the disco which was blasting out the nearby bar. He looked at the screen. Andrea had written back!

# 5

THE PAVLOV DOGS fought for their territory. The city where they had been destined to live struggled with such poverty that nobody wanted to feed the four-legged animals any more. Thrown out into the street, they tried to eat scraps found in trash cans but the bins were already occupied by packs of the homeless – people or dogs. Poodles, Pekingese, and Terriers died, torn apart by the fangs of hungry Alsatians, Dobermans, and the fiercest of street brawlers – Caucasian Sheepdogs. Small dogs made poor food but large dogs used them for training a certain movement of their heads – a quick shake – followed by silence as warm blood dripped from their jaws.

Following the dogs as they dragged him through the stinking side streets of the city, Jonathan wrote with his knees pulled in under a small table that, instead of the usual four legs, had three annoying posts. He spun a different story in his messages to Andrea. Her replies acquired, in the heat of the badly ventilated room, the proportions of visions tempting Simon of the Desert. Racked by the impossibility of fulfilment, unable to believe she would agree, Jonathan finally suggested to his lover that she should come to Warsaw for a weekend.

She replied with a brief "yes." He leapt from the table, bruising his shin, closed down *The Pavlov Dogs* on his laptop and left the room. He walked against a stream of children, bumped into windbreakers and rubber dinghies, rubbed against heated bodies in flip-flops. He scanned the family schedule in his mind: on their return from the seaside, they were going to leave the children with Megi's mother and go to the Masurian Lakes for a few days instead of taking the diving course he'd so much wanted to attend.

He stopped outside a bicycle rental shop, leaned against a pole in the provisional fence, and started to mechanically peel away remnants of bark.

"Bike for you?" A youngster in a red baseball cap struck up the conversation.

Jonathan shook his head. He could tell his wife he wanted some peace to write, and move into his father's apartment until the latter returned from Croatia. His mother-in-law could help Megi with the children and he'd spend the time with Andrea.

"If you don't want a bike why're you hanging around?" The boy's voice rose strangely toward the end of the sentence.

Mute, Jonathan automatically thought and returned to his recollections of the morning: Megi had snuggled up to him, encouraging him to enter her, but he'd pretended to be asleep. She'd curled up on the other side of the bed. From beneath half-closed eyelids he saw her hair and detected the neat snip of the hairdresser's scissors. All of a sudden, he passionately longed for the sight of his own hands ruffling Andrea's hair as they made love.

A stocky man in Hawaiian shorts, with a tattoo of a mermaid fighting for space among the tuft of hair on his back, peered out from the hut bearing the sign "Bikes for 5 złotys."

"Can I help you?" he asked.

"Megi, Megi ..." The wheel in Jonathan's head picked up speed, words merged as though on a roulette wheel.

"If you don't want a bike why are you hanging around? Move away from the fence!"

The youngster, emboldened by his boss's presence, took a step forward.

"Right!" he added from beneath his peak.

"What do you mean 'right'?" Jonathan rebuked him before walking away.

If Megi had cried with disappointment or become really angry, it would have been easier for him. But she merely said, "If you've got to write, you've got to write." He almost yelled, "I don't have to, fight for me! Let's leave like we'd planned."

She helped him pack his laptop and clean clothes; she even asked whether she should drop some dinner off to him when she was in the neighborhood.

"No!" Jonathan blurted out.

She looked at him amazed; he leaned over to fasten his bag, saying, "I've got to tear myself away from reality."

"I understand." He heard the amusement in her voice.

The hardest thing was to say goodbye to the children. They gave him a quick kiss, wanting to hurry back to their granny, who was teaching them how to play poker, but Jonathan clung on to them, hugged them until Megi shouted and laughed, "Maybe you'll stay with us after all?"

Jonathan stood Tomaszek on the floor and slung the bag holding his laptop over his shoulder.

"May the Force be with you!"

Jonathan gave Megi a kiss on the top of her head, waved to his mother-in-law from the door, and left without delay.

His father's apartment was a collection of treasures from the former, socialist regime – a fake samovar with flaking patches of "silver," curtain rods to which the clips would cling for good, a drying fern on the sill. The arrival of another woman in his father's life – perhaps there'd been more after Jonathan's mother disappeared from his life and his son had gone to school in England – had left no mark on the apartment. Perhaps because his father's partner of several years, Helena, had two rooms on the same housing estate, thanks to which they could be together while retaining their independence.

On seeing the practically unchanged colors of the walls and fittings that had greeted him when he visited his father during the holidays, Jonathan suddenly missed home. He walked up to the window from which stretched an uninteresting view over the other blocks. His mother's apartment in London, the different rooms of the boarding school, his father's apartment, the rented studio in Warsaw where he and Megi had first lived, even the apartment they'd bought with their first earnings, didn't seem close enough to him to call home. But now, unexpectedly, at the sound of the word "home" the façade of their Brussels apartment building appeared in front of his eyes.

He drew the curtain, from late in the Gierek era. The patter of a dog running downstairs, the scrape of the rubbish chute lid, the groan of the lift starting up – all resonated with the memories of childhood.

Andrea didn't want him to pick her up at the airport so they arranged to meet on Krakowskie Przedmieście, where he counted on not meeting anyone he knew. People from Warsaw didn't venture along the Trakt Królewski, but left the attraction to visitors.

Before going out he phoned the children to ask them about their plans. He was afraid Megi's mother might decide to remind the children of their national heritage and take them to the Old Town. He replaced the receiver, went to the bathroom, and scrutinized his reflection, fragmented by the edges of the mirrors on the cabinet doors: did his father experience similar moments here? Did he stand here tentatively studying his features, a little similar to Jonathan's?

He glanced at his watch and picked up the shaving foam. Everything he did – daily, trivial activities – today seemed like a transgression of boundaries, an entry into a mystery or sacrilege. Covering his cheeks with foam, he clumsily knocked off his glasses, which fell on the bathroom surface. "Pan Hilary," the poem his mother had read to him when he was little, leapt at him from somewhere. "*Pan Hilary zgubił swoje okulary...*" Mr Hilary lost his glasses ...

A drop of blood appeared on the white froth. "And what if Andrea's got HIV?" He swore out loud, held the shaver beneath running water, and sat on the edge of the bathtub. Enough! Enough worrying and guilt! He was going to screw the woman – that was all.

She walked into the café and he burned. The men stared at her as usual but she took Jonathan's upturned face in her cool hands and kissed him where he'd once kissed her, that first time, almost on the lips.

A couple of hours later, he lay with his eyes open. Suddenly conscious of his own body, he listened to it, discovered it anew. Usually he fell asleep shortly after ejaculating; now he lay next to Andrea and contemplated the gulf of orgasms, stroked her body and his, and when she fell asleep, he stroked her harder, jealous of time lost in sleep, the looks not given him, angry at time wasted.

Then the alarm clock rang and Andrea had to leave. She hastily gathered her clothes and threw amused glances at him from over the mug of coffee he'd prepared in his father's worn espresso pot. She pointed to the built-in room-divider shelf, saying, "Oh, it's like those in the photo of my mother's apartment in Prague!" and to the radiator with the words, "Dad said things were better in Poland but all this looks just like Czechoslovakia."

Jonathan told her that things were better in Poland because he was only in primary school when the tanks had appeared on the streets. He hardly remembered them; it was not really his generation's experience but that of people who were a few years older, students at the time. The first free elections, seven years later, had been more important for his generation. He hadn't been in Poland at the time but he knew about the events from news in France where he'd been studying. He'd itched to return to Poland, especially when the Berlin Wall fell, but had been in love with Petra, a Swedish girl, and couldn't imagine leaving her.

Andrea told him about how, after her father's death, she'd visited Czech villages in search of distant family. Her father had been eighteen when he ended up in a camp for dissidents. He was not allowed to study, even though he painted beautifully. For the rest of his life he had to be treated for a lung disease he'd caught in prison. She hadn't found any relatives; all she took with her from Czechoslovakia were handmade lace curtains.

"Your tanks, my tanks," Jonathan whispered into her hair.

"… our tanks," she concluded with a smile.

Jonathan loved her all the more for it. They resembled each other – they spoke other languages, easily found their place in other countries, their thinking was not determined by any national reading list. They never said, as did Megi, "because back home" or "look how they …" Jonathan and Andrea knew what it meant to think in two or three languages at the same time. They knew what parting meant, and how painful coming back could be.

It was thanks to their conversations that Jonathan realized that, just as half of him dwelled in England and France, so his childhood was only here, in Poland. And Andrea had clearly understood that boy's soul because she leaned over him before leaving, looked him in the eyes, and said, "Oh!"

After she left, Jonathan spent the entire day without leaving the divan. Images surrounded him like mock-ups; when he dozed off they became more tangible. From time to time, he picked himself up and went to the kitchen to make himself some tea but he couldn't eat; not a mouthful would pass his throat, not a word.

That day he didn't send her a text. She, too, didn't write yet. He wasn't in the least worried. Was it possible to exchange more than they already had over the past day and night? They were a joint, consummated dyad – mutual owners of each other's interior lives.

The following day he got down to some writing but his thoughts were still tangled around their bodies. He tried to shift them on to the track of the Pavlov Dogs but they came back; light and fluttering, they flew above his dark head, over her raised thighs.

He didn't phone home until three days later, when Megi sent him a message, worried whether everything was all right, whether he was eating, whether he was inspired, and whether he missed them a little. Jonathan felt a pain as though someone were forcing an extracted tooth back into his gum. He put his phone aside and, after a moment's hesitation, phoned the children.

From then on, he talked to them every day until their voices ceased to sound alien. Finally, he started missing his routine – putting Tomaszek and Antosia to bed, reading them stories – and went back.

# 6

IN THE MORNING, Jonathan felt himself to be part of the Brussels landscape. He joined the flow of fathers and mothers and proudly led his two children, asking them about their day, smoothing down their hair, and gently pulling them along by the hand, weaving in and out between rushing pedestrians. Fluorescent waistcoats flashed along the cycling paths; with a briefcase in their front pannier, a toddler in the seat behind, parents hurried to nurseries and work.

Motorcycle headlights reflected in cars; someone was walking their dog; the warm September wind tore at tricolored flags suspended from windows. The people opposite waved to him. The older man, already in a suit, was finishing his coffee; the younger, in jeans and a pale T-shirt, was starting work later that day. Holding on to Antosia's backpack as it slipped off her shoulder, Jonathan greeted various neighbors.

He rarely thought about Megi now. And when he did it was to find fault in her and blame her for the routine that he considered was causing their infrequent and poor sex of the past few weeks. He grew stiff when with her – not from desire as before, but from alienation. He was repelled by her naturalness, her fluids, secretions – everything that he adored in Andrea. He avoided his marital duty, angry at the world for having delegated it to him. "People are divided into those who are sexual and those who are asexual, and the latter rule the world. Or those who want to be taken as such," he bridled. "They're the ones who demand sex be kept out of sight, and when it shows shout, "Pervert! Whore!"'

In the meantime, the Pavlov Dogs changed into a pack of unruly mongrels. A new element had crept into their territorial wars – the fight over bitches. Jonathan had planned to describe the laws governing dog gangs with greater insight, to sketch more clearly the characters of the dogs who survived by using the intelligence of tamed animals and awakened ancestral instincts. He wanted to describe how efficiently they terrorized the city but the only thing he thought about of late was making love; which is why the tale veered off course and Jonathan, happily enchanted by love, ceased to envy Andersen his ability to change personal failures into the sad stories of his fairy tales. The Pavlov Dogs leapt at each other's eyes, while a certain supple bitch, that looked like an Alsatian, stood on the side, beneath a tree, and gave herself to as many dogs as managed to cover her.

Stefan pressed drinks into the hands of new arrivals, chatted, and turned lame phrases into jokes, marking his path with spontaneous outbursts of laughter. People were drawn to him, forming a buzzing crowd while he, the good host, kept appearing at the door to welcome more guests.

Jonathan had lost Megi in the crowd a long time ago and headed toward Andrea. As usual, the men had formed a circle around her, from which they emerged – capering knights – more confident, defterm and wittier than usual. Had Jonathan been himself, he would have stood at the side and watched but, when it came to Andrea, he had long ceased to be an observer, which is why he squeezed in between Przemek and Rafał and stared at his lover.

She smiled at him as she did at the others. She shared her attentions fairly with those to whom she spoke, thanks to which they blossomed like northerners under antidepressant light bulbs. Simon's appearance disturbed the balance. In his brilliance, the brilliance of a bulb marked "authority," the conversations grew heavier and bristled with facts. Those gathered in a circle now weighed their words, wrapped them in the cotton wool of phrases such as "I don't know what you think but ..."

When Stefan's son, Franek, sent by Monika with a tray of canapés, stood next to them, an apparatchik with a strong French accent came to life: "Do you like the *Teletubbies*?" he asked the boy.

Franek looked at him, confused. He was too old for stories aimed at two-year-olds.

"Are you also in favor of censoring the program?" A journalist from a British newspaper turned to the Poles in the circle.

Przemek made an effort to laugh.

"We're in favor of censoring what some of those in government say."

"You've got to admit, it's an excellent publicity stunt, electing twins for the highest positions in the state," jibed Simon.

"Isn't one of them gay?" asked the journalist.

The smile on Franek's face kept appearing and disappearing. He didn't understand what was going on but tried to guess by the way the men spoke.

"Wasn't he the one who detected homosexual undertones in kiddies' *Nightie Night*?" the bureaucrat with a French accent enquired.

"*Hello, Dr Freud!*" The journalist raised his hands.

Everybody laughed. Jonathan gently pushed Franek toward some other guests.

"Interesting," he mumbled. "My friends from Poland heard about all this from the BBC. There was practically nothing about it in Poland. The statement was treated like political folklore."

"I bet your friends don't read Polish newspapers."

"Why shouldn't they? They're Polish."

The journalist waved it disdainfully aside.

"So, how many Polish friends have you got? Two?"

"I'm Polish."

The journalist burst out laughing.

"You are? So where did you learn to speak English like that? Oxford?"

Jonathan held the silence a second longer than was fitting then said politely, "In Poland."

"You mean to say," the bureaucrat with a French accent joined in, "that nobody there has heard about the proposal to take off the kiddies' TV show because of hidden homosexual undertones?"

"Only those who read a tiny item stuck in the middle of the most trivial news from Poland," retorted Jonathan.

"It's not such a small issue since the whole world is talking about it."

"Depends what the world wants to talk about."

"But we're not just making it up," said Simon.

"Of course not," Przemek joined in placatingly.

"Facts are facts," interrupted Jonathan. "They can be blown up or ignored."

"Isn't that a bit of a conspiratorial way of thinking?" Simon tipped his glass.

"Typical of those from the old Soviet bloc?" Jonathan's voice sounded surprisingly sharp.

Przemek opened his mouth and immediately closed it; Andrea raised her hand as if wanting to speak. Simon was still looking at Jonathan with the same smile. Perhaps he was waiting for Jonathan to turn everything into a big joke, as they had both been taught to do by the English education system.

But it was too late. Something had opened in Jonathan, something that deformed his words and drew the muscles around his lips, which refused to respond to Simon's smile. They were kinsmen, brought up in the same country; and yet Jonathan was seeing himself as others viewed him – coldly, from the outside – and what he saw was the perpetrator of a social gaffe, a serious Pole who had lost his temper.

"My son's informed me that you're talking about queers," Stefan's jovial voice resounded behind them. "At last something I know a bit about!"

Rafał quickly started chatting to the British journalist; Przemek drew the bureaucrat with a French accent aside; Andrea whispered something in Simon's ear. Jonathan turned to Stefan and rolled his eyes, at which the latter, as if conspiring, pressed a packet of cigarettes into his hand.

The terrace was deserted, the rain having chased the smokers inside. Jonathan rested against the railings and clicked the cigarette lighter.

"Gave him a piece of your mind?" Stefan stood next to him.

Jonathan took a drag and without a word blew out a cloud of smoke.

"Don't worry, it's just the usual hiccup after ditching a girl. It doesn't normally happen to me," Stefan explained, seeing that Jonathan wanted to say something, "but I've seen it happen to others."

He leaned against the railings then after a while added: "Anyway Simon had it coming. He didn't invite you to that party. He thinks that since you're a nobody in the Commission … You've shown him that's not the case."

"What's not?" asked Jonathan in a drab voice.

"Well, that if you're not in the Commission it doesn't mean you're not important."

Jonathan stared at the garden stretching out in front of him.

"Stefan," he said clearly. "I'm fucking his wife."

"Still!" Stefan tore his hands away from the railings. "Even though she didn't invite you to their party, ignored you, and after everything else you said?"

Jonathan stamped out the cigarette butt.

"Right, that's not the point," Stefan said, more to himself.

When the terrace door closed behind him, Jonathan rested his back against the rough wall. In the light seeping from the apartment, he could see the rain cutting through the air. He turned his face to the sky. How far he'd gone! He loved Andrea even for her faults. He was hurt, yet happy. Is this the essence of love, he thought. Pain?

All at once, he longed for his calm love of Megi.

*"What are they talking about?" wonders Megi, looking at Jonathan on the balcony. "Exchanging rude jokes, what else?"*

*She turns her eyes to Andrea. She's like a stone chafing in her shoe. Megi tries to shake it out of her mind – in vain. If it was a man who'd so irked Megi, she would confront him. But Andrea is a woman.*

*She remembers the dream she had that night: she was standing at a party like this one and talking about something unimportant. There were fewer people than here which was why she was surprised nobody had noticed a bear slip in through the door.*

*It was beautiful! Its coat, almost black, glistened like a pitch-black stream, fur swaying in rhythm with its gait. As it passed Megi, it didn't slow down but walked between her legs at the same steady pace. She shuddered, clenched her glass tighter and, with an apologetic smile, looked around at the faces of the guests. But they seemed not to notice it, perhaps they had not even noticed the bear's presence at the party.*

*She'd woken up, flooded with an irrational feeling of happiness: the bear had chosen her, passed between her legs! She burned with shame, exciting shame.*

*Megi runs her fingers through her hair and her eyes return to the circle of men swaying around Andrea; she watches Andrea make room for them, invite them to be the center of her interest. With her attention, her eyes, she extracts from those she is talking to whatever they believe is the best in them; she is their mirror; the canvas for their self-portraits. She merely retouches a little and immediately they appear better – are "the real thing!"*

*Megi shrugs. She doesn't believe in Native American male friendship. Brought up by women, she knows that nothing can equal their power. Which is why, when women turn against her, Megi feels lost.*

# 7

As HE WALKED next to Stefan, Jonathan remembered that, according to Megi, the more time he spent with his friend, the more Jonathan became part of Stefan's dog team and, like a good Husky, took on some of his friend's personality for a time: the way he spoke, some of his gestures. "It's easy to guess who you've just seen," she laughed. "Do I also pick up other people's traits?" Jonathan worried; he didn't want to be a chameleon. "No, no," Megi reassured him. "Only Stefan's."

Stefan was less susceptible to Jonathan's influence and Jonathan consoled himself that even though his friend's personality may have been more dominating, he, Jonathan, had more empathy. Does that mean I'm more feminine? The thought flitted through his mind, but he quickly rid himself of it. "Masculine" and "feminine" were so flexible and kept on changing; he himself was the best example of this. He didn't bother to put a name to it. He had already been an outsider in life; he might as well be avant-garde.

This time, as he walked down the street with his friend, Jonathan felt, for the first time, that he was observing him. He studied Stefan's body language, the glances he threw at passing women, his half-smiles, the way he turned to look – at that woman for example, older than them, classy.

Once she'd passed by, Stefan didn't even interrupt what he was saying, as though separate cells in his brain registered aesthetic and sexual events without disturbing those responsible for the coherent spinning of a story. Yet the woman walking away must have thought Stefan was still eyeing her because when Jonathan glanced back, he saw that she was trying to step lightly in her stilettos over the uneven pavement.

The street traced a gentle arch. Brussels, he thought, a sexy city where people look at each other and this mutual attention warms them as if they were lying in a beach shelter. A city where Megi had one morning dared to say, "Why clitoris? It should be tickloris."

They passed another girl at whom Stefan cast his approving eye.

"Not bad," he muttered.

"Young."

"What do you expect? Thirty-year-olds are desperate. Marriage and babies – that's what they have in mind. Forty-year-olds are great but they scare me."

"Twenty-year-olds in bed are like broth from a stock cube."

"But you can screw them," sighed Stefan.

Jonathan stopped short. Stefan walked on a while before realizing he was talking to himself. He turned and looked questioningly at Jonathan.

"She wasn't even twenty," Jonathan indicated behind him.

"What's up with you? I haven't raped her!"

"You're forty and dribbling over a girl half your age. Are you retarded or something?"

Stefan cast his eyes around as if to seek understanding from the waiters watching for customers at the Italian restaurants.

"What's …" he began but Jonathan hissed through clenched teeth, "You don't like Andrea, do you?"

Stefan stared at him goggle-eyed.

"You don't like her because she's just like you," continued Jonathan, speaking as if he were also listening to himself. "She eyes men in that same way and then …"

Stefan stepped up to him, slowly, as if he were an injured bird.

Two waiters stopped talking; their coal-dark eyes glowered beneath the awning.

"Why do you leave them?" Jonathan jabbed Stefan's chest with his finger.

"Who?"

"Those birds of yours!"

Stefan gazed at him and, tilting his head to one side, said slowly, as though to a toddler, "Because I've got a wife."

Jonathan shook his head.

"No, no! I mean why do you pick them up? Why do it at all? Understand?"

Stefan walked up to him, sheltering them both from the waiters' sight.

"Sorry, old chap," he said quietly. "But I don't understand."

Autumn smelled of flowers and it wasn't clear where the scent was coming from since leaves were rustling in the trees, fumes drifting from cars and police horses, leaving odors more suited to a nineteenth-century street.

With the start of a new school year, Jonathan returned to his routine: he drove the children to school, wrote, fetched them and, when Megi came home and began preparing dinner, took his gym bag and left. Andrea already waited for him in the church. They went to her place and made love on Simon's bed.

He couldn't settle his thoughts for a long time after his return; they skipped in euphoria and made him want to run, hold witty discussions, learn Spanish. In order to cover his tracks, he tapped the keyboard while allowing images from an hour ago to scud before his eyes: Andrea snuggling on top of him, her slender thighs wrapped around his hips, his eyes and lips covered by his lover's dark hair.

In October, Simon left for a whole two weeks. Jonathan wanted to make the most of the time, even though his going to the gym every day might have appeared suspicious. Andrea was the one who showed caution for them both and, as was her wont, was sparing with herself and forced him to wait for her invitation.

He was furious. Why hold on to the rhythm of their first dates? The speed at which they see each other ought to have equalled the strength of the emotions which carried him. He pressed her because she was now the only one he wanted to make love to; her body seemed semifluid and unearthly, their fucking ecstatic.

He stopped enjoying Megi. He waited for his wife to fall asleep at night and only then went to bed. He lay there, still feeling the weight of Andrea's head on his shoulder, recalling the murmur of their whispering, the tangle of words, the moisture of their tongues, the merging of English and Polish, French and Swedish.

Once, when he'd had enough of waiting for Megi to fall asleep, he silently picked up his phone, which at night he kept beneath the bed and, hiding it behind a bottle of water, started to leave the bedroom. Suddenly, the light of a message flashed on the screen and, magnified by the plastic bottle, fell on Megi's face.

Only after a while did he dare to look at her. She was asleep … But if she had woken up then, if she'd read what was painted on his face, illuminated by the bluish glow, he would have answered with sheepish simplicity: "I love her. I want to be with her."

The Pavlov Dogs yapped in Jonathan's head even as he jogged around Cinquantenaire Park; and – wonders never cease – the point at which he usually grew tired was when he passed one of Brussels's strange statues, the statue of a dog. The subject was attracted to him like filings to a magnet – Antosia told him how her friend's bitch had run away during a walk and come back pregnant, then Megi came across a second-hand clothes shop right next to the statue of a dog like the one in *Tintin*. Their daughter begged them to take in one of her friend's puppies when they were born; his wife was fascinated by the fact that the bronze dog was peeing.

Jonathan absorbed the information and, although not everything suited his story, something filtered through; be it the nervy peeing here and there of the leader of the mongrel pack or the polygamous personality of the prettiest bitch. Something even made him call one of his chapters "Pushing to get down in the gutter."

His students appeared after the holidays in practically the same line-up. Cecile said it was rare for people to go back to writing after the holidays, just like when learning a foreign language.

Jonathan entered the building with a certain thrill. The stone statues in little hats seemed to greet him; the man sitting in the glass-fronted kiosk marked "Information" welcomed him as one of his own. A moment later, gray-haired Geert, sun-tanned Ariane, Jean-Pierre in the immortal jacket that served him throughout all the seasons of the year, and British Kitty, now with longer hair, walked in; only the oldest participant, Nora, was missing. Jonathan asked whether they'd written anything during the holidays – they answered with smiles full of embarrassment, and Ariane pulled a thick notebook bound in cream canvas from her bag.

"My daughter gave this to me," she said. "I've been writing in it for some time now."

"What are you writing?" They leaned toward her; Ariane opened the book. The sentence on the first page looked like embroidery on a kitchen wall-hanging.

"What's that maxim?" asked Kitty.

"It's a sentence from *The House of Spirits*. I love that book!"

They leaned over the entry.

"… 'if you call things by their name, they materialize…,'" Geert translated the beginning.

"…'and you can no longer ignore them because…'," continued Kitty.

"'If,'" Ariane corrected her. "'If, however, they remain in the realm of words unuttered …'"

"'… with time they may vanish into thin air.'" Geert adjusted his glasses.

They fell silent. A tram rumbled past the window.

"That fits in with the former subject we studied." Jonathan smiled. "To 'The Semantics of Love.'"

"Former?" Ariane pulled herself up. "But that's why I'm writing in this book!"

"Really?" Jonathan was pleased.

Ariane answered with a smile; Geert nodded.

"But isn't it a stupid subject?" Jonathan let out.

Jean-Pierre stopped sprawling over two chairs and sat up straight.

"It's broad," he said after some thought.

Geert agreed.

"A lot falls into place because of it. I hear more, feel more."

"Me, too." Kitty laid her hand over her pretty bust. "After all, you did tell me to write with tenderness."

"Buy yourself something like this." Ariane leaned over to her, indicating her notebook. "No, wait, I'll buy it for you!"

"But going back to that quotation," said Geert, "I wonder… What if things that have been given a name do become real?"

"I've got a practical question," said Ariane. "Does anyone know where Anaïs Nin hid her diaries?"

"In a bank safe," replied Jean-Pierre. "Before that idea occurred to her she used to keep her secret one somewhere at home covered with an "overt" one. But later on, when she had piles of them – and some of them almost got lost during her travels – she decided to keep them in a bank safe."

"And Henry Miller, where did he keep his?" asked Ariane.

Jean-Pierre looked at her derisively.

"Wherever he pleased. What did he have to be scared of?"

Megi leaned over the dark desk; there were a few dents in the wood. The shadow of swelling veins slowly appeared on her hands.

"No," said Jonathan. "I don't want old furniture in my home."

Megi tore her eyes and her fingers away from the texture of the surface. Tomaszek's squeals as Antosia tickled him came from another part of the shop.

"Why not?"

"I've already told you." He looked around because a thud had reached him from the corner where the children were. "Buying antiques is for the senile. Look around, who comes here to buy anything? Nobody but old fogies."

"Who, please God, don't speak Polish."

"It's a different matter if the piece of furniture's been in the family for years. But I don't intend to bring home something I know nothing about."

"Don't you think it's mysterious?"

"About as mysterious as second-hand underwear."

The search for desks had already taken them two weekends. Jonathan was annoyed, not so much by the antiques to which Megi persisted in returning as by having to drive around instead of resting. A side effect of moving was the need to throw away old things and buy new ones, just as one of the consequences of having children was constantly having to provide them with something new because they kept growing out of their old things. Jonathan was ground down by the cogs of small necessities.

"Let's go to IKEA then," sighed Megi, settling in the front seat of their car.

"And didn't I say so from the start?" muttered Jonathan, at the last moment pulling out a half-empty carton of juice from beneath him.

The aisle in IKEA led them relentlessly through areas packed with wardrobes, beds, chairs, picture frames, while the children managed to find ways of disappearing in one place and leaping out from another. Megi, in the meantime, filled the yellow and blue bag at an alarming rate with what, in Jonathan's opinion, were unnecessary objects.

"You said you didn't want any Swedish artificial egalitarianism at home." He ruffled his hair as she threw a bathroom rug into the bag.

"Jonathan, those old rags on our floor…" she retorted, assessing the shade of the towels stacked nearby.

He turned so as not to look at this when he heard someone calling him. Kitty stood by a shelf of vegetable graters and next to her were a stout man and a chubby child in a buggy.

"We're looking for a high chair for Emma." Kitty indicated the little girl who raised her eyes and studied Jonathan intently.

Unknowingly, he answered the child's gaze with a smile. Little Antosia had stared like that when she was a baby. "Studying objects," he and Megi used to call it, admiring how she turned a building brick or spoon in her hands – a miniature scientist.

"And we're looking for desks for the children." He waved toward Tomaszek, who was swinging on some curtains. Antosia was not in sight, hiding behind bales of material no doubt.

"Let me introduce you," he turned to Kitty as Megi approached. "This is my wife. And this is Kitty who comes to my writing course."

"My wife," he repeated, introducing her to Kitty's partner.

Once they'd parted ways, Megi forged ahead without a word.

"Megi," he called, seeing a desk he thought might be suitable for Antosia. "Wait!"

She turned with a long face.

"What's up?" he asked.

"I began to think you might have forgotten my name."

He pulled himself up, looking at her helplessly.

"'This is my wife,' 'my wife,'" she continued, mimicking him. "Have you forgotten what I'm called? I'm Megi!"

She cheered up only once they'd decided on two small desks and were headed to the check-out. On the way, she stopped at the mirror department; he walked up to her and put his arms around her, stroking her hair.

"Well," he murmured. "That's out of the way. We coped. As always."

He looked at her face reflected in the mirror, then took in everything, the two of them, the furniture shop.

"Yes, as always."

He ran his hand over her cheek, turned, and called the children. He kept calling them even though they'd heard him a long time ago. He called to deafen the thought that had jabbed at him unexpectedly as he gazed into the mirror. *Even when you're old, I'll love you,* he'd thought. *Even when you're old, Andrea.*

They circle each other on the pretext of talking; the air sparkles with tension. He comes up to her, pulls up her skirt and caresses her naked butt. His cock presses against his trousers; he swiftly sets it free with his other hand and rubs it against her buttocks. She turns her head and searches for his lips – there they are, the hungry cavern with sharp teeth tears at her lip. She turns and adheres to him with her whole body, slips off her skirt, shakes off her shoes and stands before him in her stockings and summer top.

They move away from each other and, feigning cool, go to the bedroom. Beside the bed, she unbuttons his shirt and licks his chest; he impatiently throws off his trousers, slips off his boxer shorts. He forgets that the socks should go first, then pulls them off, holding on to her hand like a blind man. He kneels in front of the triangle of hair, catches her labia in his lips, slips his tongue beneath them and licks the hollows. He is in her groin, smoothes her clitoris, teases her pussy with his tip.

Juices run from her when he grabs the muscles of her thighs. He strokes them gently; they shake beneath his fingers. He sits her on the edge of the bed and with one hand on her hips, parts her thighs with the other. He licks her there, listening to her sighs; her smooth thighs tug at his ears.

She lies on her back; shudders run through her body; she tingles right down to her toes. She tells him this but the words become incomprehensible; the explosion of orgasm leaves her wordless for a few seconds. He licks her belly, sides, breasts; gathers all of her, submissive and hot, and lies on her. Nothing separates them, except his cock between their naked bellies.

She pushes him on his back and wraps her thighs around his hips; the tip of his penis jabs her groin. "Sit, sit!" he begs her while she lowers herself with teasing slowness, her hair hiding her wide-open eyes and falling over her lips. She rocks rhythmically until the muscles in his stomach grow tense. He has to get out of her, cool off a bit.

He enters her again, smoothly, from the back, he draws the shape of her butt with his fingers, harder and harder. "I mustn't have any marks," she pleads breathlessly, and lies on her side while he, behind her, enters and pulls out, a sweating automaton. He turns on his back and scoops up her butt; she sits on him backward; her gently muscular back arches beneath his fingers. He slides his hands down to her hips and leads them up and down, spears her so her head sways, her face turns to the ceiling – until her groan bounces off him.

He pulls her damp body on top of him, turns her lips to his lips and slips into her from beneath; slowly he pushes his tongue into her mouth. The head of his cock, hard as stone, rubs against her inner lining; and finally shudders convulsively. As he injects his charge of sperm into her, Andrea bites his lips. They bleed, but Jonathan doesn't feel it.

# 8

WHEN HE RETURNED from Poland after Christmas, Jonathan understood why people in the north didn't know how to flirt while those in the south seemed constantly aroused. The secret lay in the amount of clothing. As soon as he left the plane in Brussels, although busy gathering the children and suitcases, and finding a taxi, his eyes veered toward several girls; he did what he hadn't done for a long time – he undressed them with his eyes.

A perfectly real question – what a woman wore underneath – started to prey on him, not sparing even the mothers he met at school when he fetched the children. With a new proficiency, he divided the women into categories so as not to bother eyeing those in tracksuits, those who dressed sensibly, or those who were too tall or plump.

Showiness ceased to offend him. If a woman emphasized something with what she wore – or didn't wear – she must obviously have something to show. He rejected Megi's comments – with which he had until recently agreed – that an attitude like that was crude and followed the line of least resistance. He was now a turned-on teenager and a self-confident man. To his satisfaction, there was no woman who didn't feel this – even through layers of winter clothing.

When he walked down the street with Stefan, their heads now turned in rhythm: a woman – turn of the neck – another – a fawning glance – a chick in boots – aaah! The last remnants of embarrassment dissolved, and Jonathan rode the wave of spring that overtook the winter and set itself free from the shell of ice in a stream of smiles, glances and flutterings, until he felt a whirlpool of heat within.

"What is it?" he asked his friend once when they'd popped into a bar for a beer after the gym.

Stefan followed his bright eyes.

"An umbrella stand," he explained.

"I wasn't thinking about that. Are you having something?" Jonathan broke off because the waiter they called the Lion King, due to his mane of hair, stood beside them.

"All that exercise has made me hungry, I think I'll have a croque monsieur." Stefan flicked through the menu, undecided. "Or no, I'll have a croque madame. *Pour moi, le croque madame, s'il vous plaît.*"

Instead of listening to Stefan who was telling him all about Przemek's maneuvers to settle into a government position in the future, Jonathan immersed himself in recollections of the previous evening.

The lights on the sound system glimmered, music seeped slowly, the sound of horses' hooves came from the window.

"Mounted police," whispered Andrea and huddled up closer in the crook of his arm.

"They won't find us." He smiled in the half-light and kissed her hair.

The squeaking of trams and the distant wail of a fire engine woke him at dawn. For a moment he didn't know where he was. He stared at the colorful stripes of the sheets, the books piled up by the wall, the navy-blue alarm clock, children's drawings. He peered over his shoulder – next to him lay Megi.

He curled up into a pretzel. He was in his apartment – this was his home. He called this period in time home because during it there was room for his family, Megi, and Andrea. His home was large, sunny, and full of love …

The waiter placed a plate with a hot sandwich covered with minced meat in tomato sauce and melted cheese on the table. Jonathan, with difficulty, shook the recollections aside.

"… the option of going back to Poland." He heard Stefan's voice. "And then he might propose that Megi should carry on working for him. What do you think about it?"

"About what?" Jonathan drank a little of his beer, the pleasant coolness tickling his throat.

"Going back to Poland."

Jonathan looked at Stefan as if he were intending to lip-read from now on.

"It probably won't come to it, they're only rumors." Stefan patted him on the shoulder and bit into his croque.

"Based on what?"

Yellow ribbons of cheese stretched from Stefan's mouth. The thought of cutting it from the croque flashed through Jonathan's mind.

"To Poland?" He half stated, half asked.

"Mhm." Stefan shook his head in all directions.

"Impossible." Jonathan leaned forcefully back in his chair. "I'm not going anywhere."

Stefan nodded enthusiastically.

"Anywhere," repeated Jonathan.

"Of course." Barely concealed compassion appeared on Stefan's face.

Jonathan leaned forward then back, and forward again – he rocked like someone autistic. Stefan pushed the plate aside and put his arm on Jonathan's shoulder, but Jonathan brushed it away.

"I'm not going anywhere."

*Megi thinks she's running out of eye cream, Tomaszek's voice is hoarse, the emails are piling up, and she doesn't know where to buy the small celery she needs for a stock. Oh yes! And the dry-cleaners – she has to drop off their spring jackets. And buy some pretty underwear to surprise Jonathan.*

*The sun is shining over Brussels like a light bulb over the chaos of a bedroom, laying bare tricks of make-up and worming its way beneath warm clothes, making people rub their eyes and untie their scarves.*

*Megi enters Exki and picks up a sandwich labelled "Romeo et Juliette." As she makes her way to the check-out she hears someone calling her. The trainee is waving to her from a table; next to her sits a long-haired girl. The girl turns and Megi sees it's Andrea.*

*Something skips in Megi; her sandwiches grow sweaty in her grip. She doesn't know if she should go up to them; in the end, she forces herself, even manages to say something. Andrea reaches for a serviette; her nails are painted a cherry brown, a color Jonathan associates with old hands. Megi has short nails with a touch of natural varnish. She sees now that they lack expression.*

*They leave together and bid each other goodbye beside a window displaying underwear. The trainee says something about the Spaniard. "Jacinto" – the name rasps on her lips with its foreign sound; Megi's nervousness explodes in a torrent of hysterical giggles. She muffles them; it's ignoble to laugh like that and she stops her mouth. She's made a fool of herself; the trainee looks meaningfully at Andrea.*

*But suddenly Megi sees that Andrea's lips are quivering. Or maybe she's imagining it; maybe Andrea wants to yawn or say something. The laughter dies in Megi. The trainee walks away and, a moment later, Andrea also says goodbye. And Megi struggles with herself. She's itching to call after her, to look into her face.*

Jonathan felt guilty that he was sparing with sex with Megi so as to have more to give to Andrea. So for several days he fumed, waiting for Simon to get himself off to England, while Megi, in the meantime, was making it increasingly clear that he wasn't devoting enough time to her. Initially, she was nice to him, cuddled up, and even paid him compliments – which surprised him because he'd thought that that stage in their relationship had passed irrevocably – and, although he was still blinded by his desire for Andrea, Megi's fawning behavior had an effect. This led to a frightening emotional complication – he felt guilty for being tempted to fuck his own wife; in his eyes this equalled a betrayal of his lover.

Yet Andrea kept calling off their meetings. She wrote about an overload of professional duties that required her attention; her emails became rarer and rarer. Jonathan justified this by saying she was busy, but one night he woke up, needled by the thought that he'd jumped to her every beck and call, regardless of professional deadlines.

Again he was in the grip of jealousy and suffered like an old man riddled with arthritis. Lack of sexual fulfilment added to his tension. How he missed the feeling of satisfaction in his body, the delicious pain in his groin that came from screwing Andrea. Didn't she miss it, too? The image of his beloved woman in someone else's arms extinguished his joy in life.

He recalled their last meetings, searched for a place, a situation in which he might have offended her, said or done something untoward. He blundered on – for her sake. Waiting for stupid messages, suffering so much pain, uncertainty, imagining a younger, more attractive, better dressed, more successful ... oh!

One day, when he got back after dropping the children off at school, he found Megi at home.

"Don't you feel well?" he asked when he saw her pottering around in her dressing-gown, making coffee.

"Do I look ill?" She smiled flirtatiously; her hair was slightly damp after her morning shower.

Jonathan put his bag on the floor and studied her.

"So what makes you stay at home?" he asked.

"I wanted to surprise you." She nervously tightened the cord of her dressing-gown.

He walked up to her, put his hands on her shoulders and kissed her on the head. Megi sighed and returned to brewing coffee.

He sliced the bread, she laid out the butter. As they prepared breakfast, they exchanged comments and joked. Jonathan told her that Cecile had offered him the course next year with extended hours; Megi summed up Przemek's strategic maneuvers in two fields – to get close to the politicians who looked as though they might win the next elections, and to get a girl.

"Both long-term strategies?" Jonathan bit into his sandwich.

Megi pulled a plate from the cupboard and handed it to him.

"His problem with women is that they instinctively sense what's most important to him," she replied, sitting down on the high stool. "Meaning power."

"In my opinion, his problem with women is that he's hideous."

"And yet he does have girlfriends." Megi's dressing-gown slipped open a little; a long thigh showed beneath the towelling.

"A good subject for a nature program."

"Some find him attractive," she muttered.

"Get real. Would you like to have it off with him?"

She laughed; her leg slipped out completely from beneath the white towelling; Jonathan's eyes rested on the smooth skin. He wondered whether she had any panties on.

"You don't understand what makes some men attractive, that's the whole problem."

"It would be a problem if I did understand."

"Don't you fantasize about doing it with guys?" she asked.

Jonathan shook his head, staring at the band of skin above her thighs. He moved closer.

"And with two women?" she questioned.

"Mmm!"

"A propos, I met Andrea recently. We bumped into each other in Exki."

The sandwich shot out of Jonathan's hand. He bent over, apologising under his breath. "We," in a sentence where his wife put herself in the same category as his lover, upset his balance, and not only mentally. But he was struck by something else in what she'd told him.

"When did you meet her?" He picked the bread up from the floor and threw it into the bin; his face pulsated.

"I can't remember." Megi shrugged. "Last week? Two weeks ago?"

"Two?"

"What's the difference?"

He spun on his axis and swiftly began to clear the kitchen surface.

"Aren't we eating any more?" Megi was surprised.

"I've got to go and write, the Pavlov Dogs are being dogmatic."

He made toward the hall; Megi pattered behind him, her dressing-gown hanging off her slender shoulders.

"Are you going out? You just said you were going to write."

"I'll be back in a minute. The printer's run out of ink, I'm going to get some more." He pecked her on the cheek and ran downstairs.

Andrea didn't want to let him in but he sat out in the hall and stayed there until she poked her head through the door. Seeing him hunched there, she told him they had to stop seeing each other.

"I know what happened," he said, getting to his feet.

She stepped back and shook her head.

"I know, I really do know," he whispered, slowly coming close to her.

Again she shook her head but he stretched his hand out to her and gently immersed his fingers in her hair.

"Andrea …"

He took her by the head, then by the hands. He cuddled her as they stepped over the threshold, crossed the living room; he laid her on the bed. She didn't look at him, said nothing, her lips and fists clenched. He stroked them until they began to yield. He licked and kissed her fingers, one after another, carefully, tenderly. He held her in his arms, rocked her until she no longer curled in on herself.

Then he started to stroke the whole of her – from her smooth hair, down her shoulders, breasts, belly, hips, thighs, and knees. He slipped off her socks, caressed every toe, licked the spaces between them, kissed her toenails. When she groaned, he rolled up her skirt, lowered the rim of her panties and entered her, without undressing – only his cock and her pussy. Andrea arched and started to cry but he scooped her beneath him and came without a single thought, his face wet with happiness and fear.

# 9

Jonathan stood behind the glass and watched the group of children practising aikido. Little hands parried blows; this child and that tumbled under sudden swings. Tomaszek brandished his limbs enthusiastically; Antosia carefully copied the instructor's moves. Her precision, his spontaneity, Jonathan's and Megi's genes merged.

He glanced aside checking that nobody had caught him in his rapture. But other parents were gazing at their children with similar bliss. Jonathan smiled to himself – they were shameless! There was a time when he hadn't been able to understand it, but now, along with other parents, he allowed himself to be carried on the wave of indescribable happiness that moments such as these brought.

Megi kept saying that the instant she first saw Antosia, and then Tomaszek, when the tiny babies lay on her belly in the delivery room, was the very essence of life for her. She said that never before or since had she experienced anything so strong.

He believed her; he'd been there with her, seen her reaction. He'd experienced it differently. What he most remembered of the births was his own helplessness, the fact that he couldn't help his woman, had nothing to do, nothing concrete, nothing he was good at. When he took the three-kilogram bundle into his arms, he wept with fear – the newborn was so fragile.

Later, he changed the diapers with Megi, got up in the night, fed the babies, and taught them how to walk, but in truth it had taken him longer to be ready for fatherhood than it had taken her for motherhood. Now, he watched Antosia and Tomaszek through the glass and thought that moments such as these were the sun of life, fragments from a limited series, treasures.

"It's a shame adults don't enjoy themselves," he thought, observing the children. "Adults plan and execute."

Andrea appeared in front of his eyes. From the moment he saw how humane she was and realized that, in spite herself, she was trying to break it off with him because she did not want to take him away from his family, he loved her even more. She was a beautiful woman and a wonderful human being. The thought of her brought on an erection and tears welled in his eyes. When he'd taken her – that time after finding out that she and Megi had bumped into each other – she'd written to him saying he ought to leave her. "How can I leave you," he wrote back. "You're in me deeper than ever. Can't you see what you're doing to me? I want to fuck you and kneel before you. I can't believe that you, *you*, are with me."

He looked at the children again. Such strong emotions had sprung up within him lately. How he'd matured as a father, as the man of a beloved woman. Once he'd thought that fresh experiences washed away the color of previous ones; now he knew they deepened them.

*Megi runs doubled over beneath her umbrella as hail pounds the fabric and the rain spits even beneath it; but when she stops outside the shop the sun is already shining to the accompaniment of birdsong. A mannequin stands in the display window in front of which she and Andrea had parted a few days ago. Today it is dressed in a silk vest. Not only Jonathan but she, too, associates silk – especially imitation silk – with old age.*

*Megi pushes the door and walks alongside the row of hangers. Something sexy but not kitschy. In no way must Jonathan laugh at her. She wanders around, restless as a bee, until she grabs a bra and pair of panties and dives into a changing room. The black triangles of underwear contrast sharply with her pale skin. Megi joins her hands and unconsciously rubs one against the other.*

*"Is the size right?" the saleswoman asks from behind the curtain.*

*"Yes, yes." She rubs her hands harder.*

*A memory comes back: they used to rub their hands like that at the summer camps then shove them under each other's noses saying, "Look! That's how corpses smell." Megi smiles; the mirror registers the change. She bends over and pulls her phone out of her bag. She'd told her mother of her suspicions about Jonathan and Andrea – she's close to her mother – and they both decided that Megi should phone Andrea to sense whether the panic in the latter's eyes had only been an illusion.*

*She dials Andrea's number, which she obtained from the trainee, and cringes. What's she going to talk about? The smell of corpses? What's Swedish for "corpse"? Or Czech? She knows nothing about this partner of Simon's.*

*"Hello? It's me, Megi."*

*"I'm sorry but is it urgent?" replies Andrea's official voice. "I'm just recording."*

*Megi hangs up.*

*"Is that your size or shall I bring another one?" the shop assistant enquires from behind the curtain.*

*Megi doesn't reply. She stands in front of the mirror; the black lingerie is draped over a hanger, next to it her own clothes. She gazes at the triangle of pubic hair. Should she shave? That's what they'd done to her when preparing her for the operation. The smell of disinfectant and a bald pussy. She hated them for reducing her, a woman, to a little girl.*

*And now she's cold. She quickly pulls on her clothes and leaves the shop, buying nothing.*

Jonathan's thoughts returned to the previous evening. They'd watched a couple of episodes of *Sex and the City*, Megi had borrowed them from Monika, who loved the film.

At first, Megi had watched the series as she would a spider behind glass.

"A woman's sexuality can't be based on a coarse reversal of roles, especially in the Casanova myth!" she'd fumed. "There's a rhythm in the way a woman matures. There's a time for everything – on a monthly, yearly, and ten-year scale. I can see that men might want us to be available nonstop but it can't be like that! And something like this" – she'd pointed to the screen – "is made to sell things to the ever-ready female, crotchless panties and other shit. There's no truth, only business."

"Celibacy was introduced for similar reasons." Jonathan smiled. "So as not to pass church property on to children. That's business, too."

He'd thought she'd laugh but she got to her feet and angrily switched off the television. It suddenly hit him that she hadn't laughed for a long time. He couldn't make her laugh any more. Was it like that ever since Andrea had arrived on the scene; was it then that the thread of understanding between him and his wife had started to grow weaker?

Watching her, he was again haunted by beginnings. As if there was such a thing as a beginning! Yes, he'd met Andrea, accidentally kissed her, but they must have been waiting for each other. There must have been a vacuum in him somewhere for the moment to have shaken him so much. Because when had Megi last shown herself to him in a bra and panties? She used to show him her new clothes, ask his advice about whether they suited her or not, to which he used to reply, "Yes, wonderful," "No, take them back," "Not bad but a bit too sensible." They'd acquired the habit in their first years together when Jonathan, asked for his opinion, had pulled the new garb off, had her, and only then expressed his opinion.

The good old days! They'd enjoyed each other, laughed together. She'd thought Jonathan's fascination with the female metaphor of taking off the armor of the office day so funny. He'd latched on to the phrase. Megi, home from work, would say, "I've got to remove my bra," and he, returning tired, would throw himself on the sofa and, glancing at her, murmur, "I've not even got the strength to remove my bra." They'd joked that they were moving with the times because taking off a bra was on a par in their home with loosening a tie. And then daily life had teemed with chores to be done immediately so that, one day, when she'd appeared in front of him in her underwear – he couldn't remember exactly when – he'd merely nodded his approval and returned to the computer. Poor Megi had stood in the doorway for a moment then turned, embarrassed; Jonathan had leapt from his chair, put his arms around her, and given her some good cunnilingus. She'd stimulated him until she squeezed a few drops from his cock, like an icicle melting in the spring sun.

Now, Jonathan turned to the table and began to tap at the keyboard. The Pavlov Dogs didn't romanticise beginnings; they lived in constant continuity; their lives were continuous. And when there was no constancy they allowed something else to take its place. Such was the law of nature, a dog's law.

# 10

SOME TIME AGO, when Latin American literature was in fashion, Jonathan found the verbosity of its prose annoying. He'd been a fan of Nabokov then, of his precision, spiced with an ironic style. Now *Love in the Time of Cholera* drew him in like music pulsating in his belly. He asked his students what they thought of Márquez and saw that his admiration alone didn't render Márquez objectively admirable. Ariane said she'd already been through it – just like bell-bottoms. Jean-Pierre sniffed at the lack of refinement in the overly long stories. Geert, a poetry lover, mumbled that so many words between two covers overwhelmed him. Only Kitty admitted that Latin American novels were not a bad vintage.

"Because what's so literary about the sentence: 'He finally understood something that, without knowing it himself, he had felt numerous times before: that one could at one and the same time and with equal pain, love many women simultaneously, without betraying any'?" asked Jean-Pierre.

"That's not any good." Ariane settled herself more comfortably on the chair.

"In what way?" asked Jonathan.

"It's too …"

"Immoral?" Kitty broke in.

Ariane shook her head as though something buzzed around her.

"Too simple! Simple as …".

Jonathan was about to throw in the missing word but realized he didn't know the English word for "*cep*" [blockhead].

"Didn't I say so?" Jean-Pierre took possession of another chair and turned it into an elbow-rest.

"What's simple about it?" Kitty was surprised.

"It's a round sentence that doesn't clarify anything," snorted Ariane. "Where is human emotion?"

"In the rest of the book?" risked Jonathan.

"What I mean," Ariane seemed irritated by something, "is it lacks life's reality."

"Literary novels aren't nonfiction," muttered Jean-Pierre.

"Reality is integral to the story," she explained almost angrily.

Jonathan thought about it afterward when sitting in church waiting for Andrea. But only for that moment because next they lay on the carpet in her living room, Jonathan with his hands around her waist, Andrea snuggled in the saddle of his hips. As she raised herself he took her apple-shaped backside in his hands. He adored her sticking it out; he could admire her pussy for hours.

On his way home, he decided to keep both Andrea and Megi. He wanted them both; the symbiosis was essential to him. Vibrating with love, he thought about the chain of sexual moves – he licks Andrea, Megi sucks him, Andrea Simon, and he, Jonathan, takes Megi from behind.

In all this, he felt wanted, desired, and loved. When he left home, Megi admired him; when he went to Andrea's, she huddled up to him. He wallowed in caresses, blossomed in their love, discovering ever better sides to himself. People he knew and people he didn't know flocked around him now, women accosted him with their eyes, men phoned about professional matters until he was afraid that one day he would wake up and find that it was all too good to be true.

At such moments, when he was horrified by how far he'd blundered, he tried to weigh out the failure of his "real" relationship – or at least the one that others considered as such – his marriage. And yet the word "failure" didn't fit because although he had turned his world upside down in his thoughts, undermined its foundations, and vigorously thrown everything away to be with Andrea, in reality he defended that world. He didn't even think of leaving Megi – his best friend, his family. And under no circumstances his children. No such script existed.

Jonathan thought that the contrasts provided by the evening were the stuff of writers' dreams. The three parties he and Megi had attended were like going from one funfair mirror to another, one making you thin, the next making you fat.

They started with a party held by a couple of Megi's young colleagues. The hosts were good-looking, served imaginative dishes, made sure their guests had enough to drink; their fair-haired daughter played with a fattish Golden Retriever. After an hour, Jonathan had said practically all that could meet with favorable answers. When the conversation moved to comparing life in Belgium to that in their fatherland – with an emphasis on the superiority of cucumber soup over the local speciality, *carbonnade* – Megi leaned over and whispered in Jonathan's ear: "Can't they see that there's no conflict between liking what's here and what's there?"

"They're defending their own yard." He shrugged.

"Brave Snail that kept to Polish soil," she snorted.

"What snail?"

"Required reading. The peasants resisting foreign powers in the nineteenth century. You were doing Shelley at the time."

Next was a pub – somebody from Megi's work, who'd been transferred to another EU country, was holding a goodbye do. Jonathan stepped into a world of cigarette smoke and tipsy men with marks left by their wedding rings. Seeing some dancers place their hands on the intimate parts of their partners, Jonathan signalled to Megi that it was time to go.

"If that was hell and the other was heaven," he muttered, "what's in store now?"

Simon, the host of the third party that evening, had not omitted to invite them this time. Andrea greeted them at the threshold. Jonathan was speechless, she looked so beautiful in her tight dress; which is why he was relieved that, after taking their coats, she mingled with the crowd.

The apartment seemed entirely different than the one he knew from their secret trysts. He had generally put the meticulous appearance of the place down to Simon; now he was unpleasantly surprised to discover that the bourgeois love of order was no stranger to his hostess either.

The food was served in family porcelain, the knives and forks arranged in neat rows, next to which lay ironed fabric napkins.

"Most ambitious," muttered Megi, squinting at the cutlery trestles that had no right to be there because everyone was walking around carrying their plates.

Despite the pomposity, the guests were circulating casually, raising serious issues in the kitchen, making drunken passes on the dance floor, petting each other and smoking on the balcony. The door handle to the bathroom was loose so that women went in pairs – one went in, the other stood on guard. It occurred to Jonathan that they always went to pee together, and that the lock must have broken that day because the previous day, when Simon had returned from London, it had still been working.

Above the heads of the other guests he caught sight of Andrea dancing with the journalist who'd been unpleasantly surprised when Jonathan had lied that he'd learned English in Poland. Jonathan turned and went out onto the balcony. He helped himself to a cigarette from a stray pack and blew the smoke into the air. A moment later, he heard a creak – in the balcony door stood Andrea.

He glanced at her over his shoulder then stared at the street full of respectable apartments. Suddenly he felt her fingers on his lips. He backed away but he'd already picked up the smell – the smell of her pussy.

Anger clenched his jaws, but his cock swelled in his trousers.

"Kiss it," she ordered.

*"Megi?" calls Martyna. "Have you been here long? I didn't see you!"*

*"I didn't see you either." Megi stifles a yawn. "Where were you hiding?"*

*"In the kitchen!"*

*"The kitchen, you?"*

*Martyna smiles, pleasantly tickled, she likes to stress her dislike of "a woman's chores".*

*"We were talking about this exhibition that has just opened in London. Did you see it?"*

*Megi shakes her head. She has just been to London but what she remembers most is the airport and the fact that she had masses of work. Martyna doesn't work; she claims to hold an artistic salon that Jonathan calls her "narcissistic salon." Martyna now starts to pour out a stream of words and Megi automatically stops listening. She recalls a conversation with Przemek, or rather information slipped in between the lines about his designs on a government position in Poland and the hint that he'd like to see her with him. Now Megi shrugs – she can't imagine leaving Brussels. She feels at home here; here, she has a choice at every corner. Besides, the children really like their school, and Jonathan ... where is he exactly?*

*Megi stares enquiringly at Martyna's moving lips.*

*"We've got to go." She makes a move to pass her interlocutor.*

*"Are you looking for Jonathan? He's on the balcony, at least that's where they were a few minutes ago."*

*"They?" Megi freezes.*

*Martyna looks at her in a way Megi doesn't like. She looks like a puffball close up, she thinks.*

*"With Andrea," says Martyna and adds, "I also saw them in the street together."*

*A frame from a Polish film suddenly appears in front of Megi's eyes – a Polish soldier being killed by a German. That tilt, the way they focused on the tilt of the body as it fell backward, drums the thought in.*

*"I once saw them leave a church together." It's Martyna's voice again. "I'm not the only one to have seen them."*

*Megi tilts her head and the world is crooked. She holds her face in her hands and rearranges it, back to its former expression.*

*"And now I saw them as ..." Martyna raises her arm, there's something black beneath it.*

*Moles, birthmarks, or has she got something stuck? The weasel of a thought runs through Megi's head.*

*"Goodnight," she says loudly and runs out.*

*They're not on the balcony. Nor in the room with the bottles. Megi tugs at the bathroom door, the handle remains in her hand.*

*"Don't worry." Simon laughs and takes the door handle from her. "Are you off already?" He, too, looks around but Jonathan isn't anywhere. He indicates the coat stand but Megi rushes out in nothing but her dress.*

*She races alongside the respectable apartments, or rather skips oddly, rubbing her arms; it's a cold evening. She can't remember where they parked. Something blinds her and makes her eyelid pulsate. She presses down on it with her fingers, which makes it harder for her to see anything – how's she going to find them now?*

*She sits on a bench in the bus shelter, shivers so much that a black boy stares at her anxiously. Megi opens her handbag – only one tissue, one sheet of paper for all this fear.*

*"Why doesn't Jonathan want me?"*

*She raises her head just as she did when she kissed the other man. He was taller than her, even a tiny bit taller than Jonathan. One business trip, two nights during which they didn't leave the bed. At one stage he'd kissed her labia and in his English, weighed down with an Austrian accent, asked, "What do you call it?" "Cipka," she answered. "Cipka," he repeated without understanding.*

*He didn't laugh at the word, he savored its sound. And at that moment she reclaimed them – both her pussy and herself – because she liked this Megi who arched her back, sticking her butt out to her lover so that he could slip into her smoothly and rub her inner walls. She loved the rhythm of the moves, the slapping, his hips and her buttocks, her arms resting on the edge of the bed, her head hanging, swaying with the rhythm of fucking. What had she thought about then? Only one thing – his cock with its pulsating head, the ingeniously formed instrument as it slipped in and out, caught at her insides and teased her, rubbed her, aroused her …*

*After two nights her pussy was so chafed that, on returning home, she was irrationally relieved that nobody penetrated her (Jonathan was not reaching for her then). Her groin could cool down, and she had time to be with herself.*

*A couple of days later, as she was going to meet her lover, Jonathan slipped his hand beneath her skirt by chance and discovered she was not wearing any panties. It excited him, she barely escaped, said she had to fly to work.*

*That day she'd had them both.*

*After some time, she made a decision – she broke off with the other man. She returned from their last meeting in tears; the car coped with her as a carthorse does with a drunken carter, while she arranged points worthy of a lawyer in her head:*

*1. Thunderbolt, that is, infatuation.*

*2. Longing to meet, childishness.*

*3. Happiness reciprocated.*

*4. Lows of uncertainty alternating with flights of euphoria.*

5. *Impossibility of being in the same place at the same time in public because the chemistry is impossible to miss.*

6. *Phase of blindness due to reciprocation, savoring each other, growing admiration.*

7. *First cut.*

8. *First quarrel and reconciliation.*

9. *Deepening of feelings but also moments of hesitation over whether to back out while there's time.*

10. *Blundering on nevertheless.*

11. *Deepening, getting to know each other better, adapting to each other, trust.*

12. *Jealousy.*

13. *Tiredness.*

14. *Increasingly serious consideration of whether or not to change one's life for that person. At the same time, small disappointments.*

15. *More and more shortcomings can be seen. Helplessness because feelings put one at somebody's mercy. Aversion to the person who has such power.*

**book three**

*Brussels, autumn 2008*

AN EX-MODEL IN JEANS, black sweater, and suede shoes approached the spick-and-span Land Rover parked in front of the toy shop in Waterloo. He let his children in – they had the same features as their father, the same movements and clothes. Packs of toys landed in the trunk. "He's going to his trophy wife. And, in the evening, to his lover," thought Jonathan and pulled out a lollipop stick from his pocket, a present from Tomaszek. His eyes fell on another man leaving the shop. "Poor creep," he pitied the flabby fifty-year-old. To his surprise a herd appeared behind the man, a Girl-Guide-like wife and a file of boys identical to their father.

Jonathan climbed into his Toyota and drove away; only when nearing home did he realize that he hadn't bought what he'd set out to buy – presents for his children. He did a U-turn on the Avenue de Fre, glancing at the residences concealed in the parks. "They belong to those who made their fortune in the Congo," his dentist, a Lebanese who'd comfortably found a clinic for himself near a wealthy clientele, had informed him. His fillings were unreliable so Jonathan had stopped going to him.

As he passed the windows of the Lebanese clinic, it crossed Jonathan's mind that it was people who hated it who lived in the heart of Brussels. Hatred, the other side of love. He was the same – like a ball-bearing in a bagatelle, he rolled from side to side. Now that Andrea was pregnant, he loved her, hated her, hated her, loved, loved …

# 1

*Brussels, autumn 2007, a year earlier*

HE EAGERLY AWAITED their trysts, like a believer awaiting Holy Communion, equally unsure whether he was worthy. Neatly dressed, he left his gym bag in the car, entered the darkness of the church and sat in a pew. Slowly, his thoughts unfurled.

Although he tried not to meet his lover always in the same places, he grew to know the people there. He bowed in greeting to the thin man with the hands of a pianist, who spent his time in the church on St Catherine's Square; nodded to the gray-haired, neatly dressed woman in St Michael's Cathedral; and the homeless who sat beneath the temple walls, he recognized by their dogs – all the homeless had dogs.

He soaked in their phantomlike presence, collected fragile events until Andrea appeared. She tore the silence with the tap of her heels, turned the darkness inside out with the scent of news which permeated her to the marrow. Still shaking after an interview, high on television adrenalin, she approached and took him by the hand. She wanted to leave immediately. She disliked the stagnation of churches, the smell of wax, stillness.

He held her hand, warming her as though wanting to pass on to her something she didn't understand. He had a fleeting hope that Andrea would ask him about the elderly woman whose eyes were glued to the altar, or the man with the fingers of a pianist. But she was already swiftly whispering about the latest moves of Commission officials. He got up and held her – wanted to lift her above the scum of current affairs, throw her a rope with an anchor so that she could grab the carelessly bypassed, fragile manifestations of life.

Once, after an exceptionally beautiful session of lovemaking, in his elation, a fairy tale's "Over the mountains, over the seas, there lived …" ran through his head. He asked whether she ever thought of traveling some more, whether she'd like to move somewhere else. She adamantly denied it: Brussels was populated with sources for her, and her television career was forged among its officials.

"It's my job," she said. "I love it. I'm happy here, everything's all mixed up, Brussels is a huge pot of languages. Here the gender of a man's cock is feminine, *une verge*. A vagina is masculine, *un vagin*. I don't want to leave."

He took her from the churches and made love to her on Simon's sofa, on his floor, between his sheets. He immersed himself in Andrea and thought he could be with her there or anywhere.

This time, after Megi's abrupt departure from Andrea's and Simon's party, he had barely managed to convince his wife of his innocence. He explained that he'd gone – alone – to buy some cigarettes. How was he supposed to have known where Andrea was at the time? "Don't be childish." He gazed into Megi's worried eyes. "Do you take me for an idiot? Why should I risk, destroy everything I've built up over the years?" Megi left the room; he raised his hands, which had gripped his thighs and left damp patches on the corduroy – it looked as though he'd wet himself.

They'd promised to be careful. And this excited them all the more; they screwed like mad, hugged in parks, petted in the car. He slipped his T-shirt beneath her butt because juices ran down her thighs when he licked her and made the seats sticky. When he returned, it was as though he were drugged. The following day, he woke up in the morning unable to believe what he'd done.

Bad dreams and strange thoughts tormented him. He couldn't imagine daily life without her, even a brief parting.

Pride in being able to satisfy both Andrea and Megi had long evaporated. He didn't want to make love to anyone apart from Andrea; the very thought of wrestling with another woman was as grotesque as inflating a frog.

He kissed Andrea and penetrated deeply or plunged shallowly, until she wriggled her hips impatiently. "Do you really want it?" he asked and rocked her from beneath while she clung to him or threw her arms out.

Although women provoked him with their eyes more and more frequently, he had stopped playing the wise guy who stood up for polygamy. The time of unbridled thoughts about numerous lovers, the time of reading Anaïs Nin, had passed. He was experiencing a wave of monogamy – with Andrea.

When he saw her at his door, alone, without Simon, he couldn't control himself and in a gesture unbefitting the greetings of a mere host, his lips touched hers. Andrea recoiled. For the first time, he saw her thrown off balance.

"Andrea!" He heard Megi's voice behind him.

"Simon couldn't come."

"I know, he sent me an email. What would you like to drink?"

"I, too, hate being asked, 'Where's your husband?'" The voice of his wife, as she walked away with his lover, reached Jonathan. "As if a woman without a partner was a table with a missing leg."

A moment later, Megi loomed up in front of him again, reminding him to look after the guests' food and drinks. He uncorked a bottle of wine and circulated with it, a little disorientated that some people were sitting on his sofa, spaced out and irritable with jealousy because Andrea was acting as if he wasn't there – tilting her head back, running her fingers through her hair and laughing at the jokes of guys showing off in front of her.

"Jonathan, could you fetch some ice from the freezer?" asked Megi.

Stefan turned up the music; some guests started to dance. Rafał stretched out his hand to Andrea in invitation. She knew the impression she made when she danced, they'd talked about it once; even so, Jonathan stood in a group with some other fools and stared at her.

"Jonathan!"

"Yes?"

"The ice! That's the third time I've had to ask you."

Megi's face seemed paler, tarnished, like an ancient teaspoon. He tore his back away from the wall. Rafał, in high spirits, tried to spin Andrea but was so overwhelmed he turned a pirouette himself. Jonathan leaned against the edge of the freezer and pressed the ice to his forehead. It excited her when men couldn't take their eyes off her, salivated about her, especially when Simon wasn't there. She sensed her power and bandied it around. She was just as they made her out to be; he was the only one not to see it because in the churches, in bed, they were one to one. There, she looked at nobody but him.

"Who's the chick?" started Jean-Pierre when Jonathan appeared downstairs with the ice.

"Which one?"

"What do you mean 'which one'?"

Rafał had let go of Andrea's hand and she was now walking toward them, hips swaying. Jonathan, without much thought, pressed the ice into Jean-Pierre's hands and blocked her way.

"Andrea," he said, although she was looking at him as though he were nothing but mist. "Couldn't we be ... together?"

*Megi's hands shake, the thought coming to her is tangled, with frayed endings: how could he ... how could he?*

*She retreats, a floorboard creaks beneath her foot. The man lifts his head from the hips of the girl lying on the pile of coats, his chin glistening like a dribbling baby's.*

*"Who is it?" The nervous giggle of the girl patters across Megi's spine like a little mouse.*

*"Never mind," mutters Stefan indistinctly.*

*Megi takes another step back, this time noiselessly.*

*"Have you seen Stefan?" she hears behind her.*

*Monika looks tired but smiles her eternally polite smile.*

*"Ha!" says Megi. What else can she say?*

*Monika's lips turn up more in a tic than a smile. A guttural sound comes from the room behind them.*

*"Stefan's downstairs." Megi closes the door and pushes Monika ahead.*

*Later, when the guests depart, she lies in bed next to Jonathan but can't fall asleep, her throat is tight. She goes downstairs, chooses a record. She needs a woman's voice. She lights a half-burned-down candle.*

*So, Stefan too! Drunk, at a party. What's worse – that or Jonathan and Andrea's balcony scene that Monika had told her about? Jonathan had justified himself while she looked in silence as he sat in front of her, downtrodden, yet attractive, with his slender hands digging into the corduroy of his rough trousers. "I'm not an idiot," he'd repeated. "What does Andrea need Jonathan for?" Megi had thought at the time. And finally she'd believed him.*

*Her thoughts of six years earlier – before she'd decided to return to Jonathan, before she'd broken up with the other man – were evidence of panic and her sense of guilt, interspersed with flashes of rebellion: "My body belongs to me." How she had deliberated at the time, how many thoughts – both her own and those of others – had she mulled over! She'd even bought a book about polygamy.*

*She didn't like a culture that shaped everyone to the pattern of "good-bad," "black-white." She had read and analyzed; it had felt as though she were regaining her sight. She thought she'd finally discerned a scale of tones; instead of judging, she graded. She ran up and down the grades, flew and plummeted.*

*A person who is free falls in love, one who is not free betrays. Why had she betrayed Jonathan? Because he didn't want her? Why didn't he want her? Had he been struck by the Madonna-Whore curse? Had he seen only a mother in Megi at the time and, for the love of God, didn't want to see anything else?*

*Beginnings, beginnings!*

*She remembers when she told her mother that she was tired, that she felt like a wound-up robot. That she was missing the anesthetic, childish infatuation. Jonathan.*

*Half a year later, she had told her that she was in love. With another man.*

# 2

JONATHAN SLIPS into the lining of Andrea's vagina. "Jonathan, Jonathan!" the cry reaches him, but he rushes ahead, forward, rubs persistently, until her muscles clench his cock. Andrea weeps but he pushes right inside, into the depths of her belly, somewhere higher than her navel.

"Oh God!" Megi would have said but this isn't her, it's Andrea beneath him. Rumpled like a rag doll, she doesn't mention God, only laughs wildly.

"Something like that, something like that," she pants, the whites of her eyes glistening, her bare teeth clenching and unclenching.

Jonathan presses his tongue between them. He doesn't drill hard with it – now, after it all, he has no strength left to push it down her throat. He runs the tip over her lips, caresses her gums, licks the inside of her cheeks. And she carries on laughing and wiping tears away.

When they get out of bed, Jonathan holds her rump from below. "The perfect shape of an apple," he says in English and Polish. She replies in Swedish and Czech. Now Jonathan laughs. Andrea tenses; he ruffles her hair, hiding the rest of his smile in it. The same things excite them but "*restaurace v cipu*" doesn't make her laugh.

Suddenly he asks her if she doesn't want any children. Andrea looks at him, her heart-shaped face framed by dark hair.

"No," she answers after reflection. "I don't like children."

Jonathan draws her to the rumpled sofa again, turns her on her back. It's better like this, now he can lie on her, simulating intercourse, which makes him grow stiff again.

"But you'll want them someday?"

Andrea slides from beneath him, picks her bra up from the armchair.

"Maybe," she says slipping her hands through the straps.

"When?" Jonathan, lying on his back, stretches himself.

Andrea turns to him and, carefully arranging her breasts in the bra cups, says, "You mean because I'm over thirty? Men have been ramming it into my head that I'm old ever since I was seventeen. The boys in my class pointed to fifteen-year-olds and said, 'Look, fresh goods!'"

She reaches for her panties; the colors of spring flash in front of his eyes, disciplined by lace trimmings.

"They did it because they couldn't have me. It was their way of punishing me."

Jonathan draws himself out on the bed, crosses his hands behind his head.

"May I smoke?"

Andrea shakes her head. She is just going to leave the room but turns at the last moment, walks up to him, and takes his hand. Slowly, millimeter by millimeter, she starts to pull off his wedding ring. The metal resists so Andrea puts Jonathan's finger into her mouth, moistens it with saliva without looking down to where an erection is slowly swelling.

"Andrea," groans Jonathan. "Stop…"

He is engulfed by flames, the heat of wet dreams spreads through his groin, tickles thighs, licks testicles coarsely, like a cat.

"God!" cries Jonathan. And spreads his arms, legs, lips.

They never went back to the question that Jonathan had asked Andrea at his party. "Couldn't we be together?" still hung in that room, that time, pressed in between the cubes of ice and Jean-Pierre panting behind their backs.

Jonathan was now writing a good deal. He woke up in the mornings and rearranged paragraphs of *The Pavlov Dogs* in his memory. There was a lot of material; this time he was not writing a children's book. A novel for teenagers was growing, perhaps even one for adults. He scribbled notes on loose pieces of paper because he didn't like notebooks. His world had narrowed to sentences on his laptop, and maybe that's why he saw the question he'd asked Andrea so clearly. He hadn't demanded an answer; on the contrary, he was pleased there wasn't one, tossed as he was between "I want to be with her," "But what about the children?", "How can I live without her?", "But Megi ..."

On his way to fetch Antosia and Tomaszek from school, he played with the chestnuts they'd stuffed into his pockets. The chestnuts had lost their charming smoothness and color had seeped away from them, but wrinkled they looked wise.

The children were very happy at the school here; they had a lot of friends. Jonathan arranged with their mothers for the kids to visit each other's houses, but found it hard to switch to concrete facts. "I'll take them after school; yes, I'll feed them; no, he's not allergic to anything," he yapped. The family machinery was well oiled, self-help books on parenting would have been proud of him.

Until one day when Tomaszek refused to go home. In a room covered with cushions, the tots had built a castle and ran around barefoot, tearing off their jackets and T-shirts. A few parents were standing at the door hurrying their children along. Jonathan, who had a date with Andrea that afternoon, shifted from foot to foot like the others, sweating in his winter jacket.

"We're going, Tomaszek," he said yet again. One of the parents took up the cry and, as in Chinese whispers, names changed, languages mixed, but the message remained the same.

The children, however, didn't listen to anyone. They barricaded themselves in the castle of cushions and ruled fairly and unfairly, pinching and shoving each other, leaping with joy and squealing in pain.

"Tomaszek!"

The school clock showed it was too late for him to have a shower before seeing Andrea.

The circle of parents around the door undulated; they, too, had started to look at the clock. Some of them had pulled out of polite conversations and turned directly to the castle, which was pulsating with life.

"Marika, come here!" "Bea, put your shoes on!" "Esme, we're going home!"

But the children blocked the entrance with another cushion and, giggling, started to collect ammunition: ping-pong balls, badminton shuttlecocks, building blocks, and balls of paper.

"Sean, please!"

"Charlie, do you hear?"

"Maura, I repeat!"

Jonathan glanced at the clock again, and was overwhelmed by the heat. They would be stuck in the traffic soon, the road – down to one lane – would be packed, he wouldn't have time to defrost the chicken, Andrea would have to wait …

"Tomaszek, I'm going!"

The castle grew silent, then giggles broke out again. Jonathan turned on his heel and started to go downstairs.

He was halfway down when he heard a commotion. First a growl then a scream – only one – that, a moment later, was joined by others. The laughter that had drifted in the air had turned to crying. Jonathan heard a stamping and turned – Tomaszek was running after him, his bare feet slapping the cold stone splashed with autumn mud.

"They've knocked it down, they've knocked it down!" he sobbed uncontrollably.

Jonathan stood still, his eyes fixed on his son's screwed-up face.

"What?"

Tomaszek tripped. Jonathan caught him at the last moment and the little body clung to him, snot smeared over Jonathan's jacket.

"Tomaszek?"

But his son tore himself from his arms and pounded Jonathan's jacket rabidly, his fair hair flying above his wet face.

"They ruined our castle, ruined it," he wept. His words broke off, their endings fading away. "They came and spoiled everything, everything! And you weren't with me!"

Jonathan wrote a description of birth in *The Pavlov Dogs* that turned out so powerful that he had to leave his laptop, pace the room, and clear his throat until the lump in it disappeared and allowed him to breathe again. He didn't tell anyone, not even Megi, although he knew she'd understand.

She was the one who'd told him how everything had welled up in her when they'd put the wet Antosia on her belly, how the newborn's breath had become her breath, and how, suddenly, in one moment, she'd become vigilant. She'd clutched the three and a half kilograms of life and looked around attentively, like a bitch.

Jonathan had been moved by Antosia's birth, although he resented the baby a little for squeezing her little head, covered in sparse hair, between himself and Megi. He'd watched as the child sucked his woman's breast, and experienced a strange tingling under his tongue. Sometimes he had felt separated from them by the growing wall of used diapers, the sleepless nights, and the squawking, of a bundle that had neither his nor Megi's features, even though everyone tried to convince him the opposite was true.

After his son had run after him barefoot from the nursery class, Jonathan had taken him by the hand and together they'd gone back to the cushions that had just a moment ago formed a picturesque castle but now lay strewn across the floor. There were snivelling tots all over the place, pulling on their shirts and shoes. Jonathan, Tomaszek's hand in his, had gathered the remnants of the castle and secured the scattered ammunition in a corner of the class. Together they had put the toys away in the baskets and Tomaszek told him about his idea for a catapult.

Jonathan sent a message to Andrea from the car. He apologized for having to cancel their meeting – for the first time since they'd met.

# 3

THE QUILT OF FROZEN TWIGS, leaves, and mud crunched beneath the wheels of their bikes and gave way with a spring. Crystals of ice sprayed with an angry *hrrt*; steam burst from their mouths and rose above their heads. Jonathan tried to overtake Stefan on his bike.

"There's a good bar not far from here," he roared. Stefan's earmuffs had fooled him; he thought his friend couldn't hear well because of them.

"Forget it," grunted Stefan. "I've had too much beer this week. Time to work it off."

"You've worked enough off; we've cycled the whole of Tervuren! You're steaming so much, you need a horse blanket."

Jonathan finally passed Stefan and surreptitiously maneuvered him toward the little eatery. They leaned their bikes against the wall and walked in. It was quite crowded inside; elderly women straight from the hairdresser's flashed eyeglass frames, the younger generation disciplined their children, waiters served chocolate desserts and wafers.

"Two beers." Jonathan held up two fingers and wiped his steamed-over eyeglasses.

The rustic interior was a trap for fat, middle-class mice; remnants of a laid-back atmosphere survived in a television set flickering above the bar, in front of which some elderly men leaned on the counter, watching a match.

"England versus Germany?"asked Stefan, just as Jonathan said, "I saw her on television."They simultaneously, spontaneously leaned back, as though they'd accidentally bumped foreheads.

"Have you got Swedish channels?" asked Stefan.

They made themselves comfortable by the fireplace. Stefan yanked his pullover off. In just his vest, he upset the harmony of the Sunday-best aesthetics.

"I've got the one with her program," replied Jonathan.

Stefan looked at him without a word and Jonathan quickly added, "Only for a month! She's great," he sighed. "Professionally speaking – don't look at me like that – I'm speaking objectively as a former journalist. Drop in and have a look." Stefan picked up his glass of beer.

"News in Swedish? Not for me, thanks."

"She really is good – professional, stunning."

"Aneta's not bad either."

Jonathan froze, his glass midway to his lips.

"Aneta?"

"The trainee."

"You've fucked her?"

"That's not the point," began Stefan.

"What's she like?"

"Oh, I don't know." Stefan frowned. "Like a bun from the Co-op – sticky on the outside, insipid on the inside. But she tastes of holidays."

"Aren't you worried she's going to go and brag to Monika?"

"Why should she? She's got a boyfriend!"

"Have you already forgotten your madwoman with the eczema?"

"It wasn't eczema but psoriasis," Stefan corrected. "Apparently it got worse when she got stressed."

"I dread to think what she looked like after talking to Monika."

"You've always got something against my chicks," Stefan flared up. "And all yours are Madonnas, I suppose? Holy Megi, divine Andrea! Oh, never mind." He waved it aside and reached for a cigarette. "Whatever! I've seen the way Andrea looks at you when she thinks nobody's looking."

"She's been so devoted lately." Jonathan cheered up. "It scares me at times."

"No need to be scared. She's not going to want to change anything officially, if that's what's worrying you."

"What makes you think that?" Jonathan bristled.

Stefan leaned across the table and lowered his voice as though announcing something highly confidential.

"No offence, you're a really nice guy and all that, but to her you're also … from Poland."

"Everybody's from somewhere." Jonathan shrugged.

"You've no professional standing in Brussels."

"Maybe that's what she likes about me?"

Beads of sweat appeared on Stefan's forehead.

"You do realize who Simon is, don't you?" he asked.

"Yes."

"Well, and you're from Poland."

Jonathan leaned toward him; they now looked like conspirators, two puffed-up cockerels.

"You think you're better, don't you, because you went to school abroad, and don't have a Polish accent, in your element wherever you go?" Stefan threw out. "But for people here, you're still one of us, a Pole, a cousin of the lad who carries bricks, the guy who can give you the number of a cheap, hardworking Polish cleaner. You've got so many advantages but aren't doing anything with them. You don't care about work or a position, you don't want to show that we, Poles …"

Jonathan stared at him in silence.

"You think we enjoy all this?" Stefan said, riled. "That life's easy when colleagues laugh about Poland being ruled by the clergy and a couple of twins, and lunch in Poland means vodka and sausages? If anyone's got the strength they challenge it, if not they watch Polish television and keep inviting their family and friends to visit. And why? So that they can see for themselves what a civilized country looks like. And bring poppy-seed cake."

Stefan leaned back, wiped the sweat from his forehead with his wrist.

"That's what life's like among strangers. Understand?" He reached for his beer.

Jonathan said he did but a moment later asked, "What strangers?"

Jonathan walked home, pushing his bicycle. Although blue with cold, the city had miraculously retained its coziness. Cinquantenaire Park seemed vaster than in summer; the sky broke through the leafless branches on which green parrots swung. Usurpers in a world of satiated starlings and sparrows, forbidden goods which had given a smuggler the slip, they had multiplied and adapted to their new environment. Now they flew in green flocks, squawking, and sweeping their long tails. Only the emerald of their feathers linked them to the "lost little parrots." With hooked beaks they hammered the local birds on the head, not afraid of even the magpies.

"You live in a world of fairy tales!" Stefan had thrown at him before they parted ways. They had quarrelled, not for the first time, but so fiercely that Jonathan was deeply stung.

"So what?" he'd fumed.

"So," Stefan had yelled heatedly, "they're not Polish fairy tales!"

"Are you mad?" Jonathan was stunned. "And Andersen's tales are Danish, are they?"

But Stefan had only waved it aside. The splash of nationalism he'd spilled on the table of the Belgian eatery was an unknown aspect of Stefan. Jonathan had suddenly seen the hard face of a football fanatic before him.

The deeper he went into the park, the more vengefully he thought about his friend. Was Stefan jealous of his love for Andrea? He lived from fuck to fuck, just like his father had and his grandfather.

Jonathan stood still and studied the criss-crossing alleys of the park, their geometrical forkings, their evenly trimmed hedges. Did Andrea also think of him as a Pole? And what kind of a Pole: one proud of his history or one who represents a nation of collaborators, like some people from "the West" considered Poles to be? He'd been made aware of this variant by a certain American woman who, when he'd taken offence, had patted him on the shoulder and said, "Don't worry, the French also collaborated with the Germans."

As he strolled down the alley, he thought anxiously that, after all, Stefan and Andrea were similar in a way. He reset his mind with a grind, trying to see Andrea from a different perspective. If he closed his eyes to her beauty, education, the fact that she knew several languages fluently and coped perfectly well with working abroad, who was she? The daughter of Czech immigrants, one who associated churches with empty shells of the past. A child with a key around its neck, running around between blocks where an apartment had been allocated to refugees. The poorest girl in class who never felt at home in sated Sweden and was fed stories about a distant revolution by her parents. An ambitious scholarship holder, curious about the world, aesthetically in love with the apartments of Brussels, a snob collecting English tea sets and cutlery, the partner of a financially and professionally well-placed Briton, head of cabinet for the Commissioner, the trophy wife of a charismatic fifty-year-old.

He stood still. Holding on to that perspective, who in that case was he? A writer untainted by official connections, an artist and outsider, "a warrior's respite." an idealist thanks to whom she returned to the dreams of her past? No, no, that's how he liked to think of himself when looking at himself through the eyes of his Andrea. But now he wanted to look at himself through the eyes of Stefan's Andrea. Was he for her (whoever she was) a handsome, trouble-free lover, but also – and here in a rather secondary guise – a Pole?

A couple of hours later, the children already washed, he came downstairs. Megi was still reading to them and, while waiting for their evening together – two hours blissfully vegetating with an unambitious film and pistachios at hand – he opened his computer. Stefan had emailed, explaining that he'd lost his temper and shouldn't have yelled like that. He attached "something as an apology."

Full of foreboding, Jonathan moved the mouse to "attachment." Enormous breasts filled the screen, gaudy advertisements floated across the nipples. Half-blinded, Jonathan searched for where to click to turn them off but the mouse froze, fixing the arrow at the groove between the breasts.

"Right!" He heard his wife's voice behind him.

"Ay, ay!" Jonathan nervously rubbed the mouse over the table surface.

"I knew it." Megi put her hands on his chair.

"And you still stand there," groaned Jonathan. "As if I wasn't humiliated enough! A moment later and you'd have caught me with my hand down my trousers."

"I wonder," Megi kneaded her chin and bent over, squinting, "what it's really advertising."

"That's what you're wondering?"

"Some sort of liquid no doubt. Yes!" She pointed to the writing. "There it is. Liquid for washing car windows."

Jonathan clicked on the cross, the breasts vanished and Megi straightened herself, giggling.

"You caught me out," Jonathan said without guilt.

"Good thing it was only that," she muttered, moving off to the kitchen.

Jonathan unwittingly froze, then reluctantly made after her.

"Good thing it wasn't the same as Stefan ..."

Jonathan slipped his hands into the pockets of his jeans.

"Okay, we've got the background, we've got the suspense, now let's have the climax," he said.

Megi rested her elbows on the work surface, which extended into the living room. Jonathan was tickled by the thought that she must have known how good she looked in that position. The breasts on the screen were nothing compared to her tits, as shapely as apples, and her butt – a little flatter than Andrea's – took on womanly shapes when she bent forward.

"I caught him red-handed with Aneta," she whispered secretively.

"No!" exclaimed Jonathan.

Megi scrutinized him; finally she poked an accusatory finger at him. "You knew! You knew and you didn't say anything! I always tell you!"

"Why do you tell me now, years later?" countered Jonathan. "Stefan's already managed to tell me himself."

"I couldn't any earlier!"

"Why not? Bound by oath, were you?"

Megi lowered her eyes.

"I couldn't because I was worried."

Jonathan gave her a searching look; a moment later, he burst out laughing.

"I almost believed you!"

"No, really," Megi defended herself but his smile was infectious. "I really was upset. And on top of that, Monika came up and I had to deflect her."

Jonathan walked up to the fridge and extracted two bottles. Later, they sat on the floor drinking beer, chatting a little, laughing a little. Jonathan stroked Megi's hair, thinking she was dear to him even though he couldn't watch porn with her or visit the red light district of Amsterdam.

Before putting on a film, he told her about his argument with Stefan, how his friend had suddenly brought up the subject of being Polish. Megi listened and stroked his hand; the threads of understanding tickled pleasantly. Then, of her own accord, she started telling him how much she liked Brussels where even Masses were celebrated in five languages, and subtitles in three languages were projected in theaters so that everybody could understand.

"And as for being Polish …" She lost herself in thought. "We're the first lot to have been able to leave Poland really out of choice. Not because of money but because we're curious about the world."

"Stefan says that those who are here miss Poland."

"Nah." Megi tipped the beer bottle. "Ask any of them if they'd go back. Just ask!"

*Megi watches Jonathan walk up to Andrea, start to undress her. He rubs against her olive skin with teasing slowness, drills her groin with his tongue, examines her nipples with his fingers, sucks her ear lobes and whispers something, but what? Megi can't hear because she's saying something herself.*

*"Jo … Jon …" Megi's words turn to dust, choke her; she spits, "Yyyyuuuuck, eeeh!"*

*"Shhh, shhh," she hears the voice on the other side of the bed. She sits up, drenched in sweat. Above her is the window, a calendar hangs on the wall, days ordered into a uniform grid. There's no way to say whether one is better than another, she is the only one who knows – once they've passed.*

*Megi lies on her back; anger runs through her body, explodes in her lower belly. She's the one he should be making love to in that way! Megi wants him to put it in her pussy and press his hips against her buttocks. That's what she wants!*

*But how can she get through to Jonathan when he's asleep, lost in dreams about himself – everything's about Jonathan, through Jonathan's eyes. Hey, I'm here, too, listen to me, hear me, be – obedient!*

*But he sleeps on, his mouth half open, his breath stale, as happens at night, down below an erection, perhaps. A dark shape, a man.*

# 4

THE GRASS SMELLED GOOD in Geert's story. Jonathan read the beginning several times and each time was struck by the fact that there was no continuation.

"What happened next?" he asked yet again; Geert looked at him helplessly.

"That's the best question possible," sighed Ariane, straightening herself on the chair.

Jonathan thought that if texts were to reflect a writer's personality, hers ought to be full of details, although a little angular. But when he picked up what she'd written during the Christmas break, he couldn't conceal his surprise. Something tender had crystallized, which he'd have believed more likely to come from Kitty had she been more daring in her range of subjects. Because this one was strong: the story of a dying peasant who reaches the decision to reconcile himself with his son.

"Ariane," he said, placing the pages on the table. "This is something entirely new to you. Where did the story come from?"

Ariane smiled, pleased. Jean-Pierre observed her with curiosity, Kitty with attention.

"Did writing a diary help?" Kitty asked affirmatively.

Ariane nodded her head again.

"In what way?" Jonathan glanced at the text. "Surely this hasn't got anything to do with your own experience."

"That's exactly why," said Ariane. "I had a lot of personal stories in me and finally found a place for them. But not here." She indicated the pages in front of Jonathan.

Geert opened his mouth as if wanting to say something but decided against it.

"Your grass smells good," Jonathan addressed him.

"And if something smells good to you it means you love it," added Kitty.

Jean-Pierre laughed; Ariane tossed back her thick hair.

"It's true," she joined in. "As long as you want to kiss someone, there's feeling. The smell is what's most important."

Jean-Pierre looked at her hesitantly; in the end, he reluctantly agreed.

"That's why Geert finds it hard to continue," concluded Ariane. "When you love something, you don't know how to write about it."

"You think so?" asked Jonathan.

"Look at my protagonist," Ariane joined in. "I don't love this peasant, he's an old tyrant."

"But there's tenderness in the text," noted Jonathan. "It's clear that you're indulging the main character, there's no straightforward 'you I like but you I don't.' All the arguments are in the son's favor yet it's the father we pity."

"According to your theory," Jean-Pierre spoke out, "Geert ought to fall out of love with his Congo."

"That would be ideal," replied Jonathan. "But the rule's hard to apply when it comes to childhood memories. You can't avoid love there. It's present, childishly stubborn."

"We haven't been of much help to you," Ariane addressed Geert.

"Thanks to you I know why grass smells good," he said quietly.

After his class, Jonathan made his way through the park as usual. He pondered what had been said at the lesson. Would he be able to describe Andrea? And the trees in Brussels? He looked at his cell and, with a sigh, slipped it back into his pocket. She hadn't sent a single message in the past few hours.

When a message finally did arrive, Jonathan's mind had initially fixated on trying to understand how he'd never thought about what would happen if they were caught. All these months he'd subconsciously ignored Simon's existence. As for Megi, there was a place assigned for her in this whole configuration. In his eyes his wife was understanding, as if she knew what was happening to him, and had accepted both him and the situation in which he found himself – and that he'd found himself in it because he had no choice. She was his friend. He'd always told her so many things. And what he didn't say, she ought to understand.

Simon was beyond the scope of his feelings and, therefore, predictions. Jonathan rarely came across him because Andrea liked to go to parties by herself, which made her seem all the more available. When they made love, she belonged only to him, everything was theirs, nothing of her permanent relationship infiltrated, so that he began to suspect that Andrea's marriage was celibate.

The message which arrived just as Jonathan was about to insert the key into his front door consisted of three words: "Simon's found out." For a moment, Jonathan stood rooted to the doormat, listening to the familiar sounds within: Antosia chasing Tomaszek because he'd swiped her eraser, Megi shouting over both of them, her voice mixed with the clatter of pans. A moment longer and a frying pan would go crashing or she'd scream.

Jonathan turned and quietly descended, not waiting for the noisy finale. He rested against one of the trees in the street. The buds would blossom when the time was ripe, over one night. When, at Megi's request, Jonathan had finally taken a photograph of the flowering trees, he'd noticed that each tree carried a tiny shield. Like numbered pedigree dogs, the trees stood and blossomed obediently. Then their petals fell in order to turn the glory of color over to other trees, planted on neighboring streets.

But now Simon had found out! Jonathan imagined his children and Megi in the impending snowstorm and was overcome with fear. "Ay, ay!" A lament rose within him, and an invisible punch below the ribs deprived him of breath. What had he done – what on earth had he done?

"Simon's found out," Jonathan threw at his phone.

"Wait," grunted Stefan, his voice disappearing somewhere.

"What are you doing?"

"Lifting weights," he panted. "Repeat what you've just said. I can't hear anything, they've got MTV on nonstop."

"Simon's. Found. Out."

Pounding music and the squeaking of machinery came through the telephone.

"Now, did you hear?" Jonathan turned in the street like a spinning top.

"But how?"

Jonathan thought he should have phoned somebody quicker off the mark.

"I don't know how, what's it matter? What matters is what he's going to do about it. Because if he phones or writes to Megi ...'

"Hey, hey, hey!" Jonathan could almost see Stefan lifting his hand like a policeman stopping a speeding driver. He stopped obediently. Branches swollen with buds hung over him, sheltering him from his family – they were on the first floor, he in the flowery basement.

"And what would you do if you found out Megi was humping someone on the side?" said Stefan. "Write letters to the guy?"

"Well, no. I'd go and ..."

"That's why I'm asking how he found out. If he's in England the first blow will have been cushioned."

Jonathan nodded to a passing neighbor.

"I'm not worried about him punching me in the face," he retorted, wrapping his hand around the phone. "Only that he'll tell Megi and create such a stink the kids will find out."

"Hey, hey!" That afternoon, Stefan's vocabulary was not impressive. "'Create,' 'tell,' what are you talking about? What guy's going to brag about his old lady making a cuckold of him?"

Jonathan abandoned his nervous pacing. Inexplicable relief made his knees go soft. "What guy's ..." he silently repeated Stefan's words.

"So what's he going to do?" Jonathan's mind clammed up, suddenly unable to make an effort.

Stefan was glugging something that could have been an energy drink.

"He'll break up with her?" he asked joyfully.

That evening Jonathan behaved like an automaton and, when his expression started to worry Megi, locked himself in the bathroom on the pretext that he'd eaten something that had gone off. Staring at his own reflection, he reviewed the options. If Simon broke up with Andrea, what was he, Jonathan, to do? Only now did he realize that it was too soon for him to know what he wanted from her. He didn't envisage her in his everyday life, that was for sure. Every time he attempted to imagine this possibility, sex came to mind. The surroundings grew blurred; there were no familiar objects, rituals, points in time, even habits he could hang on to. He tried to remember what her clothes looked like, her wardrobe, but instead he saw her naked. Was that supposed to be their future?

Over the next day and night they didn't write to each other; in the end Jonathan couldn't stand it. "What's happening?" he asked. Andrea didn't reply for a long time then finally sent a message: "What's the strategy?" He stayed silent. This time it was she who couldn't stand the wait: "Do we deny it? Do we deny everything, then?"

He lived the following days in a simulation of rejection. He kept glancing at the phone and, when there wasn't any message, writhed inside with pain. In the end, they bumped into each other at a Commission party – she glued to Simon's arm, he barely able to stop himself leaving Megi. He tried to get near to Andrea but she wouldn't leave her partner's side. It was impossible to read anything in Simon's face. He greeted Megi as if nothing had happened, nodded to Jonathan.

His fear of Megi finding out disappeared. His wife was the same as always, kind to Andrea, witty in Simon's presence. Seeing this, Jonathan finally believed Stefan – the old trouper had figured Simon out. There was to be no trumpeting around or abrupt action; instead there was a mature calm, beneath which no one knew what lay. Or rather did know, judging by the barely noticeable trace of servility in Andrea's behavior.

Watching her gaze at Simon, Jonathan was doused by a wave of jealously, despair, and disgust. She'd only recently bestowed similar looks on him, laughed at his jokes. Now she seemed to forget the whole world, as she gazed into her senile, self-important sun. Even her admirers noticed and, that evening, focused exclusively on Simon as though his beautiful partner didn't exist.

Jonathan woke at dawn again and contemplated what he should do, thrashed out scenarios – the deeper into the night, the more pessimistic. The fact that the matter hadn't exploded with a bang, that Andrea had deflected the blow (how?), ceased to bring relief. The absence of his lover became so painful it obscured everything else. And yet his imagination still refused to envisage a life together with Andrea – he couldn't arrive at such prosaic questions as where they would live, or, even more importantly, how they would tell their partners everything.

His mind, however, became truly powerless when he tried to think about his children in this context. Daily life without Antosia and Tomaszek was unimaginable. Again he realized how much his contact with his daughter and son had evolved during his paternity leave in Brussels. He no longer understood the phrase "leave home." He was aware that the signal his body gave out – "I'm hungry" – had over the years changed to, "Have the children eaten yet?" "I'm a parent," he noted, half with pride, half with surprise.

Which did not mean that, now he had stopped seeing his lover, he was good to his children. On the contrary, the chaos they created annoyed him, the quarrels, demands, and constant need for attention irritated him. Nevertheless, he didn't flee, scared he would do the worst thing possible – stand beneath Andrea's window.

When Stefan phoned to ask how the situation was developing, Jonathan couldn't give him any concrete details. Numb, he listened as his friend reassured him that he hadn't heard any rumors, meaning Simon hadn't let on and the only thing that had changed was Andrea's behavior. Stefan's experienced eye noticed that the woman had lost half of her characteristic drive for independence. She wasn't even flirting.

"Look on the bright side," concluded Stefan. "You had the chick, that's what counts!"

"I did," replied Jonathan flatly.

"And what did you expect? That she'd leave the loaded high-flyer and get married to a house husband?"

"She didn't even consider it."

"Maybe you should have proposed?" snorted Stefan.

Jonathan slowly hid his cell in his pocket. It wasn't surprising she hadn't reacted to his question, "Couldn't we be together?" He hadn't known himself what he had in mind at the time. All the guys had been staring at her, lusting after her. So he'd pressed the bag of ice at Jean-

Pierre and isolated her from them, wanting his question to close her off in the embrace of a promise. She had smelled a rat. She didn't want to belong to someone again.

Over the following days, Jonathan played with building blocks, solved jigsaws and daily puzzles. Only when drunk did he gawp at Andrea and ridicule what the officials talked about. Pushed aside by them – the circle had the invaluable ability discreetly to spit out inappropriate interlocutors, typical of people whose priority is power – he sat in a corner following his lover with his eyes.

Megi retreated into herself, reminding him of Andrea at the start of their affair – subdued and sad. Andrea, on the other hand, was resuming the colors of a hummingbird. Still very attentive to Simon, she moved further and further afield and even began to send out furtive signals that infallibly drew men to her. Simon looked on with tolerance, whereas Jonathan unexpectedly discovered in himself a deep disdain for a man who remained with a woman despite knowing she'd had another.

In the end, he stopped going to receptions where he might come across them, then, when Megi returned from the parties, picked out scraps of information about his lover. In this way he learned that Andrea had come to a party alone for the first time since the crisis, and danced with a young, gifted lawyer recently employed by Simon. Toward the end of the party, apparently, they'd disappeared in the garden.

When he heard, Jonathan got up and excused himself for a moment. He texted Andrea from the toilet, with the noncommittal suggestion they meet. She wrote back after a few minutes saying she was very sorry but a girlfriend was visiting and staying overnight. Jonathan slammed down the toilet lid.

"Everything OK?" asked Megi from the stairs.

He hated her for her concern, for decently blabbering everything out.

"Oh, and there's one more piece of news!" she said. "Andrea mentioned she and Simon are thinking about a baby."

"Whose baby?" Jonathan didn't understand.

"Theirs." Megi yawned.

He ended up beneath her window at the fall of dusk. He told his wife that he was going for an impromptu beer with Stefan and wrote to his lover that unless she came down he'd stand there until Simon saw him.

For a good few minutes she didn't text back, but finally she appeared in the window. The light from the street fell on her simple vest and panties, slid down the contours of her naked hips. Andrea disappeared into the depths of the apartment; after a while she emerged from the house and stood opposite him, dressed in a pale coat tied with a belt.

He took her by the hand and led her to the nearest church. She entered the dark vestibule first; he followed, unable to chase away the thought of whether she had anything else on beneath her coat apart from underwear. They sat down in a pew. For the first time, Andrea was not in a hurry; Jonathan, on the other hand, wriggled around. He gazed at her, took her hand, stroked the skin of her forearm as high as the sleeve of her coat allowed.

In the end, Andrea whispered, "Let's go."

They made love on the bed. No traces of tenderness remained; they tore each other apart, bit each other's tongues. He sniffed her neck and licked away the damp, glued his hips to her buttocks, searched for what was familiar and for what was unknown.

When finally he rolled over to the other end of the bed, Andrea spread her arms and legs; they lay in silence like pale stars.

"What did you tell him?" he asked in the end, and immediately regretted it.

"That you're one of many."

"Screwing you?"

"Who'd like to."

"And he still wants a child with you?"

"He does. Because he loves me."

"The way you are?"

She got up and wrapped a sheet around herself, tugging a resistant corner out from beneath him.

"Andrea." He curled up on his side. "I'm taking risks."

She clicked a cigarette lighter. She didn't smoke but clearly must have done at some stage since she kept lighters in the house.

"What do you want from me?"

He groaned as if she had set fire to him.

"You."

"You want me?" she hissed. Her glistening hair swayed in the darkness.

He looked at her shoulders, at the flickering flame of the cigarette lighter.

"I'd like to have you both."

# 5

FLUFFY PETALS fell from the trees to the pavement, their cool touch brushing the tips of shoes. Once again, Jonathan sneaked out and, wherever possible, rocked and caressed, whispered and kissed. The angry Andrea grew increasingly docile, consoled. He went to her, and it was as though they had a home. Flower pots stood in the windows, books on the shelves and, next to which, photographs. They had their favorite tastes and colors, films and rituals, declarations of love and trivial resentments. He felt that now Andrea had really fallen in love with him, the game was over. She took his face in her hands, looked him in the eyes, and said, "I love you." She licked his cheeks, lips, chin, and everything swelled within him, from his erection to his heart. He was managing to be a lover, father, writer, and husband all at once. "People ought to be able to live like this," he repeated, powerful. If he'd had a tail, he would be constantly wagging it. He'd choose a shaggy one, like a Setter's.

Andrea spread herself beneath him and said he was the one with whom she wanted a child. She'd never thought about it before but now something had come over her. "Pour it in, come inside me," she meowed, presenting her wet pussy. He went crazy with desire, but with what remained of his willpower, pulled on a rubber. She threw herself at him, like a mongrel at a bowl of food – bit him, sucked, licked, almost lost consciousness so that he was a little scared of her. Yet he couldn't not take her in that state, couldn't not make love to her. He wrestled with her until they fell off the bed, rubbed her clitoris, immersed his cock to its very roots. Until one time he couldn't wait and came without a condom. He had never yet experienced such a strong orgasm.

"Good thing you protect yourself," he tossed, rolling on to his back.

"Not any more," she said lightheartedly. "But don't worry, my period's just due."

He gave no more thought to it. He lay down to sleep next to Megi and dreamt of Andrea's thighs; he cooked what his wife liked, fantasising about his lover's rump. That's the way he was now – and he couldn't help it.

Yet, somehow, he ceased to be in a hurry to see Andrea. He cuddled the insecure and sad Megi, stroked her hair when they lay on the sofa together, gazed at her blonde bangs, and it wrung his heart: she felt so safe with him. He also missed the children. Although they didn't notice his actual absence, they must have sensed a distance because they approached him a little warily, as if he smelled of something unfamiliar. In the end, they'd let themselves be cheered up and the three of them would sit down to a game of *Battleship* or go on bike rides.

Now Andrea didn't take well to his "returning home." She inundated him with messages, disclosed her feelings, and demanded replies. Half-amused, half-troubled, he wrote back, a little surprised by her passion and his own distance. He didn't know whether he fully believed her but was so moved by her eagerness that he responded in the same vein.

Sometimes they argued, like the time when, furious at some triviality, she screamed, "I'm not any 'love' of yours!"

"Aren't you?" He was astonished.

"At best I'm what you imagine love to be. You're deaf to me, to my needs!"

A few hours later he was busying himself around Tomaszek, who was throwing up half the night. Meanwhile, Andrea sent passionate messages. Jonathan cleaned the floor and the soiled sheets, fretting that his lover was worried about not getting a reply.

"Damn it, why did I give him those tomatoes for supper?" Megi held Tomaszek in her arms. Everything stank, yet, out of the blue, a thought crossed Jonathan's mind: Andrea had entered his life because he'd opened himself to the love of a woman. Where had Megi been at the time? Andrea had entered smoothly and deeply; if she were now to leave him, his blood would flow.

When he later analyzed this period (in no great detail, rather a general summation in order to understand what really had happened) he had the impression he was playing with pictures in a memory game. He is standing in front of Andrea's apartment, demanding she see him. He leads her to the church in the opposite direction to the one they usually take; she lies beneath him and asks for a baby; he returns home and strokes his wife's hair on the sofa; Andrea reproaches him saying he has less and less time for her; he reproaches her for having used him to provoke Simon's jealousy and to finally make her husband declare that he wants a child by her.

Then his lover stops finding even the smallest gap in her daily schedule into which to squeeze their secret trysts; she starts flirting with other men in front of his eyes again. Jonathan is furious. Andrea writes, "I'm nothing but your toy!" He stops sending her messages.

And later Andrea goes away without saying a word. Jonathan learns from Stefan that his lover has been in Sweden for a week.

"Didn't you know? What's happening with you two?"

Jonathan waves it away – there are no words for this infernal circle.

"Surely it's obvious what you don't want to do," says Stefan in the end.

Jonathan looks at him hopefully.

"You don't want to leave Megi."

"I don't?" He looks as if someone has just called him a piece of celery.

"Because what would you do without her?"

"Which one?" Jonathan is lost.

Jonathan throws himself into a whirl of activity: he prepares for the end of term at his writing course, drives the children to their friends' houses, rushes to school meetings, visits the gym. At times he feels cleansed of desire: he no longer wants to fuck Andrea, is free of those dreams. He strolls down the streets of Brussels, the wind sweeps over him, the balmy temperature soothes his inner seething – perhaps it will transform the lava into petrified peace, a beneficial numbness that won't upset his daily life.

When, with its recurrences, love destroys the peace he's had such difficulty in attaining, Jonathan uses his willpower to recall how Andrea courted Simon, how she wormed herself into his favor, how she had seen in him – what, in fact? With every couple, however guarded they may be, something pokes out from beneath their tight uniform, an unruly shirt, a partially ripped lining. Jonathan and Megi also showed the world how

much held them together. How much? Perhaps too much, given how
Stefan had summarized it.

There are a number of things that have an adverse effect on the decision
to break up, thinks Jonathan: geographical distance, time span, and
perhaps something else. He's plagued by them all, even those without a
name. He's doing everything he can so as not to give in to temptation –
he runs (flees), closes himself in at home or in his writing, meets people
(cycling expeditions arranged by a circle of fathers he'd found on the
internet), goes for a beer with Stefan.

In the end, he can't bear it and writes to her again.

Andrea doesn't answer. Jonathan waits until morning then texts her
in desperation: "Will always love you and will always be stiff for you."
It is his sincerest declaration and she knows it. Several hours later she
sends a smiling face. Nothing else.

Jonathan groans internally as his thoughts circle: how indifferent
she must have grown if she's waited so long to reply! Or perhaps she
was busy? Jonathan scans the television and online news – there weren't
any important events that night – so what was she doing? Suspicion
grips his throat. Something had happened, something that rendered his
declaration unimportant.

He's almost sure of what she was doing that night. Even so, he waits
for at least one denial from her.

But no, she remains silent.

He pretended to be on form. "She's too vanilla" – he turned over in his
head his mother's saying about a certain friend who had gone to the
States, become a housecleaner, and then married the man whose house
she was cleaning. She had a degree in physics, like Jonathan's mother,
but didn't have enough luck to work in her field in the West. She became
a perfect lady who lunched. "Why do you keep in touch with her?"
Jonathan would ask his mother when Daisy (formerly Danuta) came to
England for a few days. To his mind, Daisy resembled the cow on a Swiss
chocolate wrapper; the description "vanilla" suited her dress sense and
lack of sharp opinions. She came to his mind because he felt as though
reality were attacking him like a piece of blunt glass. He wanted to be
vanilla now. Not to know and not to feel.

They don't go far, just to Normandy. Megi doesn't want to go to Poland this time. Packed to the roof ("we'd pack any car up to the roof"), they say goodbye to Reyers Street. They fix their eyes on the apartment with sunken windows, pass the roundabout where there's always a pink bicycle with a pannier of planted flowers. Once someone had stolen the flowers, but the following day new ones had already been planted; nature abhors a vacuum.

When Megi goes with the children to the bathroom at a service station, Jonathan checks his cell: no messages, Andrea is silent. As he gets further and further away from Brussels, so she, no doubt, is returning to Simon. Meanwhile, Megi appears through the sliding doors, Tomaszek wielding a balloon with the service station's logo, Antosia scratching at the price of her new hairbands. Some southerners stare at his wife.

Jonathan takes her by the hand. Now is the time to mend everything – they're on leave, she is here and so is he. Making sure that the children in the back are engrossed in their film, he places his hand on Megi's knee. He is bubbling with desire. But as soon as his palm touches his wife's skin, the tingling in his balls subsides. What does he feel? Barely tenderness. "That's always something," he would have thought, had he not remembered their trips together interrupted by intercourse on the lay-bys.

"We're so good! Why aren't we sinful?" Images explode in his memory: Andrea leans over him, teases his lower belly with her hair. Jonathan unwittingly squeezes Megi's knee, she looks at him with devotion. Jonathan pulls his hand back with an apologetic smile, as if he'd jostled an old woman in the bus; the smell of old powder on old skin, or maybe talc, almost pervades him. "From talc we come, to talc shall we return." He used to cover his tiny daughter's bottom with the white powder. "Who's going to help Antosia when she's old?" groans Jonathan's soul, which is no doubt destined for damnation.

"Look!" Megi's voice tears him away from his pondering.

An Audi with an elderly driver stands in the lane next to theirs, the interior full of hanging puppets; the dolls swing as the car moves on. Shivers run down Jonathan's back. This is a strange journey; thoughts teem, scramble over each other, circulate around real beings, bring into existence those unborn. Because if he were to fulfil Andrea's wish and give her a child, where would they be now? What car would he be sitting in, whose knee would he be stroking, from what would he be running?

"That's too much," snorts Jonathan soundlessly and switches lanes, but his thoughts continue along their old track: so, he has a strong desire, but not for his wife! Jonathan grows angry. He's giving so much of himself to his family, looking after them. And what about his needs? Resentment wells within him: he's sacrificed so much.

"Am I Jesus?" He shrugs so that Megi looks quizzically at him.

He shakes his head without turning his eyes on her. Before Tomaszek was conceived, Jonathan had felt as if he was living with a ghost. Work had sucked Megi in, just as maternity had done before. And although she sometimes prepared supper and had her mother come around so that they could go to the cinema, Megi had been so absent he'd stopped believing in her corporeality. It was not until he once discovered she wasn't wearing any panties beneath her skirt that something had vibrated between them. How long had she been walking around naked underneath, waiting for him to notice?

She'd opened up in Brussels again. She wanted him, so when he was less in touch with Andrea, Megi stepped into her place. Jonathan – lashed by a bad conscience, that far-reaching Christian scourge – wanted to offer her that place with his whole heart. He gave it and took it back because even now, as he repeated to himself that he'd sacrificed Andrea for the good of his family, he was scared. Because what if he suffocated the love in him, destroyed part of his life, part of himself – and his wife turned into a ghost again? What would Jonathan be left with?

The cliff bit into the water coupled with sky, the horizon was rough with clouds. The cow in the far distance shrank to the size of a pin and the vastness pressed Jonathan's dilemmas into thin slivers. Maybe he'd even be able to cut them and throw them into hot water like the dumplings his grandmother – his father's mother who disapproved of "bought" dumplings – used to make?

Megi strolled next to him, wind billowing her jacket. She stopped next to a rose bush.

"Hawthorn," said Jonathan automatically. "A hedge like the one that grew around the castle where, pricked by a spindle, slept …"

"Look." Megi squatted.

A flower was growing next to the bush, a bee buzzing among its open petals, stamping the stamen with its little legs.

"I've always wondered what that princess felt like after a hundred years."

Megi embraced him unexpectedly, kissed him; he felt her tongue between his teeth.

They made love a few more times during their stay, but only that once, on the cliff, belonged to Megi. On the other occasions, Jonathan slipped into her body but his thoughts were so much with Andrea that it amazed him he came at all.

Despite the cold of Normandy, Megi didn't wear underwear. When he cycled off somewhere leaving her with the children, she sent him messages he'd have liked to receive from Andrea. It was such a paradox. When, a few years ago, he'd dreamt of a little tenderness from Megi, she'd been silent. And now she was in love with him once more.

*Megi gazes at the ocean. She had been happy a couple of years earlier – she'd loved two men. She'd blossomed so much she'd even wondered whether to tell Jonathan about her lover. But no! Others would have explained everything to him in no time – he wasn't able to satisfy his woman so he wasn't a man. And as for her, what a slut!*

*Only in a culture where machos are tolerated are men cuckolds, she thought. A crude culture, where there's no place for wise women, no respect for them. And then it turns out that the macho men only shit their pants from fear of their moms.*

*Her mother had once said that the one feeling not worth cultivating was guilt.*

*Megi didn't regret either the relationship with her lover or her decision to leave him. Her body had enthusiastically taken in another man, even searched for him. From then on she'd thought about herself, about her pussy, and the fact that he'd given it a name. Her lover hadn't laughed at the word, took it the way it sounded. And for her the familiar word had begun to bring to mind something different, something bitter and juicy.*

**6**

THE DOG HUNG ITS HEAD over the small opening and barked from time to time. "Woof!" wrote Jonathan, and the hound in his imagination moved away from the hole, lowered itself on its front paws as if it were a puppy, and jumped away only to sniff at the ground again.

"What do you want?" muttered Jonathan with hostility as he got up from his laptop to stretch his arms.

Objectively, he could send his protagonist wherever he wanted. Subjectively, he could do fuck all. The dog kept watch over the hole, wagged its tail, curled its lips in a silly half-smile not in keeping with the dignity of the leader of a mongrel pack.

"Why the hell must you go down into that gutter?" Jonathan clicked his cigarette lighter and blew the smoke out on to the terrace.

He stood at the railings and gazed at the city. Brussels was built according to a medieval principle; façades faced streets set slightly at an angle to form triangles of green garden spaces at the back of the apartments. It reminded Jonathan of London, the area where his mother lived. When he got home from school, he used to take his bike and cycle around the area, root around the local haunts, find his way through the gardens and, in the evening, return to a house like so many others, in front of which stood a dustbin instead of a garden. It had smelled of washing indoors; his clothes hung on a wooden drying rack. He'd once caught his finger in it and his nail had fallen off.

Brussels was cozier. Some of the gardens, shaped like triangles of Brie, were like neglected forests where lilac boiled over; others, carpeted with lawns, were an oasis for local cats. They came here to bask in the heat; their howling reached as far as the apartment lofts. The cats bawled in early spring when the urge to rut hit them, and throughout the year when they chased each other away, fighting for their territory. They had the skill of squirrels in climbing trees and could drive their rivals to the very tip of the birch that rose above the gardens.

The other inhabitants of the gardens were birds. They overran the highest branches and the stone recesses lined with wild vines, which, in autumn, flamed a vivid red. The green parrots from the park rarely came here, frightened perhaps of the true rulers of the territory – pigeons beneath whom branches cracked now and again because they were so huge.

It was they who guided Jonathan to the mysterious door that became the breakthrough in the stories of *The Pavlov Dogs*. The walled-over entrance between one garden and another bothered Jonathan until one day he confided in Megi.

"There must have been a gate once," she said after some thought.

"What do you say?" He wanted to laugh. Megi, the lawyer and realist. Her feet were firmly planted on the ground, true enough. But then somebody had to be in this house.

Jonathan brought the mysterious door, alias "there must have been a gate," into his story and in this way enriched the space with a nebulous zone where the priniciples of firmly fenced-off pieces of land did not reign. The place, however, was not generally accessible – sometimes it was closed, not allowing entry to those who wanted to go in, however high-ranking.

That was why the huge dog, the leader of the pack, was now rooted with his nose to the hole, sniffing, trying to get through to where things were happening, tantalisingly packed away. Since "there must have been a gate here" didn't want to open for him, he had to try to slip in a different way. The gutter, perhaps? He was shaggy and enormous, yet he tried to squeeze through.

After several days of writing, Jonathan began to study the apartment, as if looking for faults. The state was familiar to him – reality, resentful at being dethroned by fiction, was demanding attention. He let many things go when he was at home alone, and copped it when Megi tracked down the damage.

He went downstairs and threw away the stale bread. He was on the point of opening the washing machine – something was rotting inside – when the telephone rang. His father was passing through London and asked if they could meet.

Two days later, Jonathan settled into a seat on the Eurostar. He loved traveling by train. Ever since childhood, he had found that airplanes disrupted the healthy pace of life; two hours between London and Warsaw seemed a cheap trick, the mind found it hard to accept the change in reality. The gray barracks visible on landing at Okęcie was superimposed over the colorful streets of London. The face of his mother seeing him off at Heathrow all too quickly turned into that of his father greeting him with a wave in Warsaw.

There had been years when he had practically not seen his father because it had been impossible to travel freely to Poland. His mother had been petrified that, although he'd have no problems going in, they wouldn't let him out. He'd lived in England for years and still the same nightmare haunted her: she was back in a country whose borders had just been closed.

Jonathan didn't have dreams like that. He was happy both in England, where he had his mother and his friends, and in Poland, in the tiny apartment of his father, whose bachelor existence was sometimes warmed by the presence of his grandmother who cooked *pierogi* and *gołąbki* for her grandson. He had resented his mother for not wanting him to visit his father. He just couldn't imagine that a country could be closed. With the blitheness of a teenager, he shrugged off her fears.

When he was older, he had bragged in school about the martyrology of his parents' fatherland. He corrected the British pronounciation of "Wałęsa" and mouthed off on the subject of "Solidarity," which impressed the girls. Only when he returned to Poland after his studies and started living with Megi did he fall out of the habit of joking about Polish history. He almost mocked it a couple of times because of his English sense of humor, and his wife's uncle, the one who emphasized how much "patriotis" meant in a person's life, started spitting with indignation when Jonathan cheerfully poked fun at the Pope.

The Eurostar rolled into a tunnel, the interior of the train reflecting in the windows. Jonathan's face: the high cheekbones and dark hair of his mother, behind glasses the eyes of his father.

An hour later he was at Heathrow, looking out for passengers arriving from Warsaw. There were quite a few people apart from him; they obscured the exit so that although he had glimpsed his father, the latter had still not seen him. Pulling his wheeled suitcase, his father was skimming his eyes tentatively over the faces. Jonathan stood on his tiptoes and raised his arm. That was how they used to greet each other at the airport: his father had raised his arm just as Jonathan was doing now.

They greeted each other awkwardly. He was taller than his father and towered over him in such a way as embarrassed both of them.

"Janusz. How you've grown!"

Their regular joke. Jonathan straightened his back but soon slouched again. He took his father to the hotel and from there they made off for their tour of Jonathan's childhood haunts, along paths trodden with friends during the holidays when he couldn't go to Poland. Toward the end of the day, seeing that his father was tired although not willing to admit it, he accompanied him to the hotel.

During the night, Jonathan, curled up on the sofa in his mother's living room, ruminated over the moment in front of the hotel when, saying goodbye to his father, he'd felt the urge to ask his advice about what he should do. "I've got two women, Dad, two loves," he would have said. But he didn't because he'd never confided in his father.

His mother … When she was still married but had already fallen in love with Nick, how had she felt? He'd never asked her somehow. He'd found a ready-made world: his father in Poland, mother in England with Nick, and he, Jonathan, in a boarding school. A gap had formed where the stories of his parents met, his own kingdom so envied by Stefan. "You had freedom," his friend would repeat. "And I'm only tearing myself away from the leash now."

Jonathan lay on his back and breathed deeply. It was stuffy; the size of London apartments was nothing compared to those of Brussels. He was amazed how very detached he'd grown from what until recently he'd considered his own. It had sufficed to leave and be happy somewhere else.

London, that of today and that of a few years ago, the crossing paths of father, mother and son, all this formed a strong knot in Jonathan. That gesture of the hand, for example, shooting up so his father could find him and follow him into an unknown world – Jonathan's world.

Returning to Brussels, he clung on to hard facts: Megi was to come back the following day with the children. All of a sudden, he was seized by the fear that he wouldn't be able to bear it and would end up writing to Andrea. He grasped the telephone and dialled Stefan's number.

Brussels was hot and humid, and Stefan, at the Poseidon swimming pool, looked like a sea lion, especially as he'd grown a moustache during the holidays.

"What's all this with the facial hair?" Jonathan struck up a conversation when they sat down on the wall having completed several laps.

Stefan stroked his dripping moustache. Jonathan glanced at a passing girl in a red swimsuit. He couldn't see her face clearly without his glasses but, as Stefan would have said, that wasn't the point.

"Did you want to look like a political leader?" continued Jonathan after a while. "Evoke noble principles? Maybe Solidarity's, with its peasant leaders? Emphasize bestial masculinity? Divert attention away from the broken tooth?"

"Leave my moustache alone."

"Where do they sell them, Carrefour?"

He fled underwater before Stefan's fist reached him.

An hour later, they were sitting in front of the St George brasserie on the corner of Emile Max and Victor Hugo. The outside tables stood next to a small roundabout; avenues, full of trees and apartments in the shade of the leaves, branched out in five directions.

"The world has five directions," Jonathan wondered. "Do you think it's only like that in Brussels?"

"I come here when I want to escape," replied Stefan, not following the subject.

"From?"

"Monika."

Jonathan looked at him in surprise. Stefan's relationship with Monika was like a mathematical calculation: it gave Stefan relative freedom, Monika status. The condition of it lasting was discretion and assumed ignorance, meaning the prewar recipe for a successful marriage.

"She's started arguing of late," muttered Stefan. "That I get home too late after work and so on."

"Why do you get home late?"

Stefan twitched his moustache as if to check whether it was about to fall off.

"I come here to escape," he squealed, "and you spout the same things as her!"

He controlled himself and added after a moment, "She carps on, even though she shouldn't. She's just found something to do. She tutors children for charity, you know, the poorer ones who have recently arrived and don't know the language, whose fathers work on a building site and mothers are out all day cleaning."

Seeing the waiter who looked like the Lion King coming toward them with a menu, Stefan waved his hand to say no and raised two fingers.

"I've been to London to see my father," murmured Jonathan.

"And Andrea?"

"So as not to see Andrea. Megi's given me time to write in peace. Her mother's helping out with the children. They're back tomorrow."

The Lion King stood two glasses of beer in front of them.

"I envy you Megi," sighed Stefan, settling more comfortably in his chair. "A man can grow with such a woman."

"A woman like that can't be deceived," interrupted Jonathan. He was feeling increasingly on edge.

Stefan raised his glass and eyebrows simultaneously.

"Even recently, in London," continued Jonathan, lighting a cigarette. "I met an old friend at Heathrow when I was seeing my father off. We exchanged a few words, she told me about her kids and husband, I did the same, then she said she's divorced."

"And you?"

Jonathan moved away from the table; the chair scraped across the pavement.

"And I nothing."

"Not one secret for another?" risked Stefan.

"I ran when she started putting her hand on my arm."

"That's quick."

"Don't rub it in."

Jonathan glanced at the Lion King who, with infallible instinct, was walking in their direction again, this time with a snack menu.

"You're honest," said Stefan, unconvinced.

"With who?" mumbled Jonathan.

He returned home tipsy, thoughts melting in the pot of memories. Megi – even that rascal Stefan envied him. Hardly surprising, she was so clever and pretty! His best friend – not his father, not his mother – only her. When she made tea, she also brewed some for him. In the mornings, she laid her head in the crook of his elbow so that they could get up and support each other when it was still dark outside. Megi – so good, so humanly good.

And Andrea? She flirted with whoever was there, screwed left, right and center. And who fucks, fucks, and will go on fucking; such was the truth of folklore and the objective truth.

Jonathan lowered his head, full of invective, and noticed with amazement that, despite the weakness that came with alcohol, he was swelling in his trousers. He hissed, looked around and discreetly adjusted the tip of his cock upward. He even had to take his cell out of his pocket; there was no room for it. And when he took it out, he wrote without much thought, "Kisses from Brussels, what are you doing?"

The intercom woke him in the morning – the organ-grinder asking for money. Jonathan refused and went to the bathroom. He found it hard to arrange the blocks of the coming day. He was to collect Megi and the children from the station, do the shopping before that, and set the apartment to rights. And see Andrea. He shook his head, spraying drops of water across the bathroom. He glanced at his phone – the envelope was pulsating, within it the hour and place of his tryst with his lover. Jonathan looked at his watch. He had less than an hour. If he managed to sort himself and the neglected apartment out on time, he would just be able to see her before collecting his family.

Fernand Cocq Square, usually buzzing with life, was exceptionally deserted, even though awnings tempted with their shade. As he saw Andrea approaching, Jonathan impulsively regretted his scruples. He'd had the house to himself for a few days; he could have had her there! Instead, he had sat and written.

"*Ahoj*," said Andrea in Czech.

Something clutched at him. She looked tired from close up; pallor broke through her olive skin.

"*Cześć*," he replied in Polish.

Her eyes turned to him but her face expressed no amusement.

Not knowing why, Jonathan remembered an occasion when they'd lain in bed. "You're a sexavore," he'd said, and she'd laughed. He'd asked whether it was true, as rumors had it, that she and Simon were swingers. "My sweet, bourgeois hypocrite." She had stroked him behind the ear.

"I've missed you," she said now as she sat in the passenger seat.

He touched her hair, tucked a stray lock behind her ear. She shook her head – he'd forgotten she couldn't stand having her hair behind her ears. He withdrew his hand and rested his back on the seat.

"And I was in Normandy."

For a moment, he thought she was going to get out. He turned to her and already his lips were embracing hers, he was sucking the softness of her tongue, slipping his hand beneath her skirt, and finally touching her pussy. He groaned – she was not wearing any panties.

Later they sat dazed, sweating. Jonathan's thoughts drifted above Fernand Cocq Square, Ixelles, Brussels. "The cock and the vagina are both feminine in Dutch – *roede* and *schede*," he recalled. Geert had once explained to him the intricacies of Belgium's second official language. He'd said that the older generation still knew the gender of specific words, but the younger had to search in dictionaries. "Genders are getting blurred," Geert had concluded.

Jonathan glanced at Andrea – he knew she would have found it funny. But she was so serious now he didn't dare mention it.

"I've got to go," he said instead.

She sat as if she hadn't heard him. Her lips were swollen, her neck covered with dark marks left by kisses.

"I'm going to the station," he added. "The kids are coming back from holiday."

He cast his eyes at her hands. She held them strangely, palms upward, like the hard-worked hands of a peasant.

"How was Sweden?" he asked, his voice unexpectedly sharp.

"We mustn't meet any more," she said.

A gust of wind ruffled the branches on the trees, the church bells chimed. "Twelve," rattled in his head.

She got out without saying goodbye. "There must have been a gate here, there must have been a gate here," pounded in his head. It didn't make sense to him, nor did anything that day, that year, even what his life had brought. All around him rose vertical walls and he obediently climbed them and slid down, climbed and slid down. When he reached the station, he was a wound stitched together in haste.

*Megi holds the receiver close to her lips.*

*"You know what he comes out with? That I 'don't share his passions.'"*

*"What passions?" asks her mother.*

*"Exactly, what passions? The need to go diving?"*

*"Let it go, don't take it to heart. It's just a man digging around in the mire of his moods."*

*Megi's thoughts return to their meeting at the station. From the moment she got into the car, she'd felt that something wasn't right.And in the evening, even though they hadn't seen each other for a week, Jonathan hadn't reached out for her. He'd settled on the other side of the bed, neat and tidy as a newly pressed pair of trousers, distant in his smoothness and creases. Only toward morning did he huddle up to her back and then penetrate her in this one, embryonic position.*

*Suddenly, Megi is dangerously close to going through his cell.*

*"Don't lower yourself," she growls to herself. "Nosey parkers get bloody noses."*

*If Jonathan had checked her phone six years ago, would she have been able to end the affair in that early stage of besotted madness? Even if she had, Jonathan might have let her down. Not been able bear it. And they wouldn't be together now.*

*Megi forbids herself from making assumptions.*

Jonathan rested the back of his head against the window of St George's brasserie. He hoped the glass would cool his thoughts. When Andrea had told him that they mustn't see each other again, he'd fallen first into a stupor, then seethed, and finally fallen into another daze.

"Beer?" guessed the Lion King.

This time it was Jonathan who'd suggested "escaping to George's" and now he wrapped himself in his friend's optimism. Stefan poured out his troubles – his daughter, reacting to Monika's constant control, was rebelling all the more fiercely and letting off steam with numerous piercings. The girl already had rings in her tongue, nose, and belly button. He preferred not to think where else; what he saw was enough to worry him and alienate him from his daughter.

Stefan reached for his beer, froth settling on his moustache.

"I saw Andrea," said Jonathan and, seeing his friend wanting to say something, added, "Only to hear 'we mustn't see each other again.'"

"Because she's pregnant?"

Beer shot from Jonathan's nose.

"Monika said they had plans, apparently." Stefan looked troubled.

A motorbike slipped on to the roundabout, one of those little farters that shatter the eardrums. In his imagination, Jonathan ran after the bike, yanked the driver by the neck, dragged him off, and beat him up – for the "planned pregnancy," for the hunch about what had happened in Sweden when she hadn't written back, for being rejected.

"Don't take it the wrong way." He heard Stefan's voice. "But didn't she use you to force Simon into procreation? I heard him myself once saying that he had grown-up children and that was enough. A young chick made him look good. But then she decided she wanted a baby!"

Jonathan turned his eyes to his friend and, in his thoughts, sorted him out like he had the motorcyclist a moment ago.

"And don't worry about the pregnancy." Stefan waved it away. "He probably can't get it up any more. And even if the miracle of the immaculate conception does take place, then Andrea will have the baby and be hotter than ever. Married women are best. They take their moods out on their husbands. For you, they dress up, pamper themselves, buy underwear."

"Married women?" interrupted Jonathan. "So it's not Aneta any more?"

Stefan ran his fingers across his upper lip.

"Aneta, no. Martyna."

Jonathan burst out laughing. The beer made his head spin; the bubbles rose to tickle his throat. He laughed, happy for a while, and light-headed.

"You're a body-snatcher. You sniff out weak relationships," he choked out in the end.

"Not a body-snatcher but a beast of prey," corrected Stefan. "I hunt out weaker specimens. Besides, married women are safe. Trainees might be appetizing but they have one fundamental failing: they're usually free. I've had enough of worrying that I might come across some madwoman who will want me to get divorced, saying I've got her pregnant."

"Don't you know when you're getting a woman pregnant?"

"In the majority of cases, yes," Stefan agreed carelessly. "Besides, the young ones, often enough, don't get aroused. They pretend they're hot stuff in bed but they give you a blow job then think they have to run and get a yoghurt at the corner shop. On the other hand, fucking a youngster, you feel you're a right lad! A propos, did I tell you about my rubber bursting?"

"During it?"

"In my car. Going at top speed. It crossed my mind because I changed the tire in a place called Zdrada [Betrayal] near Dębki. Write it down, it might prove useful for your book."

When Andrea wrote to him suggesting they see each other, he experienced a familiar physical reaction – churning in the stomach, dry mouth, tingling in the balls. Over the past two months, since she'd told him that they shouldn't meet, he'd gone through just about everything there was to experience, at least that's what he thought. Nevertheless, he agreed to see her.

He left his car near the park where she'd proposed they meet. He was early and couldn't decide whether to go for a short walk before she appeared or stay in the car. Neither solution seemed right; if someone he knew were to see him it would have been equally hard for him to explain why he was taking a walk right there as to why he sat drumming his fingers on the steering wheel.

Ever since he'd begun to cut the umbilical cord that joined him to his lover, he'd seen his behavior in a much clearer light. Until then, the overwhelming desire to be with Andrea had obscured all risks; now he thought in universally accepted terms: he was betraying his wife, meeting another woman. The dead weight of guilt and punishment crushed his chest to such an extent that he found he was wearing a trench coat for the tryst, like a detective.

When he saw Andrea, admiration drove out self-ridicule. Her skirt emphasized the length of her legs, the blouse discreetly outlined her breasts, brown hair glistened bronze in the sun. She smiled at him through the window, then climbed in, settling in the passenger's seat as if she'd just come home.

"The park, not the church, this time?" he joked.

She smelled of wind and fruit. He stole a gulp of air with her scent and rested his back against the seat.

"I've sinned too much." She looked at him with a tenderness that slipped beneath his skin and turned into desire.

"But you're fixing your ways," he said light-heartedly.

She grew unexpectedly serious. She filled her lungs with air and let loose: "I want you to know before others find out. I'm pregnant."

Jonathan stared at her, then to the side where a man, probably homeless, was lugging two bulging sacks on his back. He was swaying in a long, too warm coat – a white-bearded comma between balls of luggage. He stopped to rest; he was the color of the road.

"Congratulations," Jonathan heard himself say.

Andrea opened the car door.

"Come on, let's talk."

They climbed the escarpment. The gray-beige man disappeared while they continued down the path, two people out for a stroll. Jonathan's head was a morass, sentences were not coming together, question marks tottered, pushed aside by exclamations.

"You opened me up." Andrea's voice came on a wave. "It's thanks to what happened between us."

Andrea stood still, he walked on. Only when several joggers and cyclists had overtaken them did Andrea finish: "It's my child. Think of it in that way."

Jonathan made as if to turn back but she caught him by the sleeve. They now stood facing each other, Andrea gazing at him, he in the place where the man with the sacks had been. Suddenly Stefan crossed his mind. Whenever he'd been up to no good, he fawned on Monika, and that's what she waited for. Jonathan looked at Andrea. She didn't apologize – she demanded to be understood.

"I wanted a child."

He nodded, his eyes fixed on the ground.

"I told you about it. Remember? Remember!"

He grabbed her in his arms and held her tight. He wiped her tears with the sleeve of his trench coat, the collar of his shirt. He must have forgotten his tissues.

"I told you." He barely understood what she was saying. "I wanted one then. Remember? We were lying on top of each other and I said ..."

He locked her in his arms and she pressed against him, so hard he stepped back.

"It was then," he heard.

He looked over her head at the view stretching from the escarpment – at the water and the swan majestically taking possession of it. Closer, at the turn of the road, stood something that looked like a pen made of bare planks; inside, a heap of brown rags was huddled up.

"If you had said then that you wanted ..."

"I do."

She curled up; he felt her slight shoulder blades beneath his fingers. She was gasping for breath beneath his arm, shaking her head until hair stuck to her wet cheeks.

**book four**

*Brussels, autumn 2008*

JONATHAN TOOK the same route through the park as he usually did when jogging. There, on the other side of the fence, his thoughts merged with the smell of jasmine toward the end of May, waves of heat in July and August, the beating of his heart, and the sweat on his face. Now the park fence was on his left while on his right was a row of spectacular apartments. One of them, on sale, was lit violet from within so that a chewing-gum wrapper pressed in a niche in the pavement glistened unnaturally white in the light.

Jonathan began to walk faster. His "disciples," as Megi called them, were waiting in the stuccoed room. He should have left the house earlier but at the last moment Tomaszek had spilled some "elixir," which he'd secretly prepared, all over himself. The child had kept it beneath his bed for two weeks and when he'd proudly presented it, the stinking mixture had spilled on his shirt, trousers, and shoes. Jonathan had stood his son beneath the shower while Megi had cleaned the floor; the stench still filled the air when Jonathan rushed from the apartment with Tomaszek waving to him from the balcony, his hair wet and, on his face, an insincere expression of guilt.

Jonathan passed the legless organ-grinder who held out a mug to him, shaking his few coins. He had been there forever, longer, no doubt, than Jonathan, longer than most of the passers-by.

The door to the seminar room was ajar; a shaft of light fell diagonally across the floor. Other classes had already begun; the security man in his kiosk was dozing, his little television flickering. Jonathan stopped at the top of the stairs and leaned against the wall near a stand of leaflets. Nobody had noticed him yet; nobody knew he was there. Suspended in the space between home and work he was suddenly thrilled with an excitement not quite erotic yet equally deep. Light fell on him, plucking him out of the dark corridor.

A moment later, everything fell back into place – the security guard smacked his lips and adjusted his cap, individual footfalls resounded in the distance, somewhere a door slammed.

Jonathan peeled himself away from the wall. They were waiting for him.

# 1

AFTER HIS LAST CONVERSATION with Andrea, he could barely perform the rituals of daily life and, when the pain became unbearable, he got up and left. Beyond the apartment, the stream of unfamiliar faces and languages, those he understood and those that constituted a rapid torrent of sounds, cooled his inner fever; he caught his breath when he was among people, at last able to ask himself whether the world really did end with Andrea. "Yes," he replied and felt something other than pain – fury.

This time he didn't stop sending her messages. He knew from experience that the worst thing he could do to himself was to condemn himself to a detox, which was why he covered the screen on his cell with endless complaints, frightened that Andrea would be consistent and back out of their contact or, like a psychiatrist, would merely grunt. But she scrupulously replied – explained, apologized. There was only one thing she didn't deny: that the child growing in her belly was not his.

"I've had enough of you. I don't like you," he wrote and asked one last question: why did she present him with a *fait accompli*; why, when she'd assured him that it was him, Jonathan, she loved did she get pregnant with Simon? "I told you I wanted one with you," she wrote back. "Then why didn't you wait?" he tapped out in despair. "For what?" she parried.

He recalled how she'd kneeled with her mouth filled with his hardness. She'd licked and blown, then let his penis out of her mouth only to take hold of it again with sadistic slowness. He'd turned her on to her back, moved her leg diagonally across his belly and entered her from above, slowly. He'd crushed her with his body until she'd stopped moving. The master of her orgasm, he'd been so aroused he'd had to slip out of her. She'd rolled on to her belly and kneeled in front of him on all fours; he'd screwed her from behind from all angles until she was wet, juices running down her groin. She'd lowered herself onto her elbows; he'd pressed his finger along the groove between her vagina and her anus until she'd squealed in rapture.

"I quite like you," he muttered later, stroking her back.

"Quite?" She'd raised her head from his damp belly. Bubbles of happiness had burst in him with a quiet "puck!" He'd started to laugh, infecting her with his laughter, and together they tumbled across the blue sheets, the white clouds of linen.

As he neared the seminar room, Jonathan thanked fate for this course, for these people. They'd been faithful to him for over two years – unlike his lover. And yet he kept writing to her, wanted her, even pregnant. Andrea's baby was growing in him, too – the fourth month, the fifth … He stroked her belly and made love delicately, didn't let her straddle him.

"Could it harm the baby?" she asked, as though he were an expert, while he slipped into her gently and rocked forward, backward.

"Break up with me!" he wrote afterward but received only smiling faces. She didn't take his words seriously. She told him she loved him and was going to have a baby, and that these were two different things. A baby meant a belly and waiting. He was her love, her difficult love.

Jonathan didn't say much but diligently covered her body with kisses. He stopped at every hollow, at every swell, gentle and tender. He didn't look her in the eyes; he didn't want her to see how much he longed to screw her – so hard he'd go right through – and get rid of the intruder inside.

At times, it dawned on him how it must have looked from the outside – he was fucking someone else's pregnant woman. But, practically at the same time, he also knew that they weren't an ordinary couple. They created their own laws, discovered new paths, made love on the flipside of legality, at the limits of society's good taste, in the maelstrom of their own scruples.

He nodded to the security guard and opened the door. Geert's eyes were drifting across the stucco, Jean-Pierre was texting someone, Ariane was leaning over the table to hear what Kitty was saying.

"… I remember, the same thing happened to me." Ariane nodded.

Kitty watched her with fascination. Jonathan couldn't fathom whether she was really interested or whether it was a former journalist's professional ability to listen. On the other hand, one couldn't but help look at Ariane. Jonathan often thought there was a little windmill in her that turned at variable speeds.

Jonathan's eyes returned to Geert, still sitting in the same position and paying no attention to the women. Neither their glances nor their outbursts of laughter disrupted his concentration.

"Sorry I'm late." Jonathan closed the door. "I don't even have a decent excuse because it won't sound credible."

"Anything could prove inspiring," smiled Ariane.

"Maybe one of us will write a story about it?" added Kitty.

"Fairy tale more like," muttered Jonathan, hanging up his jacket. "Imagine a little boy who creates an elixir out of Coca-Cola, egg shells, sunflower seeds, and dishwashing powder. Oh, and I forgot salt and pepper as 'seasoning.'"

"Who is this magician?" asked Ariane.

"Tomaszek, my son."

"He didn't drink it, did he?" Kitty feared.

"No, but he kept the muck under his bed until it turned rancid. I'd rather not talk about the smell."

"It's the egg shells." Jean-Pierre nodded like an expert. "Good thing the eggs weren't raw. My daughter used them in an experiment once."

Jonathan had already opened his mouth when he saw Geert was passing some pages over to him. His eyes skimmed over the first lines of English text.

"Mother was wearing a pair of white, open-toed slippers that glistened in the sun as it fell through the car window. Every now and again a black face obscured the yellow sphere. Mother's shoes then grew dull, surrendering the glint to bloodshot eyes and teeth. Suddenly the window cracked, the glass scattered on her fair hair. The door sprang open and hung obliquely on its hinges. One white slipper touched the dust, the other flew idly after it."

"Shall I read it out loud?" asked Jonathan quietly.

Geert nodded; Jonathan continued reading.

"The car stood inclined to the left, far from the town center, on the outskirts of Kinshasa. The boy crawled along the grass, further and further away from the rebels' cries. His mother's guttural sobs grew quieter. His father was still waiting for them there, where they had not arrived.

"The boy grazed his elbows and knees so they bled; chirping pounded in his ears; the stench of rubber reached him from afar. He had no strength left. He stopped moving in the damp grass then turned slowly; the burned-out car was growing black by the road, a cloud of smoke drifting from it.

"He rolled onto his back and stared at the sky shimmering in the heat. Somewhere over there the sun was caressing white patent slippers and the tin can of a car filled with the scent of his mother's perfume, guarding the treasures of childhood. Although aflame, it was closed tight. Beneath the lava of strange faces, what was good set within her."

The following day, Jonathan phoned Cecile. They had to publish a book of stories written by his students; the two years had matured his people's talents.

"Your people?" Discreet laughter rang out in the receiver.

He couldn't write that morning; excitement chased him out of the apartment. For the first time in a long while, he didn't feel any pain. "It seems my nerve roots have stopped doing me in," he noted on a piece of paper that he extracted from a side pocket of his rucksack. There was a drawing by Tomaszek on the back: a map of favorite places sketched in the sprawling hand of a seven-year-old. Jonathan orientated the piece of paper – and here he was, halfway down a road decorated with crooked houses, in front of him a roundabout coming into view. He knew there had to be a laundromat there, a shop selling olives and chocolates, and one of Brussels's numerous pharmacies, but it was only thanks to the little map that he noticed that the roundabout lay in the shade of an enormous tree.

He walked on ahead. Rue des Tongres started with a sweet turn, which led to the delicacies of his youth: French cheeses and wines appeared behind glass. In the next window was a meat roast like the one Nick, his mother's husband, used to prepare, while in the GB shop on the other side of the street were pickles and a mock-up of the works of art his paternal grandmother had fed him. "And dat way to films," prompted Tomaszek's writing. Jonathan looked down the street: cars glided in a narrow thread toward a crossroads where trams clattered. Beyond the crossroads the street descended more steeply but must have ascended somewhere again because at its far end towered a church – the one where he had met Andrea so frequently.

He put the vibrating phone to his ear. It was Cecile Lefebure with some good news: a friend of hers, working for a publisher, had promised to ask if they'd be interested in publishing the work of a group of beginners. The money would have to come from grants.

"So it's possible?" he asked.

She laughed, won over by his enthusiasm.

"I can't promise anything."

"But maybe?"

Because of the fuss, he lost sight of his Dogs. They had not fled completely, but he felt them scampering away and panicked that he wouldn't be able to catch up with them.

"You've got too much on your plate," Megi consoled him.

She was sitting on the stairs, her arms wrapped around her knees. It was two o'clock in the morning and he was flitting like a moth between his computer and the kitchen.

"You're editing your disciples' stories, applying for a subsidy to publish the collection, looking after the children, and still harbor ambitions to write. It's hardly surprising you're uptight."

He stopped short in front of her as if seeing her for the first time.

"I don't harbor 'ambitions,'" he let out through his teeth, angry, "only characters who are going all over the place!"

"So why did you pick ones with four legs?" giggled Megi, but seeing his expression turned serious. "I meant to say that they'll come back to you. When you whistle. *Nomen omen.*"

Jonathan grabbed the end of a bread roll Antosia had rejected and started to nibble at it absentmindedly.

"If only that were possible, to whistle and that's it," he said indistinctly. "Some things have a time and place, but if you miss them …"

Megi adjusted herself on the stairs, buttoned her pajamas higher. She sat in front of him, warm with sleep, devoted. He moved as if to stroke her but stopped mid-gesture.

She went back to bed; Jonathan remained downstairs on the pretext of gathering his notes. He pulled his cell out of his pocket and exchanged a few messages with Andrea. Unlike him she didn't need much sleep; that's where they differed. "And in many other ways," he thought.

He took a beer from the fridge and opened the window. The inner courtyard, lit by the gentle glow of windows, chirped quietly with holidays. Their Brussels apartment was unusual – if he crossed to the other side of the room, and opened the huge balcony window, the shrill sounds of the city entered, music from the pub on the corner, the din of motorbikes. One apartment with windows on two worlds.

He stood in the middle of the room, and took a gulp of Leffe. His eyes wandered over the stucco. Why had he built all of this – to demolish it? Is that the eternal meaning of constructing something? He ought to be grateful to Andrea, in fact, for not pressing him for anything. If she'd gone to Megi, like Stefan's lover, and demanded that his wife get out of the way of their love … He took a draught of beer and leaned against the window frame. The air was not cooling. It was the hottest month of the year and the city lay to its side, panting lazily.

Andrea hadn't gone to Megi asking for him because women like her didn't have to fight for anyone. They forged ahead and everybody else ran after them, catching crumbs of attention, the sweetness of their glance, scraps of conversation. He slapped his forehead and yanked the cap off another beer with his teeth. Andrea laughed whenever he did that, Megi too, although she worried about his teeth.

"You can see straight away that you went to an English boarding school," giggled Andrea, and he grimaced as if he really had broken a tooth. "Simon does it too, does he?" he asked, and when she said yes, added, "Then I'll ask them to replace my molars with a bottle opener when I'm his age."

Andrea was never spiteful about Megi. Jonathan loved her for it all the more. There was something noble about her, which he would willingly have told his friend-wife. He knew Megi would have been pleased to have her theory proved that intelligent women today fought over a position in the company where they worked rather than over men.

He spat the cap out of the window. Everything would be simpler if he could finish with the duplicity in his life. But how could he ditch Andrea? Or Megi? Harmony with Megi, passion with Andrea: the mixture gave him wings, allowed him to live life to its fullest.

Paradoxically, it was now that his relationship with Andrea had assumed an unexpected equilibrium. The fact that he hadn't broken up with her when he found out about someone else's baby like many men would have done, had started a new phase in their love. He became dear to her; he saw this and, although the man in him would most willingly have got rid of someone else's foetus, it was his humanity that won Andrea over.

Jonathan stood the half-empty bottle on the sill and stared at the lights opposite as they went off, one by one. What a brittle equilibrium! Her swelling belly and with it his pain; messages by night, life by day and, in the evenings, trips to churches where he avoided people's eyes like a vampire avoided daylight.

# 2

JONATHAN STOOD downstairs in his jacket, but Megi still wasn't coming down. Finally, he heard the rhythm of her heels on the stairs.

"I couldn't decide what to wear." She raised her eyes. "Have I put on weight or something?"

"No chance," he countered automatically.

"Is Helena here yet?"

"Mm-hmm." With his eyes he indicated a pair of golden trainers beneath the coat-hooks.

"Helena, could you give the children their supper at nine then chase them off to bed, please?" ordered Megi, catching Tomaszek's hand at the last moment as it aimed to bury itself in her lacquered hair. She kissed him carefully, not to leave lipstick on his cheek. Antosia came up and put her arms around her mother's hips, gently so as not to crease the skirt.

They were late for the concert; the seats in the hall above were already full so they had to stay downstairs and watch on the screen.

"Is there anything to eat?" Jonathan leaned over to Megi's ear.

She indicated a section of the room partitioned off by small barriers where waiters were milling around. He took a step in that direction but she caught him by the arm.

"Only after the concert."

When the barriers were finally pulled aside, a tightly packed crowd threw itself at the tables. Megi stormed the snacks, Jonathan's task was to acquire some plates.

"Got them! And look, how ingenious – palette-shaped plates!" He handed her the oval shape with a hole through which he'd put his thumb.

"It's for your glass," she snorted, "so you don't have to hold it with your other hand."

"So it's free to …?"

"Hand out business cards." Megi kissed him on the lips; he felt the moistness of her lipstick.

Martyna sprung up next to them.

"And you two are still at it after all those years! Have you heard about the pregnancy?" She transfixed a mushroom with her fork; a slimy streak gleamed on her plate.

"Andrea's and Simon's," filled in Rafał as he pushed his way toward them, grunting, "What a crowd!"

Jonathan allowed himself to be sucked in by some group, thanks to which, seconds later, he was several meters away, his salad slipping precariously to one side of his plate.

"… is pregnant although it doesn't show much yet."

"Simon's too old to be a father," replied a familiar voice.

Jonathan turned. Stefan was sweating by the meatballs; below his nose, where until recently he'd cultivated the moustache, beads of sweat were collecting.

"Why are you standing by the pots?" Jonathan indicated the steaming jaws of aluminium containers.

"Herd mentality. I wasn't hungry but when everyone threw themselves at the food, so did I. Exactly as if ham were still being rationed," grunted Stefan, adding aggressively, "But you always had all you wanted. There wasn't any martial law in England."

"English pork sausages were deadlier than communist water cannons."

Stefan's face was taking on one of his national colors when he suddenly noticed Jonathan's expression. He followed his eyes – Andrea stood surrounded by a circle of friends, Martyna's hand was on her belly, Rafał was nodding and blinking compulsively, and Monika was listening with a polite expression. Only Przemek was uninterested in Andrea and stood, crushed in with his plate, directly next to Megi.

Jonathan and Stefan moved in that direction.

"When's the wedding?" Martyna's falsetto rose high.

"I'm not good material for a wife," they heard Andrea's amused voice.

"But what about the baby?" Rafał joined in.

"Oh, come on." Monika shrugged. "Women used to have to protect themselves from sex so as not to get pregnant otherwise they could've landed up with a bastard or died in childbirth. Now we can have both a rich sex life and be mothers. Even single ones, from choice."

"It's true, damn it," Stefan whistled into Jonathan's ear. "They can have it all!"

"It's a different matter who's going to do the housework, cooking, see to the children's homework ..." Monika's voice now took on a bitter tone.

"There are cleaners and other women to help." Martyna shrugged.

"And they're meant to bring up your children, are they?" Monika was piqued.

"Look at Megi," countered Martyna. "She works and has children."

"Megi's not a single mother," clarified Monika.

Jonathan felt a jab in his side – Stefan was letting him know they should clear out.

"What's happened to her?" He ran his hands through his hair when they were beyond the others' earshot.

"She's always been like that." Jonathan clenched his fists. "You heard for yourself: 'I'm not good material for a wife.' Blah, blah, blah!"

"I'm talking about Monika. And that kid ... Is it yours?"

The volume of stories by Jonathan's protégés was to begin with Geert's piece about childhood in the Congo. After it came Kitty's short story pulsating with teenage sensuality, then Ariane's text about the old pigeon-breeder, and, finally, the amusing tale of a small-town barber under police witness protection, written by Jean-Pierre.

Jonathan spread the pages out in order on the park bench and weighed them down with his wallet to stop them blowing away. On a separate sheet, he wrote the title of the anthology, then another and another.

He tilted his head to one side and matched the motifs, patterns and specific scenes from the stories to the two words that were to announce the whole. He already felt the smoothness of the printed page beneath his hands, his nose ran along the spine.

He was pleased that autumn belonged to solid facts. He slipped the pages into a paper folder and looked around. Lunch hour was approaching, office workers loomed at the gate, an old woman perched on the neighboring bench, and every now and again a pervert emerged from the bushes near the statue. Jonathan was on the point of leaving when his eyes fell on the belly of a pregnant woman sitting on a bench nearby. His body grew unspeakably heavy.

Because here, a few meters away from him, concealed beneath a black dress and an office worker's jacket and swamped in amniotic waters, breathed a little human being, possibly sucking its thumb. Jonathan's pulse accelerated and his fingers grew damp.

But the rhythm of the child's breathing and the beating of its mother's heart radiated toward the neighboring benches, muffled the drone of cars, slowed the city traffic.

And Jonathan slowly, slowly calmed down.

Andrea greeted Jonathan in the doorway. Her belly, a shapely little ball high below her bust, was barely perceptible, her face more beautiful than usual, luminous.

"You look wonderful," he whispered in her ear and she wrapped her arms around his neck. Jonathan felt her belly press below his ribs in a familiar way.

The leather sofa in the living room stood in its rightful place, yet he looked around as if expecting something to have changed. Only when he felt Andrea's hands on his back did he bow his head, bring her fingers to his lips and lick them greedily.

This time it was Andrea who wasn't careful and although Jonathan whispered she ought to watch out "because of the baby," she sat on him back to front. She rested her hands on his shins and rode, rubbing his penis against the back wall of her vagina. All of a sudden, she reached for his hands, raised herself on them, and abruptly sank.

Later, when they lay on the damp leather, Andrea nestled her head in the hollow of his shoulder, put her arm around his belly. These gestures, so soft, so unlike her! He must have entered her deeper than his own cock since she'd wanted him so much. "Do you love me?" whispered Andrea and, when he didn't reply, muttered, "You do, I know you love me."

It wasn't until Jonathan was getting dressed that Andrea said, "I've passed the exams."

She was lying on the sofa so that he could see the curve between her hips and bust, her belly covered with a blanket.

"I've already had an interview to work for the Commission. I think it went well."

Jonathan pulled his jacket off the hanger and automatically glanced at the cell in his pocket – no messages. Of course, the "message" was now lying behind him, saying something – about exams?

"You want to be an office worker?" Jonathan hid the phone.

"I need a secure job."

"But won't you go mad working for the Commission? It would be different if you were a lawyer like Megi, that's an entirely different …"

"Didn't you hear what I said?" she interrupted.

"You once said yourself that I'd feel like a goose stuffed ready for *foie gras* if I worked for the Commission and now you … You're a journalist!"

"One can change one's profession."

"And who, supposedly, would you be?"

"Head of unit."

"Can't you hear what that sounds like?" Jonathan laughed and waited for Andrea to do the same. But she got up from the sofa and, without covering her belly, waddled toward the window as if she'd been about to give birth.

"Remember our first conversation?" Jonathan was serious now. "It was about precisely that, it was the beginning of us …"

"I think I'm going to leave Simon."

"That's why I took the writing course …" Jonathan broke off.

"I need a job that will give me the certainty that I won't get sacked when I'm walking around with an even bigger belly," Andrea explained in a teacher's voice.

Jonathan watched her draw back the lace curtains and look out on to the street. Lace strips of fabric – a souvenir of her parents' country, a communist legacy. Here, in Belgium, nobody hung things like that over their windows; people had lightweight curtains, canvas blinds, or left the windows bare according to the principle, "We've nothing to hide."

"But Simon's an immovable fixture. You're safe."

Andrea suddenly turned to face him but he stared at her belly – the navel protruded like a half-extracted champagne cork. In January, Simon would break open a bottle; not everybody managed to sow a son at Methuselah's age. Because it was undoubtedly a son, Andrea looked so beautiful.

"Didn't you hear what I said?" said Andrea for the second time that evening.

Her eyes were fixed on him and, after a long while, he said, "How do you imagine all this playing out?"

Andrea didn't answer, her fingers clung to the curtain.

A few minutes later, striding through the street, Jonathan still had the texture of the fabric in front of his eyes – loose mesh, handcrafted. His thoughts were similar, full of holes: Andrea the office worker, even though she'd encouraged him to be free; Andrea without Simon but with a swelling belly.

He still had her taut skin beneath his fingers. If he felt carefully he could make out the baby's back, touch its tiny heel. Jonathan watched his step, as the apartments past which he was walking stuck out tongues of metal for cleaning shoes. Picturesque façades slipped by, elevations interwoven with window displays.

He didn't ask Andrea about the baby; she, too, usually didn't say anything about it. Both, unanimously, seemed to ignore its existence although it breathed, snuggled up to their heated bodies, its pulse beating between their naked bellies. Bigger and bigger, it demanded its own space and Jonathan knew it would be better if he ceded it. He should leave her in peace but couldn't. Something made him run after her, after this fleeing woman who didn't want anything from him. That's why this day, when she was so close to letting him into her life, he fled like one possessed. He couldn't imagine Andrea submissive, Andrea warm and devoted.

And that belly of hers! What was Jonathan supposed to do with it – take on somebody else's child?

**3**

"IT'S RAINING," said Geert.

They looked at him half-unawares from above the texts they were editing. Jonathan hadn't yet told them that their stories might be published but arranged their sessions so they could focus on the few pieces chosen by him.

He studied his disciples and thought about how far they'd come. Ariane avoided autobiographical plots like the plague but had an exceptional gift for observing reality, thanks to which she often hit on a narrative vein of gold. She didn't always have the patience to delve deeper into fields she knew little about, which was blatantly obvious, but she wasn't discouraged, and that was the main thing.

Kitty had finally stopped writing about motherhood and had reached for her former self, searching, open, sometimes unsure or frustrated. Her cycle of stories about the dilemmas of a teenager, later a young woman, took his breath away with their committed depiction of characters and polished detail. There was something nineteenth-century about Kitty's writing, no fear of thinking and a resistance to haste.

Jean-Pierre blundered into writing his family history. Jonathan had tried to direct his interest toward smaller forms but his student seethed inside – recorded reminiscences, collected testimonies, amassed old photographs and documents. Jonathan brought him a postcard of a lorry, loaded to the brim with parcels, which had got stuck in desert sand. Jean-Pierre thanked him but didn't catch the allusion. He was sure he would do justice to the enormity of his subject.

Geert clung to his chosen path and Jonathan clung to Geert. He was fascinated by how the elderly man untangled the trauma of his childhood, how bravely he subjected it to the literary process, how he fought to keep his distance and prayed for the transformation of unexpressed emotions. This was why Jonathan pressed to publish the story, neglected his own writing, sought grants, kept phoning Cecile as if his life depended on it.

Unfortunately, the latest news of the stories' publication was not promising. A group of beginners did not arouse commercial interest.

"It's raining," repeated Geert.

Jean-Pierre glanced blankly at the window; in front of his eyes he still had the shed rigged up on an urban allotment by an old eccentric whom the inhabitants of a neighboring housing estate cursed because he bred pigeons. They claimed it was his fault they'd had to install protective nets because his birds soiled their balconies. Only when he died did they start to whisper among themselves that the pigeons on their balconies were different, gray. Someone had apparently seen white doves on the day of the breeder's funeral – they'd flown over the allotments and housing estate one last time, their wings carrying them left and right, left and right. The flock had danced to the rhythm of an aerial waltz, the sun turned their feathers to gold. And then they flew away.

"Excellent!" Jean-Pierre tossed at Ariane as he set the pages aside.

She didn't hear, immersed in Kitty's story. She smiled and grew serious in turn, referred back to previous pages, underscored. Kitty, concealing her worry, kept glancing at her until Geert's story drew her in.

"Good evening." A melodious voice tore them from their reading. "I won't be a minute, I don't want to disturb you," said Cecile, making her way toward Jonathan.

Ariane shot a meaningful glance at Kitty. The men in the room – thirty-year-old Jean-Pierre; Jonathan, not much older; and sixty-year-old Geert – had their eyes glued on Cecile. There was something in the sway of her gait, the fragility of her wrists, the statuesque shape of her shoulders, that made her white hair seem like the provocative accessory of a rebellious girl.

Cecile, as usual, looked a little embarrassed by the impression she made. She walked up to Jonathan and whispered something in his ear; he looked at her, his face brightening. Kitty winked at Ariane – Jonathan looked like a boy whose mother had just given him some candy floss. He turned his sparkling eyes on her again, then on them.

"You're going to be published authors!" he yelled.

He returned home in sheets of rain. The outline of the arch loomed unclear above the park fence, the fountain in front of it was still. His cell rang in his pocket.

"I hear Andrea's trying for the position of head of unit," Stefan said. "Poor Megi!"

"Why?" Jonathan drew to a halt. Drops of rain fell into his hood.

"She probably wasn't offered it," Stefan stated, rather than asked.

Anger mounted in Jonathan. He'd felt so good after Cecile's news and this guy dispelled all his enthusiasm with one stab.

"She's a bit broken up about it," Jonathan admitted reluctantly. "She'd passed the exam, after all."

"I might be bursting your bubble," Stefan interrupted him impatiently, "but you've got to have support in the Commission."

"Life as a transaction."

"What?"

"That hideous Przemek was supposedly going to support Megi."

"He's not big enough."

"That's what I keep telling her," triumphed Jonathan.

"I mean in influence. Especially if she gets blocked."

"Who'd want to block Megi?"

Stefan didn't say anything.

"Well, who?" Jonathan hustled him.

"Think."

"Who?"

"Simon."

The rain had stopped but the dusky city didn't come to life again. The clatter of hooves sounded through the backstreets but the horse patrol was nowhere to be seen. Jonathan raised his eyes to the arch. A souvenir of the time when Belgium was magnificent, a postcolonial monument erected with money from the Congo. The symbol of Jonathan's freedom – Jonathan, the jogger. But now, after reading Geert's short story, he looked at the construction in a different light. The pain of the child in Geert's story permeated Jonathan and remained there.

When he got back, Megi was asleep. He peeped in on the children, set their window ajar. Antosia was lying on her side, the girl-elf of Bauer's paintings; her long hair flowed off the bed, glistening in the streak of light coming from the hallway. In the daylight, it was a shade of gold, almost red, just like Megi's before she'd started "improving" it with highlights.

Jonathan turned and picked up the duvet, which had slid from the other bed. Tomaszek slept in a spread-eagle position, his arms and legs flung to the sides. Jonathan noticed how his son had grown; his shape had lost some of its roundness, his limbs had lengthened. He covered him, breathing in the puppy smell.

"My child. Mine," drifted Andrea's voice. Jonathan abruptly pulled himself up and stole out of the children's room. He slipped under the duvet and wrapped himself in Megi's warmth. But sleep didn't come. He rolled on to his back and stared at the oblique window.

Stefan appeared in his mind. His women were amazingly like each other. Clinging women – those were the ones he attracted, those were the ones he shunned, starting with Monika, through to his last whim, Martyna, the doyenne of narcissists. Stefan saw his children chiefly on weekends. He talked to Jonathan about his daughter's piercings but lacked the courage to speak to her. Franek still tried to please his father but it was clear that the twelve-year-old was inevitably beginning to gravitate toward his peers, ceasing to need his father.

Jonathan's women were different, independent, self-sufficient. He congratulated himself for not being a menace who mended his own ego by undermining their values. He wasn't afraid of strong women, nor was he afraid of children. He didn't run away from being a father – it was his right to be one. Although he sometimes growled with tiredness, these growls expressed love. If he were the father of Andrea's child, he wouldn't dodge the responsibility. If he were ...

He started counting in his head: she was to give birth at the end of January so she must have conceived in May, perhaps April. "I told you I wanted one with you," came Andrea's voice. Megi sighed in her sleep.

Jonathan sprung out of bed, ran downstairs and pulled out his diary from his jacket. When exactly had that been, the time they didn't use a rubber? An article deadline, his mother's birthday, a school meeting, but no markings for fertile and infertile days. May, May ... There was still that night in Sweden when she hadn't replied to his messages. Had that been because someone was with her?

He stepped onto the balcony, lit a cigarette, and let out a column of smoke. Constellations: Orion, the North Star. Megi didn't know much about them, could barely find the Great Bear. Andrea didn't want anything from him, she cut him off from her life. Whose was that little human being growing in her?

A bat glided above the gardens, its trajectory cut by a light, a falling star or a plane.

Who else was Andrea screwing?

Jonathan leans Andrea against the wall and slips his hands under her dress; his fingers run down her naked body, only the swell above her pubic mound brings him round. She quickly turns and sticks out her rump. Her waist is still narrow from the back, her buttocks firm and shapely. Jonathan parts them and takes a while to fit his cock into the hole. Andrea pushes her rump out further but Jonathan prolongs his manipulations. He knows how hot she is – a miracle of the middle trimester, an onslaught of hormones that sweep a woman away, telling her to get as much humping in as she can before confinement and delivery.

Slowly he inserts himself into Andrea; her pussy is hot and wet, the walls part effortlessly. She absorbs him into herself, sucks him in with her warm opening, would have allowed herself to be screwed to bits. She writhes in orgasm, although she doesn't usually come from behind. Now she howls quietly; her legs, shaking but obstinate, hold her stiff.

Jonathan helps her lie on her side. He waits until she's had enough – she'd come four times that day – but again she arches her back. Just before her wave reaches its climax, he picks up speed, the whirl has caught him, too.

Later, they lie wet, Jonathan's hand wandering up toward Andrea's hips. It comes across her belly and, instinctively, irrationally, retreats. He still can't ask about the shape that is there between them, doesn't know the due date or how the pregnancy is going.

He climbs into his car and moves away from her apartment. Around the corner he hits a traffic jam straight away – dairy workers from Germany and France are blocking the main streets of Brussels, police stand guard at the impassable tunnels. Jonathan presses the pedals one by one: accelerator – he's driving on postcoital euphoria; brake – he ought to ask Andrea openly who the father of her child is; clutch – he's afraid of what she'll say.

He goes back to the same crossroads, passes her apartment again. The hands of the clock glide mercilessly; he should have been at the school long ago but had been fucking when they closed the thoroughfares. After forty minutes, he manages to get to Reyers. The lower part is closed off, along the upper rolls a vehicle cleaning the road. The cars move bumper to bumper; police watch threateningly from beneath the plastic screens of their helmets. Jonathan, in rhythm with the frog hop of his car, searches his memory for any affirmation that Simon is the child's father. He can't remember any.

"Shit, shit!" He thumps his palm against the steering wheel; the man in the Audi next to him watches him in sympathy.

The street has already been swept but all the lanes of traffic are stuck; cars glisten as far as the eye can see. The vehicles move off slowly and again come to a standstill at the Montgomery roundabout. Tractors block the lanes around the fountain; a red, plastic cow looks on from a trailer. "Shit, shit!" Jonathan stamps the floor of the Toyota but the string of cars still doesn't move. He pulls out his phone and calls the mother of one of Tomaszek's friends. He's fallen victim to the demands made by French dairymen, has been immobilised near a red cow. Could she keep an eye on his kids?

He moves forward slowly and finally grinds to a halt in the siege of honking cars. The tractor drivers aren't there; they've gone for a beer. Only their machines are left, blocking the way for Brussels's rushing inhabitants. If the farmers were here that would be something, at least, but no! It's shadow-boxing. Sweating, Jonathan opens all his windows. He hadn't asked Andrea if he was definitely not the father. The red cow looks at him accusingly. He hadn't asked because he can't stand heart-to-heart talks; truthful answers scare him. There's no room for truth in illicit liaisons; truth might destroy the delicate construction.

Something changes in the configuration of vehicles; the gray nose of his Toyota sniffs out a thinning of the traffic and, at last, breaks out toward Avenue Tervuren. It streaks along the empty lane; cold wind and rain sweep down Jonathan's collar, veil his glasses with drizzle. Things are fine as they are, with their staggering rate of lovemaking and short moments of happiness. The child is her child and she is his love.

With bravado, Jonathan turns right into Boulevard du Souverain, passes the crossroads, and in reaction to his unexpectedly restored freedom races down the street – in the process of being repaired ever since they'd moved to Brussels. Then he speeds until he grinds to a halt in another traffic jam. Another unexpected obstacle: a fairground has installed itself on the one and only free lane.

Parents are milling around awkwardly when Jonathan arrives at the school playground, their eyes searching for their children. Dusk transforms the playground, the cheerfully painted monkey-bars and huts become forts, delighted gnomes giggle in the bushes. His heart in his throat, Jonathan looks around for his kids. He could count on Antosia's common sense but where had giddy-headed Tomaszek got to?

A mother he knows emerges from the drizzle and points to the lush hedge. He recognizes his son's voice among the cacophony of screams drifting from there; Antosia he finds on the swings. In the light of the street lamp, he sees the altered faces of parents, late because of the traffic jam. Soon, just like his, their eyes would anxiously be groping through the dusk, as they worried where their children were.

Holding their hands, Jonathan drags his kids to the car; they're with him now – two hands, two children. He has no more hands.

*Megi passes Portofino brasserie and comes to Luxembourg Square. The wheels of taxis rasp along the cobblestones, the old tenements cower in the drizzle. The corridors of the new European Parliament building hang suspended above the ground, stairs meander in glazed cages, a screen projects a circle of stars. "What a clear-cut shape," thinks Megi. "You don't have to struggle to find the Great Bear."*

*Przemek had insisted he walk her home; she'd just about managed to wangle her way out of it. She wanted to be alone after what he'd implied: that she would have got the position of head of unit had it not been for blocking from above.*

*"Above?" she'd asked. "But was it official?"*

*He'd shaken his head, looking around carefully.*

*"Who doesn't like me and why?" She'd groaned, and a moment later regretted her imprudent words because Przemek had immediately moved closer.*

*Megi shudders when she remembers that moment of physical proximity. How come some people have no inhibitions? Even men who look like Shrek try to pick her up, not giving a second thought to why an attractive woman who has a handsome husband should want to go to bed with them.*

*Megi pulls back her hair, wet from the drizzle. An unwanted admirer was nothing compared to the fact that she'd passed a difficult exam and not got the job because of someone's whim. If only she knew who it was, but it was like shadow-boxing. She guessed it was someone much higher up than Przemek, some vengeful éminence grise.*

*And later, in the ladies' toilets, she'd overheard that Andrea had got the post.*

*Her umbrella slips down Megi's back, her hair and shoulders get wet. She cuts across the cobbled square, where the little fountains froth in summer. Only the approach to Schumann roundabout left.*

# 4

WHEN ANDREA TOLD HIM she'd got the position of head of unit, he tried to assume a suitable expression. What was worse was that he didn't know which suited best. On the one hand, the new job would turn the journalist into an office worker, on the other, the post was a Eurocrat's dream because the money was secure and the head of unit was untouchable. Well, and his wife had sat up many a night in order to pass the exam and get the job, then everything had gone to waste because he, during his free time from writing, was fucking the life partner of the head of cabinet for the Commissioner. At least that was Stefan's theory.

"Congratulations, you're magnificent," said Jonathan, kissing Andrea on the forehead, which, for some time now, had been a strong rival to her lips.

He recalled the saying that people love each other as long as they want to kiss each other on the lips. But there were so many shades of love, after all; desire could evolve into friendship, into mutual respect … "Bullshit!" something cried in Jonathan, whose emotions expressed themselves in English, while common sense used Polish. Probably because when, as a boy, he'd said goodbye to one of his parents, the other didn't spare him arguments, saying that he had to come to terms with the situation. English was the language of school and peers, but also feelings. When he gazed into Petra's icy irises, he heard her hot, English declarations. Bullshit, he repeated in his thoughts.

Love was infatuation, desire, and passion, that's what his body told him, his ever-fertile body, which, having sniffed out the smell of its woman, followed her trail until he'd fucked her. Friendship, respect – those were the values the human being in Jonathan called upon, the human being Andrea had noticed when he'd agreed to be with her, even though she'd got herself pregnant by another man. But the human being in him was not constant. It took on the characteristics of a male, because how else could he explain the doubts that assailed him as to who the father of his lover's child was, the way he downplayed Simon's procreative abilities, and his attempts, underlain with anxiety, to ascribe the child to himself?

The human being in Jonathan kept being burned to a cinder by desire and from his ashes arose the male. He peed to mark out his territory, took his female, then lay on his back in a gesture of surrender – because once more the human being had appeared on stage – whom the male chased away. And so it went round and round.

"You're magnificent," repeated Jonathan.

Andrea cheered up and, in his heart, he congratulated himself on having perfectly mastered the schoolboy reflex of repeating the last sentence without understanding.

"I've got to go." He reached for his jacket.

Ever since the roads had been blocked, he left with time to spare, then sat in front of the school in a car that grew cold.

"What did you say?" He glanced absentmindedly at Andrea, as he groped in his pockets in search of his cell.

"That I want to leave Simon."

He froze, one arm in the sleeve. Something like this had already happened, this scene, her eyes fixed on him expectantly, with concealed joy. So what was that last sentence?

"But," he began, chasing away thoughts about *déjà vu*, "Simon won't let you leave."

Her face darkened. He continued nevertheless: "And what about his child?"

"It's my child."

Silence, then: "Andrea!" yells Jonathan, throwing his jacket on the floor. His cell flies from the pocket and slides until it comes to a rest by Simon's slippers.

Jonathan grabs Andrea by the elbows and shakes her. Her hair covers her face so that only her belly, that belly, indicates where her front and back are. When finally her face appears between the dark strands, her lips, twisted in fury, scream, "You didn't want to have a child with me!"

Jonathan squeezes her arms, feels her muscles tense, feels her bones as though his fingers had long ago punctured her body.

"Is it mine?" he wants to yell.

She waits for the question but Jonathan purses his lips and watches Andrea tilt back her head; her eyes are black, angry, her lips tremble. When she finally says something, her voice is sure, distinct: "It's my child."

Jonathan's fingers slacken. Andrea moves away from him.

"Mine," she repeats as if she were informing viewers of the fall of shares on the exchange. "I can afford it, in all respects."

A few hours later, lying on the bed he shared with Megi, the children cuddled up to his sides, Jonathan tried in vain to understand what Antosia was reading. The words of the story hummed soothingly, Tomaszek's eyes were closing and from the whirlpool of Jonathan's thoughts leapt Andrea's yelling. Or maybe it was he who'd taken it as yelling because in reality she hadn't raised her voice again when he left her that afternoon, only drily informed him that if she left Simon, it didn't obligate him, Jonathan, in any way. She wouldn't break up his family, wouldn't take that responsibility on her shoulders. Jonathan didn't have to be afraid either for himself or, more to the point, for her. Andrea would manage.

"Daddy, Tomaszek's fallen asleep. And you're not listening," complained Antosia.

Jonathan raised himself, carefully took his son in his arms and carried him to bed.

"You read beautifully." He kissed Antosia on the hair.

She nodded but there was scepticism on her face. His daughter's reactions were more and more mature, she didn't have tantrums like a child, only concealed her feelings like an adult. He hugged her closely so she wouldn't see his expression. He would have preferred her to remain a child a little longer, be happier a little longer.

He turned off the light in the children's room and went back to his bedroom. Megi was working long hours again; she'd phoned not long ago, explaining that she'd be late. He opened the window and exposed his face to the breeze of the evening air. Andrea hadn't explained anything, had decided for herself that she wouldn't get in the way of his family.

She hadn't asked for his opinion; she had simply resolved it should be this way.

He looked at the oblique roofs of the apartments, at the arc of his street, at the tops of the leafless trees. Everything here was mild; the November gusts were melancholic rather than sharp, the houses leaned against each other affably, windows smiled in the façades, each apartment building was different, each a little old, a little new, unpretentious, familiar.

"Don't worry." Andrea's words came back to him. "I'm not going to break up your family." Jonathan closed the window; the room turned silent. She'd made the decision herself. But then he, too, had never started to think seriously about leaving Megi and the children. It was his private taboo. And Andrea had understood that his passion for her belonged to the present – Jonathan felt her here and now – while his feelings for Megi were retained in his memories, in their watching the children together, in their plans and daily routines. And although the fireworks of being with his lover outshone daily routine, the basis of his life endured, the main current flowed persistently, linked the past to the future, waited for the moment until it could overflow and embrace the present again.

The slamming of a door reached him from below. Megi's footsteps were slow, like his grandmother's in the past when she'd walked to his father's apartment. His grandmother had tended to be tired; shopping pulled on her shoulders. Something clattered downstairs – a hanger had slipped from Megi's hands.

Jonathan quickly stripped and slid beneath the duvet. Suddenly a thought occurred to him that he hadn't taken into account before: if Andrea left Simon and he stayed here, then ... his lover would be free. A free Andrea, Andrea openly taking advantage of her freedom!

He switched off the bedside lamp, curled up on his side, and Megi, seeing him asleep, stepped back from the bedroom door and quietly closed it behind her.

# 5

JONATHAN SAT in the sauna on the scorching planks and breathed the humid air. Stefan had settled himself next to him on the wooden steps. Jonathan passed him a can of beer and opened one himself.

"How did you know Simon was blocking Megi?" he asked.

"One knows these things."

"Megi only told me today."

"And how did she know?"

"You know so why shouldn't she? She's the one concerned."

Stefan rolled his eyes; the steam was making his face turn red.

"If she's the one concerned, then everyone should know except for her," he bristled.

"What's this, 'teach yourself Cardinal Richelieu'?"

"Did Przemek tell her?" Stefan answered with a question.

Jonathan nodded.

"And did he tell her it was Simon?"

"No, not that."

Froth spurted from Stefan's can as he opened it.

"Then you've got more luck than brains." He shook the froth from his hand; the smell of beer filled the sauna. "And I'm in deep shit. I'm not sure Monika hasn't caught on I fucked Martyna because she's not talking to me. "Where's my shirt?" I ask and she says nothing. I bring her flowers, still nothing. What an atmosphere! I tell her that the children are suffering because of it but it's like banging my head against a brick wall."

"Has she done it before?"

"She used to soften with flowers."

"So what are you going to do this time?"

"I thought you'd tell me." Reproach flitted in Stefan's eyes. "I've run out of ideas. But getting back to you, what's the situation? She's pregnant, he's getting his revenge, Megi's blocked because of it ..."

"Blocked but we don't know whether that's why," retorted Jonathan through clenched teeth. He had a superstitious approach to words; he didn't like the idea that when uttered they created facts. "That's your theory."

"And Przemek's."

Stefan raised his arms; a couple of drops squirted from his can onto the wooden planks, and the smell of beer grew stronger.

"And now they'll kick us out of here if you go on stinking the place out with that," muttered Jonathan.

"But what did you tell Megi when she mentioned the blocking?"

"That it's a conspiracy theory. And that since she's passed the exam and has the necessary experience, she'll get another job before we know it."

Stefan nodded in approval.

"She won't buy that, she's too intelligent, but you showed you were trying. And Andrea? Do you see each other?"

Jonathan nodded.

"And fuck?"

"None of your business."

"Meaning you do. So nothing's changed."

"Only that Andrea wants to leave Simon."

Stefan choked; beer spurted on to the bench again. Jonathan raised his eyes without a word.

"And you haven't told me? But she's not gone running to Megi yet, has she? Shit, it's like that Ilona of mine."

"Quite the opposite!" Jonathan riposted. "Yours wanted to live happily ever after with you. Andrea is different."

"In what way? So why's she leaving Simon?"

"Says she can't go on like this. But that it doesn't oblige me in any way because she doesn't want to break up my family."

"And what, she's going to be alone, with the baby?"

"That's exactly what's doing my head in! Andrea alone ... And all those guys, understand?"

It took Stefan a while to grasp what Jonathan meant.

"You must be mad," he said in the end. "You're scared she'll make the most of her freedom? A pregnant woman, then a single mother with a small child, is going to make the most of the single life? Give me a break!"

"So what am I supposed to be scared of?" Jonathan was at a loss.

"Just that when she cracks up from being alone she'll go to Megi and create a stink!"

"That's not Andrea." Jonathan shook his head. "She's got a job, good money, she'll hire a nanny. What does she need somebody like me for?"

"And you, what do you need her for?"

Jonathan started squeezing his can; the sound rang out in the quiet sauna like an explosion.

"She keeps running away from me," he said barely audibly. "I can't leave her because she runs away and … keeps wanting me."

Stefan looked at him strangely, then asked, "And aren't you afraid she's going to land you with the baby?"

"All I'm afraid of," said Jonathan after a long while, "is what I'm going to tell my children. That's all I'm afraid of in this whole business of, as you call it, 'landing me with the baby.'"

Stefan gasped in anger, spread his hand out in front of him, and folded his fingers one by one.

"Alimony, looking for a nanny, choosing a school …"

Jonathan began to wriggle around on the bench.

"More generally," he interrupted Stefan's counting, "I'm scared of asking her whether it's mine."

"Want to know what I think? Don't!"

"But what if it is mine? Surely I've a right to know. On the other hand, what about my kids? What about Megi?"

Stefan reached for another can of beer, pretending not to see his friend's contorted face.

"Don't think in terms of 'what if,'" he said earnestly. "Do what I do in such cases: check you haven't got HIV and don't phone her any more. Then she won't leave Simon and it'll all blow over."

*Megi walks briskly past the Hotel Renaissance façade. Jonathan wanted her to buy Tomaszek a pair of trainers for his gym classes on her way back from work because the boy had grown out of his old pair. They couldn't go together because the children had swimming lessons that afternoon.*

*"Can't you do it tomorrow?" She was sitting in front of a pile of papers, finding it hard to turn her mind to domestic matters.*

*"If he's grown out of them, he's grown out of them." Jonathan cut her short.*

*Megi enters the black district; ahead of her, Chaussée d'Ixelles tempts with its lights. A pair of shoes gleam in a display she passes: red, with a huge bow at the toes, patent leather. What if she had a pair like that? And a hairpiece to go with them like the one hanging in the hair salon nearby – black, curly hair, not Afro but thick waves. Megi turns the corner. She's struck by the ad in the pharmacy window for an anticellulite cream: someone is handing a woman a brand new body, a shape on a hanger, smooth and shiny. Megi shudders. But every wrinkle is a notch made by time, a mark denoting "I've been there." What was there to be ashamed of?*

*Returning with a package in her hand, she watches men in coats and suits sneak along the walls. Of course, the time for "international relations" is coming to an end; the little hotels and brothels were under siege between five and seven when office workers squeezed in pleasure between work and family dinner. Wasn't it Przemek who'd told her that?*

*That day he'd proposed they go to lunch and she'd insisted they meet at the Exki; the speed and transitory nature of the place precluded intimacy.*

*"I've been offered a job back in Poland on excellent conditions," he began ceremoniously. "I can't tell you exactly what it involves but if I were to take it I'd have a whole team under me, and also," he smiled, a strand of rocket lodged between his teeth, "lots of power."*

*"Congratulations," she replied.*

*"As I mentioned before, I'd like to offer you a position in my future team. A lot of responsibilities, decent money, and no small influence over matters. What do you say?"*

*Megi picked up a plastic spoon. She had to weigh her words. Przemek was, above all, a player and only after that an admirer.*

*"When would you be starting?"*

*He smiled with approval. She hadn't asked when she would be starting because that would have meant she'd agreed; but neither had she said no.*

*"Early next year."*

*Getting into the metro, Megi decides not to tell Jonathan for the time being; she'll sleep on it first. When she reaches the apartment, she sees that the windows are dark – Jonathan and the children aren't here yet. He must have treated them to a hot chocolate after their swimming. Megi climbs the stairs and stands in the silence of her own home. Just like six years ago when, after having seen her lover, she returned late on the pretext of having so much work. She'd stood on the threshold then just as she did now – the threshold of happiness and scruples, sexual fulfilment and moral trembling. Or perhaps simply fulfilment and trembling?*

*And yet she'd broken up with the other man. She extends her fingers and folds them one by one, silently repeating, "One: decision to leave him; two: sticking with the decision; three: getting stuck because of panic that am killing love; four: physical low, body's mourning; five: first, tiny signs of picking up."*

*Megi walks up to the huge window and gazes out at Brussels's roofs from the dark shell of her apartment. She had coped, picked herself up. Nobody had told her how to do so, she'd got there herself. Now she is stronger, there is more of her. More of her and more about her.*

# 6

JONATHAN SENT ANDREA fewer messages but didn't stop completely. He'd worked out this strategy when he'd decided to put Stefan's advice into practice – and although he had a strong feeling that he'd been given a prescription for a different disease, he couldn't afford to turn up his nose. He needed a remedy immediately.

He reassured Andrea, hinted that at this stage of pregnancy she ought to look after herself, that he was and always would be there, but that they ought to limit seeing each other. He himself started to obsessively invest in family life. First of all, he had a blood test done.

Sitting in the waiting room, he browsed the leaflets about HIV. Dry sentences began to erase Andrea's kisses from his memory, changed the meaning of tender gestures, of his tongue's exploits in the depth of her groin. Now he scrutinized those moments with the possibility of being infected, delved into the details without his former excitement, rewound the scenes of their intertwined bodies from a medical point of view. He left millilitres of blood lighter, a venomous feeling of guilt heavier – if he'd caught the virus, he was endangering not only himself as a father but also the innocent Megi!

He decided to avoid physical intimacy with his wife while waiting for the results. But he deceived himself because, although more and more sexually frustrated, he knew that his desire was not directed at Megi. He still wanted only Andrea, even though he put himself off her in his thoughts as much as possible. He even suspected that she wouldn't notice his remoteness and if she did she would, as was her wont, allow him to distance himself more. But whether the pregnancy had changed her or whether he was not sufficiently tactful, it was enough to make her start sniffing around. So he met her in order to reassure her – in a church once more, because Simon wasn't going away so often during the last trimester of her pregnancy.

They stood, hidden behind a pillar, facing the altar, her back against his belly, his arms wrapped below her neck. He studied the stained-glass windows and thought that somebody had to break the infernal circle before it sucked in innocent people, children. He wanted to tell her this but couldn't, so his eyes merely flitted between his lover – the pregnant atheist, a Czech woman brought up in Sweden – and the motionless Virgin Mary to whom his Polish grandmother had prayed. He even tried to remember the words she'd taught him but got stuck at the beginning of the *Hail Mary*.

He held Andrea in his arms, filled to the brim with love, and then got into his car and drove away. Fewer and fewer messages came, and he was increasingly convinced that he was in a deadlock; even if Andrea were to leave Simon, he wouldn't leave the children and Megi. As it was, he'd already cut the branch they were sitting on (if Stefan and Przemek's theory about Simon blocking Megi was correct). Was he, on top of it all, to leave her knowing how much the professional setback had cost her?

At least now she had some support from him; she appreciated his looking after the house while she studied for exams, thanked him for serving her salads when she got home from work, depressed, pensive. He was pleased his wife didn't catch on to what the salads really were – part of his plan as a prodigal husband, a practical version of Stefan's flowers of apology. If he could, he would have carried her in his arms, but he couldn't touch her. Not only did he not find her attractive, he found her repulsive – so fair, so sexlessly good – different from Andrea.

He writhed with unfulfilled sex. He had under his nose a woman whom Stefan envied him, at whose sight Przemek slobbered, and he couldn't force himself to take her; instead of which he coveted his neighbor's wife, an egoist who yelled that the child was only hers, because of whom he woke up at night with a burning desire or the fear that she'd infected him with HIV. She must, after all, have had as many men as she desired.

As if this wasn't enough, she pushed him away from her life, had decided she wasn't going to be with him. And kept him in a state of uncertainty as to who the father was! Here he stopped his accusations for a moment – it wasn't her fault that he hadn't asked if he was the father but had immediately forged ahead with innocence and love. She wouldn't have told him anyway; at most she would have said that it was her child. It was herself she loved above all, and her freedom, and Simon closed his eyes to this. That was why she was with him. Jonathan was troublesome because he was possessively in love.

He later lay in his bath, gazing at his own body, that looked as though it were immersed in formaldehyde. His thoughts lost mo-mentum, got stuck. Maybe he'd done the wrong thing? After all, things were fine between them now. She'd said herself that everything was finally falling into place. He was accepting of her and an experienced father, she felt safe with him, she'd seen and grown to love the human being in him. She said that, subconsciously, this was probably what had drawn her to him – his inner youth and easygoing nature with, on the other hand, warmth, and the fact that he gave so much of himself to others. He didn't place power on a pedestal, didn't pursue high positions, didn't boast of a trophy wife. With him she would not feel as though she were "somebody's" she had grown out of that, so she said …

Jonathan abruptly sat up; water splashed on to the floor. He was killing love! Why had he listened to that idiot Stefan? He didn't understand any of it! He hadn't ever committed himself like that, not even Monika could drive him crazy with love, only to the altar; Stefan saw his marriage as a matter of honor, not a love-match. If he happened to think too much about a girl, he applied the hair of the dog. He went on about love because some chicks wouldn't allow themselves to be screwed otherwise, but he himself admitted that he needed women in the plural. He classified them according to color, shape, taste, and smell. He was married to himself, his own "other half."

Jonathan shuddered. He and Andrea were different. Their love was an exception. In any case, he had more space in his heart – and that's what he should have held on to.

But Andrea had decided that she didn't want to break up his family. He remembered how once, when she realized how crazy he was, not only with desire, but with love for her, she'd asked, looking at him with some disbelief, "But you've got everything: children, a fine wife, a profession you're passionate about. What do you need me for?" He hadn't answered. She had cuddled up to him, fawned, and then fled. What was he to do? He ran after her.

He slipped deeper into the bath, water filled his ears. Indeed, what did he need her for – in order to have something of his own apart from what he already had – a family, a tidy life? Was it the same with Andrea's child, this seed conceived by her "I want," by Jonathan not being ready and Simon's acquiescence, and which now dwelled in the waters of her belly. Was it her liberation, a living expression of her will?

Jonathan's head emerged from the water and he took a gasp of air. Thanks to her he had regained his attraction to risk. That was why he was now waiting for the results of the HIV tests.

He picked up Antosia's orange sponge. If he hadn't wanted to risk anything, he wouldn't have started up with her – Andrea, who didn't allow anyone, including him, to tame her. He wasn't longing for warm slippers. He saturated the sponge with water and squeezed as hard as he could. "Was Megi warm slippers?" he asked himself. Or maybe some force was driving her into them?

And then he stopped thinking about it all – at least, that's what he ordered himself to do. When the thought of Andrea appeared, he threw himself into a whirl of simple, daily activities. It was a good thing he didn't have to edit the little collection; the short stories written by his disciples lay on Cecile's desk and Jonathan hoped she wouldn't have too many comments. He couldn't use his head now; it was all fogged up, sentences fell apart.

He had lost sight of *The Pavlov Dogs* entirely. When he dipped into what he'd written, he didn't recognize his own sentences. Somebody else had put the story together, somebody whom the dogs liked, whom they approached, nudged with their noses, at whose sight they wagged their tails. Nobody liked Jonathan – neither his wife, whom he didn't desire, nor his lover whom he ought to drop, nor his children for whom he had no patience of late. Even the dogs had left him.

He drove the children to and from school, loaded and unloaded the dishwasher, loaded and hung the washing, lugged the shopping, took the children swimming, dragged himself to the gym, and jogged by force of will. The hours dovetailed, duties ground along. "I haven't got the strength for them," he thought. He didn't understand what he was reading, he set his social life aside because it required too much effort, he didn't let his wife drag him to the cinema because he no longer liked her. It was because of her that he'd had to relinquish himself. Now neither desire nor friendship held them together.

He trained so intensively at this time that he was finally laid low. Megi said it was the result of jogging in foul weather, Stefan that it was waiting for the results of the HIV test. At moments like these, Stefan always fell into depths of remorse in the form of psychosomatic symptoms, which again cemented his relationship with Monika who had to look after him. Had he allowed himself to think about her, Jonathan himself would no doubt have admitted that it was because he was cut off from Andrea. But he wouldn't allow such a thought. He had a strong will; he was, after all, a writer. Only his body was now weak.

He let himself fall – the pain gnawed at him and he gnawed at the pain. He wrapped himself entirely in a martyr's way of thinking; every morning began with it, and the evening ended with it. He thought about the pain and not about Andrea; about his nerve roots and not about her child; about his lumbago and not the freedom she wanted officially to regain.

He curled up in bed, barely registering the sounds in the apartment. Megi took a few days off but got up early anyway, as if she were going to work, while he lay there pretending to be asleep, short of sleep, aching, sweating. He listened to the swoosh of water in the bathroom, to the children's pattering, to their scrambling, hushed in vain by Megi's whispers. The door slammed and he opened his eyes. And again forbade himself to think about Andrea.

After a few days he started to get up, walk around the room. On seeing his own face in the mirror above the sink he thought he looked like an old druid. He hadn't shaved because he wasn't sufficiently steady on his feet to risk using a razor.

On Friday, after taking the children to school, Megi knocked on the door to the bedroom, which, for the duration of his illness, had become his own private den. He invited her in with a vague cough and she sat down on the edge of the bed.

"I'd like to tell you something," she began.

He looked at her from beneath half-closed eyelids; she appeared embarrassed. Jonathan attempted to sit up. Megi leapt up to pull the pillow higher. Suddenly, he wanted to laugh.

"Is the maiden in the family way?" he asked sternly.

Megi smiled; for a moment once more she was a student in love and not a lawyer with furrowed brow. She couldn't believe how well-read he was in Polish literature and admitted that she, like the majority of her friends at secondary school, had merely skimmed through Sienkiewicz's *Trilogy*, but then she wasn't a born humanist; which is why she loved the ancient Polish interjections that Jonathan had absorbed when he spent weeks of his holiday at his mother's.

She shook her head now, and told him about Przemek's offer – that, career-wise, she was tempted because she'd be able to learn new things, because here, after three years working as an administrator, she knew her responsibilities off by heart. Well, and, despite having passed the exams, the promotion had passed her by.

Jonathan listened attentively, from time to time a grimace of pain flitted across his face.

"And what do you think?" she asked in the end.

His eyes turned to the window. A little bit of sunshine pierced the clouds. What she was saying also seemed to come from outer space.

"To Poland?" he finally said.

# 7

THAT SATURDAY he tried to leave the house. He wanted to escape from the mangled sheets, the sound of the television, the children's activity and Megi's domestic pattering around doing household chores. He wanted to escape from the silence that had fallen over them after she'd told him about her offer.

He got dressed and barely managed to make his way downstairs.

"Are you going out?" Megi leaned out of the kitchen.

"Yes," he muttered and started putting on his shoes.

He picked up the right shoe, thinking he owed Megi the chance to return. It was because of him that she hadn't got the promotion; he saw her frustration. She was not some dozy office worker; after coming here and relishing the novelty, she had cultivated her patch without much effort and was quickly disheartened by the excess of bureaucracy that inhibited the efficiency of what they were doing. She considered herself too young to be "coming and going with a briefcase," which was how she described the fate of her fellow officials. She enjoyed challenges, problems. Sharp, she was familiar with power games but hated intrigue.

Jonathan mechanically put the right shoe down again and picked up the left. He couldn't imagine going back to Poland. It was like steering a ship back to port with its sails unfurled and instructing the crew to enjoy the flapping. Here, his children learned different languages, got what Stefan envied him. Here, they had friends of different nationalities with different roots, histories, skin colors.

He replaced the left shoe on the floor, turned with a groan, and began to rummage around in the pocket of his jacket. He searched and searched but Tomaszek's map wasn't there. He sat down, trying to remember where he could have put it. He definitely hadn't thrown it away. What if it had fallen out?

He hunched over, forgetting about his lumbago, and yanked his head up with a moan.

"Is everything OK?" Megi leaned out of the kitchen again.

He muttered something; she emerged and walked up to him.

"Too weak to go out?"

He nodded, feeling like an idiot.

"I thought so." She ran her hands over his arm. "It's too soon. Give yourself time."

And then there was the affair with the dove. Jonathan trudged upstairs, step by step, groaning like an old man. He was on the half-landing when a white bird fluttered in through the open window. Its legs slid apart on the smooth surface of the parapet but it didn't flee, merely stared at Jonathan. Only the stamping of Tomaszek's feet alerted the dove; still it didn't fly away.

It was then – as he later recounted – that Jonathan understood the bird was sick or dazed. Tomaszek stopped short and watched his father, who himself had difficulty moving, help the bird find its way out and close the window behind it. But when, some time later, Antosia ran past, she noticed the bird was still there, perched by the window-frame. She called Megi but her mother was getting dinner ready so Jonathan dragged himself downstairs.

Together with the children, he inspected the bird through the window pane, then went down with them. Together they constructed a cardboard "house," lining it with a soft rag and placing a saucer of water and some bread in the corner.

"Shall we make him a microwave as well?" asked Tomaszek.

They left the cardboard shelter outside, Megi helping them because Jonathan couldn't bend down. They sheltered the bird from the wind and rain, while making it possible for it to get out.

The following day, the children leapt out of bed and ran down to see how the dove was. But the bird was already dead. Jonathan did his best to console them but the sight of the white feathers covered with the first snow of the winter upset them all.

"And it didn't even die in the house we made especially for it," snivelled Tomaszek.

"It must have needed some fresh air," deduced Antosia.

Megi left them pondering where to bury the bird and went for a walk; a week's "leave" had left her drained.

When she got back, they were waiting for her with a white box in a carrier bag, all dressed to go out.

"What's that?" she asked, indicating what looked like a box of doughnuts from Blikle patisserie.

"The dove," replied Antosia, putting on her hat. "We're going to bury it. You've got to drive, Mommy, because Daddy can't."

"He's all twisted up." Tomaszek was more precise as he prepared to go out without his gloves.

*"I'm worried about whether we did the right thing, leaving that poor bird out in the freezing cold," Jonathan whispers into Megi's ear. "The children are taking its death so hard."*

*"And what were we supposed to do, take it to bed with us?" asks Megi in an unexpectedly argumentative tone.*

*She watches Jonathan grip the banister. He's pale; it's the first time he's going out since being ill. He's doing it for the children, so that they remember the dove's burial. Megi walks up to him and impulsively puts her arms around his waist.*

*She ought to ask him whether he's thought about Przemek's offer of eventually going back to Poland, but instead she thinks of Emile Max Street, blossoming with pink flowers. In the background flash the displeased faces of her cousin Adelka and her husband Robert. "Oh my God, and Uncle Tadeusz?" pounds in her head. On the other hand, shouldn't she go back to Poland, shouldn't she stretch herself professionally? After all, how long could she be an administrator?*

*Megi sighs and lets Jonathan go. She doesn't ask him anything. She goes downstairs and he follows, a fairy tale writer with a white dove in a Delhaize plastic bag.*

The next day, Monday, Jonathan dialled his doctor's number.

"Hello?" A Flemish accent echoed in the receiver.

"I'm calling about my HIV results." Jonathan only just managed to give his details; his mouth was so dry.

"And how's your back?" the doctor asked as she searched for his name on the computer.

"Better, thank you."

He was practically in working order thanks to painkillers and was intending to go out by himself that day, without anyone's assistance. Unless …

"Negative," she said lightly, and Jonathan sank into his armchair with a groan.

"Still hurts?" He heard her concerned voice.

"No, it's the relief."

"Everything's negative," she repeated. "Although you ought to watch your cholesterol."

He replaced the receiver and opened the terrace window. He took a deep breath of fresh air. Good news, a new beginning. He turned his eyes to a corner of the terrace – the rubber plant had not survived the winter. They'd forgotten to bring it inside and now blackened leaves hung from its branches. Jonathan stretched his arms up; when his back was better he would bin the flower pot with its label: "Rubber plant, perennial."

# 8

TOMASZEK'S MAP turned up in the backpack. Jonathan hadn't looked in there for several days. He walked along rue de Linthout, reached the roundabout where rue des Tongres joined Georges Henri, and stood beneath the tree. He wanted to walk on, following the instructions, but momentarily lacked strength. He glanced at the brasserie to which he usually went and the other on the opposite side of the street, which he considered pretentious. Surprising himself, he chose the latter.

Waiting for his coffee, he began to wonder whether the romance that had started exactly on this street, in the bakery a few meters away, had not been a typical result of coincidences: family, routine, suppressed sense of self, impaired creative expression. He thanked the waiter for the coffee, raised the cup to his lips, and scanned the winter sky. He was no good at such dilemmas, had no idea how to get a grip on the crisis in his relationship. The affair, all that, when captured in words, seemed both flat and shameful.

He smoothed out the map. "And dat way to ..."

And suddenly he saw a ginger tail in front of him, followed by another, fluffy one. They were wagging them, panting as they looked at him with eyes in which he could find no trace of guilt. So it was here the pack had moved to! He'd finally caught sight of them in the backstreets of rue des Tongres, amid the meandering walls, behind pillars. It was here they roamed, here they ran with their noses to the ground. They had been here all the time but he hadn't seen them!

The mongrel that looked like a toilet brush ran right past him, brushing Jonathan's trouser leg with its coarse hair. Another, like an Alsatian, rested its paws on a concrete trash can and was foraging for something. Finally, further down the street, Jonathan saw a familiar shape – the leader of the pack trotting lightly, his muscles defined beneath his fur, the hair on his nape gently bristling.

It seemed to Jonathan that the cars stood still and people froze at the sight of the enormous dog. He got to his feet in order to get a better view.

"Is the table going to be free?" somebody asked in French.

Jonathan blinked.

"No," he said, not very politely, and pulled a notebook out of his pocket.

When Jonathan picked the children up that afternoon, he no longer felt any pain in his back but his fingers were stiff. The story was writing itself, the coffee growing cold, the waiter had approached twice asking if he could fetch anything but didn't dare approach a third time. Left in peace, Jonathan caught the dogs, immortalising their adventures, shaking his head at their moves. What they were doing didn't depend on him; he could only watch and take note.

He might even have forgotten to collect the children from school had it not been for Megi, who called, prompted by intuition (she was handing over the domestic helm carefully, knowing how difficult it was to get a grasp of it all at once). He went for them, still agitated by his work. His mind undulated and skipped, metaphors ousting real details. A child is the fruit of the home, its content, pulp, seeds, he thought as he watched Tomaszek and Antosia playing in front of the school. It ripens, hangs, grows heavier and heavier until it falls. A certain percentage of fruit hangs on the branch until it becomes wrinkled, and even when blackening won't fall off. But a healthy fruit rolls, rolls, until it ends up near or far from the mother tree. Sometimes it will rest against another fruit – and the ground beneath the tree is sown with them – and then it becomes like the one next to it. If it rolls further away, it becomes an independent fruit. Independent to what extent?

Jonathan ushered Tomaszek and Antosia into the car, put their backpacks into the trunk then, stepping back, thumped the back of his head against the trunk. As if in reply, a thought flashed beneath his aching skull: what a good thing Andrea didn't want to break up his family!

It was Megi who offered to take the children to Poland for two weeks so that they could meet their more distant family before Christmas. He would be able to write in peace.

"I want to get a finished copy of *The Pavlov Dogs* under the Christmas tree." She pecked him on the cheek as they stood at the airport.

He smiled and stroked her hair. She'd stopped using lacquer recently and had said she was growing her hair. At the moment it was at the in-between stage with strands of hair pulled behind her ears and, although neither pretty nor tidy, it was – as Jonathan consoled her – getting there.

"Apparently it's terribly cold in Poland." She cuddled up to Jonathan.

"Buy yourself an electric blanket."

"Electric blankets are sex for the elderly. A propos, thank you for yesterday's dinner!"

Jonathan had chased the children to bed early the previous evening and prepared a special dinner, first making sure that Megi would be home at the normal time. He had, in fact, been prepared to wait even until midnight if she'd phoned, as she often did, to apologize that she was running late. He wanted to celebrate his return to writing with her, his agreement to go to Poland, and – perhaps – their first intercourse for some weeks.

"You complained that I don't cook," he now said frivolously, keeping his eyes on Tomaszek,, who had somehow found himself at the very center of a group of Orthodox Jews.

"You were eavesdropping! My mother's the only one I told, I remember perfectly well!"

"Men always eavesdrop, that's what they build their worldly power on."

"I thought it was oppression and captivity." She caught hold of Tomaszek as he ran past and told him to behave. She glanced at her watch – they ought to start saying goodbye, it always took quite a while.

"I'll just fill you in on two rumors," she threw. "Firstly: Monika wants to go back to Poland."

"Why don't I know anything about it?"

"I'm not even sure Stefan knows." Megi shrugged her shoulders. "It seems she's going through some revolutionary changes. She didn't look at all like the Monika of old when I bumped into her in the street last night."

"Daddy, can I touch that man?" Tomaszek tugged at Jonathan's jacket and pointed to a poker-faced Indian.

"No," Jonathan automatically retorted.

"Is he a fakir?" asked Antosia.

"I doubt it."

"Do you know, when I saw her," Megi continued, "I had the impression it was as if, well, as if she'd fallen in love with a lesbian."

"What's a lesbian?" whined Tomaszek, whose father was holding him by the hand to stop him running off again.

"Maybe she really has fallen in love?" Jonathan raised his eyebrows.

"It's not that." Megi shook her head, trying to find the right words. "It looks to me like one of those cases when someone who's submissive has finally called it a day."

"*Kramer versus Kramer?*"

"Yes, something like that. She was different, held herself upright. She said she couldn't find a job here, that her daughter, I quote, 'has fallen into bad company", and Franek has stopped speaking Polish. And that she wants to leave. It's a shame because she's set up such a great club for the children of poorer Poles. She's got people who help them with their lessons, computers …"

"And Stefan?" interrupted Jonathan.

"I think he's walking on burning coal." Antosia had not taken her eyes off the Indian. "Even the soles of his feet are black."

"Or he didn't wash them before going to bed, yuk!" Tomaszek rattled off, sneaking a crafty look at his parents.

"They're the man's shoes," threw out Megi for the sake of peace and quiet, then said to Jonathan, "I asked her about Stefan, too, but she only shrugged."

Jonathan scratched his head.

"I ought to phone him."

Megi looked at her watch and called, "Come on, kids, say goodbye to Daddy! We've still got quite a way to go and I bet we'll get stopped again, like last time when Tomaszek was smuggling his compass."

Jonathan picked Tomaszek up, ruffled his hair and told him to help Mommy. Antosia hugged him and asked him to feed her tortoise every day.

"What tortoise?" Jonathan worried.

"The plasticine one. He likes lettuce and jelly babies. You will remember, won't you?" She looked at him sternly.

"Lettuce." Jonathan clicked his fingers.

"And jelly babies," added Antosia, menacingly.

"Typical tortoise food."

Megi walked up and snuggled up to him with her whole body. They hadn't made love the night before but ended up talking and watching their favorite series. Jonathan grasped her tightly around the waist.

"What do you think, should I tell Stefan or not?" he asked, handing her her hand luggage. "You know, so he's not the last to know."

"He'll find out when the time's right." Megi waved it away.

"He's a close friend."

"Friendship isn't just passing on the latest bit of information."

Jonathan adjusted Tomaszek's hat, gave Antosia another kiss.

"We didn't manage to talk again, as usual," he threw at his wife as she walked away.

Megi handed their passports to passport control, let the children go before her.

"And what was the other piece of gossip?" he called.

"Oh!" She stopped. "Monika said Andrea's left Simon."

**book five**

*Brussels, December 2008*

JONATHAN WONDERED how his story about the pack of mongrels ought to end. Being superstitious, he opted for a happy ending – poor penmanship perhaps, but full of optimism. On the other hand, a dramatic ending would offer him a chance to leave the shelf of children's writers and climb to that of adult writers. "Why did you let *The Pavlov Dogs* get caught by the dog-catchers?" he imagined being asked during a writer's evening. "Because you can't live outside the law. At least if you're a dog," would be his answer.

But the dogs had had enough of his writer's strategy. They went where they wanted to go but were happiest in Brussels because here streets branched from roundabouts in five different directions or more. Jonathan could only run after them.

# 1

ANDREA GREETED HIM at the open door; the light from inside filtered through her lightweight maternity shirt. He gently put his arms around her; her belly barely fitted beneath her bust.

"You found your way all right?" she asked.

He snuggled up to her hair, which had grown even more, and into the crook of her neck. How good she smelled! She herself had a theory that as long as people were attracted to each other by their smell, there was desire; when the smell lost its fragrance, love evaporated. He took her face in his hands and started to kiss – her eyes, her nose, forehead, chin … He nibbled at her ears, licked her hair-line until she started breathing heavily.

At one point she gently pushed him away.

"We've probably got to talk first," he muttered reluctantly.

"No, no we don't," she said, took him by the hand and led him into her new apartment.

They were careful with their lovemaking. Jonathan turned her over like a newly acquired treasure; she fitted her new shape to him. If it wasn't for the fact that he remembered what time Megi's flight had been, he would have thought he and Andrea caressed with no beginning and no end. It was dark when she let him in, dark when he made himself comfortable within her, dark when he slipped out, dark when he felt the nagging in his groin again. Only toward morning did the light bring out her features and the thought crossed his mind that the problem with beauty was that it existed only here and now. That this moment, too, would fade.

Andrea stirred and stretched herself. They had only seen each other once in the morning, it occurred to Jonathan, a long time ago, in Warsaw. Suddenly he was embarrassed by this new intimacy: he briefly deliberated whether to leap out of bed and brush his teeth, or kiss her first – it was so long since he hadn't woken up next to another woman.

"Hey," she said in Swedish. The familiar word, the language of his first love, Petra, greeted him in his lover's new home.

"Hey," he replied.

The first morning after their night together, he found three messages from Megi. He rang back, superstitiously stepping out of Andrea's apartment into the street. Megi's tone was cold, the same as when she spoke about professional matters. She asked why he hadn't picked up the phone; he replied that he had run out of battery. She wanted to know how his work on *The Pavlov Dogs* was going; he lied that it was going well. Megi fell silent so he asked about the children, her mother, his father, Uncle Tadeusz, Aunt Barbara, and the rest of the family, whose names he barely remembered. Odysseus came to his mind, the hero who conquered so many women and islands that his beginnings dimmed in his memory. "What beginnings?" he asked himself, pocketing his phone.

For him, everything began the moment he'd stood at the threshold of his lover's apartment, on the top floor of an old apartment building where there was a lift with a grille like a birdcage. He had immediately taken to St Gilles, the massive church at the back of her tenement and the market with its weekly stalls.

He didn't go home after that first night – he lived at Andrea's for the duration of his stolen freedom. He bought some new toiletries in the corner shop, a few T-shirts and some boxer shorts as a change of underwear; when he put his jeans and sweatshirt into the washing machine, he couldn't leave the apartment until they dried.

Every morning Andrea left for her new job, bidding him goodbye with a gentle kiss – she wore lipstick and he knew he shouldn't hug her passionately when she was made-up, which is why he woke up very early in the morning – his erection a fail-safe alarm clock – and fucked her lazily until they were both satiated. He didn't compare Andrea to Megi, Petra, or any other woman whom he only partially remembered. He took her, his *terra incognita*, and learned from scratch on this isle of freedom – he, a human wreck with a meager supply of underpants.

They argued a great deal during those days; trivial things took on the proportions of stumbling blocks thrown beneath their four uncoordinated legs. A moment later they wrapped their legs around each other and writhed. Many words were left unsaid but this suited Jonathan, and Andrea was similar in this respect. Instead of talking, he preferred to cook her the best dinners possible. Choosing victuals, he milled around the market stalls; he didn't look around apprehensively to see if there was anyone he knew nearby. He didn't even have an explanation at hand in case he did meet someone unexpectedly. At last, he felt free – after years of fibbing and hiding, it had started to be all the same to him.

He passed a shop selling vinyl records, a bookshop and a bakery. He entered and bought almond croissants, the ones Andrea liked. And the sight of "bum" rolls, which he bought on rue des Tongres, stirred a longing in him.

He learned about the pre-Christmas party from Megi. The invitation had been emailed to her and she'd thought that since she couldn't go herself, he might want to drop in. At times, he sensed a certain alienation in her voice – she was going through something, maybe she simply suspected? It seemed more and more obvious to him with every passing day. They were, after all, like the yoked oxen which the priest had, to their disgust, evoked on their wedding day.

He left the apartment and stepped into the lift. Megi was acting just like him who hadn't yet asked Andrea if he was the father of her child. He pulled the lift doors apart and stood on the stairwell lined with nineteenth-century tiles. He nodded to the neighbor living on the second floor and asked the old man from the first floor after his health. Over the last few days they'd exchanged greetings, comments about the weather, and the negligence of the trash collectors.

He drew the winter air into his lungs. Soon it would be Christmas, presents, his birthday … He pulled up the collar of his jacket and made toward the Brasserie Verschueren. He didn't want to go to Ludwik's, who hosted the immortal Commission Christmas parties, but he didn't like the idea of Andrea going without him. He intended to arrive a little after her and have a glass of mulled wine on the corner beforehand.

When he saw him, Ludwik swept the hallway with his eyes.

"My wife's in Poland," Jonathan rattled off. What did the man expect? That she was hiding behind the coat rack?

Jonathan looked around the familiar interior – the floor gleamed with unhealthy brightness, the Christmas tree looked as if it had been bought in a shop selling appropriate accessories.

"Don't worry, we'll soon puke all over this place," he heard Stefan's voice at his side.

From the balcony where they had gone to smoke, the Eurocrats' district looked like Łódź in the previous century after its manufacturers had gone bankrupt – dark windows illuminated by street lamps, no pub music, no twenty-four-hour *alimentation générale*.

"Martyna saw you going to Andrea's apartment with her." Stefan blew a few impressive smoke rings, pursing his lips like a carp. "Apparently you were lugging a shopping bag."

"And they say I try to dodge cooking." Jonathan reached for a Gauloise.

"But is it true? I told her she must have been seeing things, I even blew up at her."

"Good." Jonathan nodded.

Nothing else came to his mind, he felt light and empty inside. Something told him that this feeling preceded another, painful sensation but he couldn't, of his own volition, leap from his balloon of indifference.

"Eh!" Stefan tapped him on the shoulder. "So how are things with you two?"

Jonathan turned his eyes on him. Megi would ask the same question when she returned.

"I'm living with Andrea," he replied.

"Does Megi know?" asked Stefan after a long while.

Jonathan held on to the barrier, pretending he was gazing at the dark street. He shook his head.

"And what's going to happen now?" His friend's voice reached him.

Jonathan shrugged. He was in no state to stammer out anything else. "I'm living with Andrea." Those four words released into a space full of guests at the Commission Christmas party, even though separated from it by a pane of glass, drained him of strength.

"I've never gone that far." There was helplessness in Stefan's tone. "The furthest I got was when that crazy woman came flying up to Monika."

"What really happened to you then?" Jonathan choked out, trying to focus on the story that he couldn't care less about right now.

"Don't ask." Stefan waved it away. "But going back to you ... Think it over carefully, old man."

"Meaning?" Jonathan gripped the barrier again, his cigarette going out several meters below them on the pavement.

"You don't really know her." Stefan's forehead furrowed. "Don't announce anything until you're a hundred percent sure."

Stefan went in, returning a moment later with two bottles of beer. He clearly wasn't himself that evening, didn't intend to circulate among people or sort out professional matters.

"Monika wants to go back to Poland, as you probably know," he mumbled in the end, tilting a bottle into his mouth. "Martyna told me, do you see? Monika hasn't said a word to me since that time and it was only when everybody started asking me what I thought about it, that I realized I was the only one who didn't know. Like a total idiot!"

He gestured at Jonathan with the bottle and added, "I even resented you for not telling me but then I heard that you're having it off with her again." He indicated Andrea who was standing next to a dark-haired stranger.

Jonathan tore himself away from the barrier and practically glued his forehead to the window.

"Who is he?"

Stefan followed his gaze.

"You know, the guy who's got three chicks here and a wife and children at home. I told you about him." He shrugged. "Apparently he's just getting a divorce."

"Does he know Andrea?"

"Oh, yes!" began Stefan and broke off suddenly.

Jonathan turned to him.

"You know something. Talk."

"Everybody knows." Stefan had the expression of a dog caught peeing. "Rumor has it that she's been going with him ever since she left Simon. But if I know him, he was the one chasing her, he's always wanted a go at her."

Stefan said no more. Jonathan stood with his head bowed; the balcony swayed beneath his feet. The horizon seemed to expand and expand in front of him and, finally, there was a vast space there. A moment longer and he would have an attack of agoraphobia.

"Why didn't you tell me?" He barely recognized his own voice.

"Because you said you weren't together any more! The last time we spoke you said you had lumbago and had ditched her, remember?"

"*Kurwa, kurwa …*" Jonathan put his hands over his face. Polish curses seemed foreign to him, he switched to English.

Stefan stood with his hands spread out helplessly, one holding beer, the other a cigarette.

"I had that whole Monika mess hanging over me."

Jonathan didn't hear him; fragments of scenes ran through his head, snippets of conversations fell into place, suddenly clear and logical: the muted ring on Andrea's cell, the conversations she ended on the stairs, a man's disposable razor in the cupboard beneath the sink, which she apparently used for shaving, although she had once told him she had her legs waxed.

He felt Stefan's hand on his shoulder.

"She doesn't know anything." Jonathan picked up four recurring words. "Megi still doesn't know anything."

"I haven't got any strength left," said Jonathan and swayed above the barrier.

Stefan grabbed him by the shirt; Jonathan straightened himself and turned. He now stared through the balcony window at the group around Andrea – Rafał was sneaking a meaningful look at Przemek, who was hiding a smirk, and only crooked Ludwik and the dark-haired man were talking, oblivious to everything, and gazing at Andrea.

Jonathan tore himself from the barrier and for a moment looked as if he was going to plunge head first through the windows of the balcony door.

"What are you doing?" He heard Stefan's cry.

"What?" Jonathan was looking at him as if he didn't see him.

"You're not going to do anything foolish, are you?"

Jonathan shook his head rhythmically in a futile search for words.

"No," he retorted finally. "I'm only fucking off out of here."

He didn't switch the lights on at home; he entered the living room in the dark and collapsed on the sofa. He slept in his jacket and shoes, dreamless, just as when he'd sat difficult exams. When he woke up in the morning, he was afraid to move – everything in him was dispersed. He cast his eyes around. The plants had dried up, the rubbish he hadn't thrown away stank, a pile of letters lay strewn by the door.

It was on this pile that Andrea's eyes fell as she stood at the threshold.

"Who let you in?" asked Jonathan. He was in the kitchen, unwashed, with no jacket but still in his shoes.

"Your neighbors. And the door was open."

He stared at her, made-up, hair neatly brushed, innocent, in a so-called blessed state.

"Stefan didn't want to say what happened but ..."

"But you guessed," he interrupted her.

He didn't invite her in; he couldn't bear her entering the room where his children sat at the table.

"One of your attacks of jealousy, is it?" She studied him tenderly, almost curiously. He was on the point of raising his arm to tell her to leave when she said, "What do you want from me? Just tell me once and for all and at last I'll know."

"Have you slept with him?"

"That's my business."

"Is it his child?"

"No, it's mine," she replied calmly.

"And who else's? Mine?"

*Andrea's hand roams toward her belly, rests on it like a shell on a shelf.*

*"No," she finally says, slowly and clearly. "I wanted it to be yours but you weren't ready. The child's mine and Simon's."*

*"I don't believe you!" yells Jonathan, alarmed by the squeaky pitch of his voice. "I don't believe you about anything, you're terrible, terrible ..."*

*He yells so that his legs give way; he sinks to the chair and from the chair, lower. He doesn't feel the touch of her hand on his hair; it's as if he is turning numb, his tissues despairing in the distress of being rejected.*

*She bends over him but it isn't concern that speaks through her. She forms questions, but so quickly that she hasn't got time to add question marks. They sound senseless.*

*"I was supposed to wait, was I," she hisses, "but what for? You knew that I loved you, that I wanted a child with you. Is it fair to want that? I can't fill in gaps with words like you; I act, it's actions with me, you don't see that, you don't see ..."*

*"What actions?" Jonathan hides his face with his elbow; his glasses are askew, the floor digs into his ribs. "Like yesterday?"*

*"What are you talking about?" Andrea wants to lean over him to hear better but her belly is too large, so she straightens her knees and asks from above, louder, "What?"*

*"You're always going to be like that, unfaithful, remote! I don't want you like that."*

*"It's not me." She shakes her head above him. "It's your lack of will. And your family."*

*Jonathan rises, first to his knees, then gets up; now he looms over her, unshaven, exhausted.*

"*No, no, no,*" *he repeats.* "*It's not my family, not me. It's you! You're the one who's like that, you'll always be like that! I'm scared of you. I don't want you when you're like that.*"

**2**

MEGI LISTENS *to the sounds of Warsaw – the screech of trams, ambulance sirens, the rattle of garbage trucks. Her city. And yet, when her cousins had asked her whether she missed the place, she'd nodded – because she did but it was Brussels she missed. Her local patriotism is muddled: she can't stand visitors speaking badly of Warsaw, she defends it, then leaves and doesn't think about it, head over heels in love with Brussels.*

*But now she feels as though her other city is betraying her. Fury mounts in her, seethes, is uncontrollable. Megi cries; her mother comes out to her on the balcony where, despite the frost, her daughter tends to sit with a glass of tea; she strokes her hair which is longer now, the highlights growing out. And Megi begins to talk: how rumors closed in on her, from Martyna's mention of seeing Jonathan and Andrea in the street, through Przemek's seemingly casual hints, to Jonathan's reaction on hearing that Andrea had left Simon. And now Martyna had phoned again, asking – as if solicitously – what could have happened to Jonathan to make him leave Ludwik's party so abruptly.*

"*That's still no reason to ...*" *Her mother tries to comfort her.*

"*He was walking with Andrea! Carrying shopping bags!*"

*Her mother runs her hand down her back, no doubt thinking that her daughter isn't dressed warmly enough – it is, after all, minus five degrees – but doesn't say anything, taking on to herself words sticky with tears.*

*Suddenly Megi pulls her head away from her mother's shoulder.*

"*I'm going to call that roach! I'll call and give her a piece of my mind!*"

*A whirl of suspicions had surrounded her ever since she'd said out loud to her mother,* "*I think he's unfaithful.*" *From that moment all the filings were drawn to the magnet – dates tallied, exchanged glances made sense, even Jonathan's T-shirt, wet along the spine, had been like that not because he'd been to the gym but because he'd poured a bottle of water down it to make it look credible.*

*"I'm going to call her, I'm going to call." Megi presses the keys on her cell but can't find Andrea's number.*

*"My God, how stupid I am," she moans and quickly wipes her tears away because there's movement in the apartment. Antosia has just woken up and Tomaszek will be up in a moment, too.*

*"Go to them," whispers Megi to her mother. "Please."*

*She turns and holds her face to the freezing wind. She is thinking about Jonathan – and is horrified by the boundless love, hatred, contempt, and admiration she feels for him. Because if he leaves them, if he follows his feelings, if he leaves his life for the other woman, Megi will hate him. Yet she will also admire him and despise herself for this admiration, for her own weakness in face of the strength of a man who has the courage to go his own way.*

*But if Jonathan stays with them, if he chooses what Megi had chosen not so long ago when she'd dropped the man she'd fallen in love with, she will also understand him. In her loathing and disgust she will understand his scruples, deep love for his own, inseparability from his children, what he feels for her. Is it just habit?*

*Megi can't think about it, it hurts too much. Was he repulsed by her, was that why he couldn't make love to her?*

*She thinks about her own affair scornfully now – there was no comparison with what Jonathan was doing to her now. That other thing was just a plain old yuppie cock-up, a typical office romance. But although Megi distils the hackneyed truth, hides behind it, she remembers that she'd been in love. If it had come out into the open then, she doesn't know how it would all have ended.*

*She knocks over her mug with her sleeve; the tea spills over the balcony tiles. Megi can't go to fetch a cloth because her face is all blotchy and Antosia will immediately know she's been crying and will ask questions. So Megi stands as the brown puddle with tea dregs in the middle freezes over.*

*Or maybe I should leave him in peace, to sort it out for himself, she now thinks soberly. Not make a middle-class tragedy of it, not make a song and dance? If she leaves Jonathan people will enjoy the game, will watch two people fight. In return they'll conscientiously condemn the person Megi loves. And she'll leap into her role as the betrayed, hurt party. Is that what she wants, other people to lick her wounds?*

*Megi, the lawyer, orders herself to be pragmatic and wraps her arms around herself because she's terribly cold. Andrea isn't one of those crafty pieces of work who use sex to get on; Andrea could only lose by her relationship with*

*Jonathan. The tea puddle glistens in the sun peeking through the clouds; Megi's eyes fill with tears again. She hates herself for this understanding of her rival. Because Megi doesn't really want to lose Jonathan. She's crushed by hard facts: his trousers rolled up at the bottom of the wardrobe although she'd told him numerous times to fold them, the sink full of stubble, which – as usual – he hadn't rinsed out after shaving. Him playing football with the children.*

*Again she's in the grips of atavistic hatred.*

*"Mom," she calls. "Mom!"*

*Her mother stands in the doorway; Megi weeps but can't cuddle her, stiff with despair.*

*"I could kill them." Her lips are contorted, she doesn't recognize herself. "I could kill them!"*

Jonathan sits on the terrace of their Brussels apartment. He is alone, in his love and in his pain. He has no doubt that what's happened to him is love – and it hurts more than lumbago. Andrea and Simon, Andrea and the prat with three women, Andrea and her Scandinavian freedom, Slavic charm, the need to please.

He dissects his lover into basic elements, after all he knows a good deal about her: the daughter of immigrants, her parents – dissident activists, refugees after Prague Spring. They lasted only a few years together once in Sweden. The mother, an ambitious chemist, couldn't bear working as a cleaner; the father, accustomed to conspiring, to manning the barricade, had lost the ground beneath his feet. They'd missed Prague and the days that had given their lives sense. Andrea was the last outburst of a love that was falling apart in the stagnation of Swedish life. She was born and the world lit up for a moment, then everything went out.

She didn't remember her father from her childhood; she'd got to know him better once she'd grown up. She spoke well of him, made excuses for him, justified him. With her mother she had a difficult relationship. Andrea had run away from her, first to university, then to work, finally to Brussels. Her father had died shortly after.

Andrea and Simon. Older than her, charismatic, handsome. And he, Jonathan, who was he in her life? The one with whom she laughed, ate with her fingers, was breathless with delight when he dressed her after they'd made love, tilted his head when he mentioned Antosia and

Tomaszek. He tried not to talk about his children because he thought he detected disapproval in her face, boredom – and then she'd told him that she wanted a child by him. But she'd said so many other things, too! That they'd go to the seaside together, that one day he'd show her Warsaw, London, Paris – the places of his youth. And that they'd go to Stockholm – Jonathan would help her get to like the country she'd been brought up in, where she'd been poor, with no money to buy the clothes that her richer, Swedish friends boasted. She wanted him to pour into her some of his admiration for Scandinavia – and much, much more.

She had another, separate world with Simon but, during those years, Jonathan had begun to treat him a little as though he were a character in a comic – a superhero, God's gift to women, a bit funny in his striving for perfection; an older guy trying to keep up the appearances of youth. And yet it was Simon who was the father of Andrea's child, he was the one out of the two of them who had, as she would say, "proved himself in action." It was to him that, as hard as she may deny it, she'd forever tied herself.

"Out of the two of them ..." Who else, apart from Simon? Jonathan shakes, his hands wander toward his face, clumsy wooden blocks. He's cold, even though the winter here is a joke compared to that in Poland and Sweden. He pulls his hands away from his face and his thoughts away from jealousy because they lead to one place only. If he were to touch them with his tongue, it would stick forever.

And yet, through his constant hardening of himself, his opening and closing of wounds, he believes the love has given him strength. Jonathan leans forwards in his chair and stares at the empty apartment opposite. The December sun lights up the sanded floorboards, the decorated walls. The room awaits furniture, movement; the floor is ready for paths to be trodden. A beginning.

*Megi wraps the children's necks with colorful scarves and waves from the window. Tomaszek skips along, Antosia is a little reluctant, she would have preferred to read, but their granny shows them something and they break into a run.*

*Megi gazes at the snow below, at the playground, and a boy in a white surplice springs to her mind unexpectedly. She'd been not much older than Antosia when she'd seen him walking next to the priest at the head of a funeral*

*procession. Her friend had told her that he went to the technical college; Megi*
*remembered his shapely mouth.*

*Like Jonathan's when he'd seen her standing in the middle of the room in*
*a corset. She'd bought it especially to please him; it had been her first outing to*
*the shops by herself after giving birth. Her mother had looked after Antosia and*
*Megi had run off to the shop and squeezed herself into the sexy construction.*
*Before Jonathan returned, she'd drawn the milk from her breasts in order*
*not to leak.*

*"It's fine," he'd said with a slight grimace, and left. She'd remained alone,*
*in the new corset, like a bride waiting to be unveiled. Except there was nobody*
*to admire her.*

*She'd gone back to work, fallen in love. There isn't only one man, there*
*are many.*

Jonathan entered their bedroom; his eyes fell on what Megi jokingly
called the matrimonial bed. It had stood untouched since she left; the
throw was still folded over in the corner, a bit of the pillow sticking out
like the inside of a dog's ear. Jonathan perched on the edge as if he were
sitting on a sickbed. In his blindness, infatuation, search for sensual
pleasure, escape from daily life – he suddenly saw what he'd done to her.
So many years, so many lies!

He leaned over, seeking the smell of Megi in the bedclothes, but the
pillow no longer smelled of her. He picked up the security pass with her
photograph from the floor. Andrea wore a similar one of late, which she
carefully placed by the mirror when she came home. Jonathan turned the
badge with his wife's photograph over in his hand. They kept returning
to each other, kept thinking about each other – positively and negatively
– running the risk of not thinking anything at all.

Passing each other, patching up, endless effort.

*Megi turns from the window. It's stuffy in her mother's apartment; heating in*
*the blocks can't be regulated. Communist levelling still holds strong. Megi rests her*
*thighs against the radiator; heat spreads to her hips.*

*It wasn't her lover who'd given her strength to get out of the stalemate of*
*rejection, the euphoria and shock of motherhood, and the sense of being socially*
*lost. She'd thought, at the time, that she was drawing strength from the illicit*
*infatuation. But she, Megi the lawyer, drew her sap from her work. She'd*

*passed the exam, gone to Brussels. Perhaps somebody else would have sucked*
*strength from love. Her fig leaf was independence.*

# 3

JONATHAN ASKED TOMASZEK and Antosia at the airport how they'd
enjoyed their stay at Granny's, whether Father Christmas had already
delivered presents in Poland, and what was bulging beneath Tomaszek's
jacket.

"A surprise!" cried the little boy, making himself comfortable in the
back seat.

Jonathan fastened the seat belt around him.

"Is it alive?" he asked carefully.

"Nah!" giggled Tomaszek.

"They almost didn't let us on the plane," informed Antosia grimly.
"Because this fathead made a collar out of Granddad's bullets."

"Bullets?" This time Jonathan didn't have to feign surprise.

"Blank ones," Tomaszek corrected. "Granddad said that they don't
shoot any more."

"But the customs officers didn't know that," snorted Antosia. "That's
why they interrogated Mommy and held us so long that …"

"That Antosia peed herself!" laughed Tomaszek.

"No I didn't!" Antosia lunged to thump her brother.

"Quiet, children!" Megi spoke for the first time since she'd climbed
into the car.

"Don't swing your legs, Tomaszek," added Jonathan.

"I didn't, I only wanted to, you idiot, fathead, twit!"

"That's enough, Antosia!"

"You peed yourself, you peed yourself!"

"Not a word from now on!" thundered Megi and the car fell silent.

When the children went to bed in the evening, Megi started to
unpack the suitcases and Jonathan went to the living room. He stood his
present, Tomaszek's surprise, next to his laptop – a dog made of colorful
rags, its throat squeezed by a collar of blank bullets. Tomaszek had wailed
so much at the airport that, after they'd carefully inspected the blank

bullets, the crew had agreed to put the dog in the baggage hold. Antosia claimed that it was because the soldier had taken a fancy to Megi, Megi assured him that it was because of Tomaszek's howling, while Tomaszek swore it was thanks to Antosia peeing herself.

Jonathan gazed at the dog, sewn on Granny's sewing machine. On an impulse, he switched on his computer, found his text, and began printing it. He was sitting on the floor among scattered pages when Megi entered.

"Are you going to tell me what's going on?" Her voice sounded hard.

Jonathan raised his head from the papers. He was overwhelmed by chaos, how out of touch he was with his text. How could he have let it come to this again?

"If I only knew."

Megi came closer, her feet almost touching the scattered pages.

"What's up with you and Andrea?"

He lifted his eyes to her. She stood there, looming over him like the Statue of Liberty; beneath her, the adventures of his dogs lay jumbled.

"What on earth is going on?" she yelled.

Jonathan knows he has to answer her.

Megi stares at him.

They argue, sharp words, hard as stones. She screams about his affair; he repeats, "It's not true, not true, not true!"

Megi's blood boils. She wants to believe him but hates him, doesn't know how much truth there is in what he says. She'll never know.

She stares at him, at what he's done to their lives; burrowing insects have caused an earthquake, and now he's surprised that their world's turned upside down. "Idiot, fathead, twit!" Antosia's words ring in her head.

She bites when Jonathan wants to touch her. Their yelling brings the children running, and when they, too, are crying, Jonathan runs out. Megi lies down on the floor; the jumbled pages rustle beneath her. She turns the only remaining thought in her head – there isn't only one man, there are many – but can't understand the phrase.

*Antosia covers her with a blanket. Tomaszek brings her some juice and puts it next to her. They lie down on the sofa, near to her and, after a while, she hears their regular breathing. She wants to get up, give them the blanket, but doesn't feel well. Beneath her eyelids she sees a tiny light, somewhere on the left, a glimmer that, as she studies it, turns into a corridor.*

*Megi is scared to go there. The light doesn't disappear so she raises herself on her elbows with a groan. Routine, right? Only routine helps in such cases. All right, she'll go and wash. She steps under the shower, runs the shaver over her shins, armpits, bikini line, listens to the stream of water. She remembers her father, the lower half of his face smeared white, his funny expressions, the shaving brush …*

*Her mother had divorced him, her father had left. Now Jonathan was leaving.*

*Megi is left alone. Megi is shaving.*

# 4

JONATHAN ROLLED OVER on to his other side. The mattress let out a puff, the sleeping bag slid down with a rustle. He kicked it aside, he was too hot as it was. He opened his eyes and stared at the ceiling. The glow of the street lamp, the texture of the stucco, four meters of space.

The apartment was empty; all that remained were the washing machine, dishwasher, fridge, mattress, and divan on which Stefan was snoring. Monika had moved out just before Christmas. The children had apparently protested, their daughter especially didn't want to move to Poland, but Monika had already sorted everything out – the move, the schools, and had even found herself a job.

"What's she going to do?" asked Jonathan as he was brewing some tea in the morning.

Stefan was sitting on the floor, nibbling a piece of toast.

"Something to do with leasing." He shrugged his shoulders.

His face was bloated. Not only had they drunk too much the previous evening, he also claimed not to have slept well, which Jonathan, who'd kept on waking because of Stefan's snoring, believed to be an exaggeration.

"And you?" Jonathan passed him the mug. Only one was left so they had to share.

A couple of hours later they were at Zaventeem airport.

"So, are we going to see each other in Warsaw?" muttered Stefan. They looked at each other, gave each other an awkward bear hug. Stefan averted his face, which sported a moustache again, and sniffled. At passport control, he turned for a moment and lifted his hand in the air. Jonathan lifted his and showed him his middle finger in an offensive gesture; Stefan cheered up briefly.

Jonathan made toward the exit. He hadn't been surprised when Stefan informed him he was following Monika to Poland. There was something inseparable in the misery of those two, an element of being condemned to each other, the sweetness of suffering in the marriage of old lags.

"She's changing," Stefan had said the previous night when they were sitting on the floor with bottles of beer in their hands. "But I'm not going to change any more. I'm not looking for anyone else."

"No?" There was doubt in Jonathan's voice.

"Well, perhaps to screw a little on the side."

"I wonder what made her change?"

"Martyna," Stefan had retorted without hesitation. "Before she left, Monika told me that when she looked at someone like that – and I quote – 'useless kept woman,' she felt sick."

Jonathan roused himself as somebody's suitcase caught on his trouser leg, followed by a vague "*Pardon*". He walked up to the door marked "Exit" but, instead of going out, stopped and pulled his cell out of his pocket.

He had two messages. One from Cecile, asking him to keep an evening in March free because she'd managed to book a room in the little mansion by Botanique where they were going to launch the anthology. The other was from Stefan: "Before you hand the keys back to the owner, chuck the cheese out of the fridge or he'll think we've mucked up the drains."

He patted his jacket and felt a hard shape in his pocket – the keys to Stefan's apartment. He had somewhere to stay for a couple of weeks until the end of the year.

All of a sudden, he turned around and fixed his eyes on where departing passengers disappeared. He was on the same side as his mother had once been. She'd no longer loved his father then, only Nick. But most of all, she'd loved him, Jonathan, as she kept telling him to the point of boredom.

How many years it had taken him to shake off his binding belief in realism. It was only recently that he'd realized he had a right to premonitions, impressions, instincts, and outbursts – even though he was a man.

It was too cold to sit on the park bench so he just stood beside it. A pigeon limped in front of him. Jonathan watched it – the bird was missing one foot. Jonathan rested his hip on the bench – he, too, was limping, inside. But he could still fly.

He pulled out his cell. "What are we going to do now? Are we going to be friends?" She didn't reply so he tapped out, "But you don't believe in friendship." "No, I don't," wrote back Andrea.

A moment later the little screen flashed again. "Neither of us will guarantee your happiness but you can count on pleasant experiences that will allow you to forget."

Jonathan put away his cell and, despite the cold, sat down on the bench. If he decided to leave, he would become a kidney stone – the family would excrete him but with great pain.

The two women he loved. His best friend and the mother of his children. His pregnant lover.

Something red appeared in the sky – balloons had escaped from a fair. He heard children's cries. They're what's most important, he thought. And women, men? That's just pumping up the ego. Which is life-giving, unfortunately.

Jonathan stands at the door but doesn't take the keys out of his pocket. He rings the bell. His daughter opens the door, looks at him solemnly.

"Have you come back?" she asks.

Behind her stands Megi, who now also stares at Jonathan. Tomaszek pushes his head between his mother and sister.

"Are you coming in?" That's Megi's voice.

Jonathan enters and stops in the hallway.

"What next?" he asks.

# Epilogue

*Brussels, 2009*

IN THE SPRING OF **2009**, the anthology entitled *About Loving* comes out. At the book launch, Jonathan says, "We built up our approach to love together – at our sessions. When one of us wasn't coping, he or she passed the baton on to the others. Our writing is a set of connected vessels."

Megi goes to Warsaw for a decisive talk concerning her work. At the same time, she receives an offer for the position of head of unit in Brussels. She returns to Brussels and, when she finds herself with the children at Zaventeem airport, unexpectedly breaks into tears.

"Are you missing Granny's house?" asks Antosia.

Megi doesn't answer, only gazes at Brussels's colorful crowd.

She doesn't know what awaits her here, but knows she'll stay.

In the autumn, Jonathan publishes *The Pavlov Dogs*. The parents of his former readers make sure the novel doesn't find itself in the hands of their children. It's the parents who lose themselves in the author's first "grown-up" novel.

Andrea gives birth to a son.

# about the author

GRAŻYNA PLEBANEK was born in Warsaw, Poland. She is the author of the highly acclaimed and bestselling novels *Pudełko ze szpilkami* (Box of Stilettos; 2002), *Dziewczyny z Portofino* (Girls from Portofino; 2005) and *Przystupa* (A Girl Called Przystupa; 2007). *Illegal Liaisons* (*Nielegalne związki*, 2010) sold 27,000 copies in Poland and is her first novel to be translated into English. In 2011 Plebanek received Poland's Zlote Sowy literary prize for her contribution to promoting Poland abroad. She is among a group of international artists whose portraits are exhibited in Brussels Gare de l'Ouest for the next decade. She writes a regular column in the Polish weekly *Polityka* and has worked as a journalist for Reuters News Agency and for Poland's highest circulation daily newspaper, *Gazeta Wyborcza*. She lives in Brussels, Belgium.

# about the translator

DANUSIA STOK has translated novels by Marek Krajewski, Andrzej Sapkowski, and Agnieszka Taborska; nonfiction books by Mariusz Wilk and Adina Blady Szwajger; and screenplays by Krzysztof Kieslowski and Krzysztof Piesiewicz. She compiled, translated, and edited *Kieslowski on Kieslowski*. She is a member of The Translators' Association / The Society of Authors in the United Kingdom. She lives in London, England.